T0301066

THE WHITE CIRCLE

Also by Oliver Bottini in English translation

Zen and the Art of Murder (2018)
A Summer of Murder (2018)
The Dance of Death (2019)
The Night Hunters (2021)
The Invisible Web (2023)

OLIVER BOTTINI

THE WHITE CIRCLE

A Black Forest Investigation: VI

Translated from the German by
Jamie Bulloch

MACLEHOSE PRESS
QUERCUS · LONDON

First published as *Im weissen Kreis* by DuMont Buchverlag, Köln, in 2015

First published in Great Britain in 2024 by

MacLehose Press
An imprint of Quercus Editions Limited
Carmelite House
50 Victoria Embankment
London EC4Y 0DZ

An Hachette UK company

A CIP catalogue record for this book is available from the British Library.

ISBN (HB) 978 1 52940 923 9
ISBN (TPB) 978 1 52940 924 6
ISBN (Ebook) 978 1 52940 926 0

This book is a work of fiction. Names, characters, organisations, places and events are either the product of the author's imagination or are used fictitiously. Any resemblance to actual persons, living or dead, events or particular places is entirely coincidental.

10 9 8 7 6 5 4 3 2

Designed and typeset in Minion by Libanus Press, Marlborough
Printed and bound in Great Britain by Clays Ltd, Elcograf S.p.A.

Papers used by Quercus Books are from well-managed forests
and other responsible sources.

Prologue

April 2004

They took the usual route, into town via Südstadt, stopping from time to time, chatting to people – "our people", as Timo always said, "our streets, our people" – chatting about football as if everything were normal. And for Timo, Stefan Bremer thought, everything *was* normal.

At around eleven o'clock a report came in over the radio about an attempted aggravated robbery, Werderstrasse, less than a couple of hundred metres away. "Finally something's happening," Timo said, switching on the siren. He liked to arrive accompanied by a battle cry.

Bremer sped up only slightly. He'd barely slept and was blinded by the harsh morning light. He'd left his sunglasses at home, having stood in the hallway for several minutes, waiting for the familiar movements and sounds that now wouldn't come. In a wave of panic he'd hurried out of the apartment without his sunglasses, wallet or mobile.

Timo on the radio, Bremer not listening.

His first night without Nicky; her warmth was gone, her body, her fitful breathing. Only her smell was still there, in the duvet and the sheet – the fragrance of springtime wherever he turned his head. At around three o'clock he'd lain down on the sofa in the sitting room, but her smell had come with him, on him, in him, in the memory of that day seven or eight years ago when they'd bought the sofa. In the images before his eyes.

Eventually he did fall asleep.

"Over there," Timo said. An elderly man was waiting by the side of the road, red-faced, his chest pumped with agitation, waving his hands about. He was wearing a green apron.

Bremer braked and brought the car to a leisurely standstill.

I'm going now, Nicky had said the evening before. He was staring at the kitchen clock, twenty-five past eight. For some unfathomable reason that was important. At twenty-five past eight on the evening of 29 April, 2004, Nicky left.

They got out. "You do it," Bremer said.

"Are you Herr Fink?" Timo said to the distressed man.

Attempted aggravated robbery, the thief – armed with a knife – long gone, routine. Bremer was going to write notes, but his hand was shaking and the white paper was painfully reflecting the sunlight. His eyes half closed, he focused on the essentials. *11.15. Prob. East European. Shoved. Knife.*

"*What* did he do?" Timo asked. After eight months he still struggled to understand people who spoke with the hard Baden accent from Karlsruhe. It was tricky for someone from Brandenburg an der Havel.

It had taken Bremer a year to understand it, a whole year and Nicky. "He shoved Herr Fink against the shelves and threatened him with a knife," he said.

"Are you injured?"

"No!" Fink exclaimed, more angry than frightened.

They entered the small shop. Newspapers, sweets, lottery tickets, tobacco, some stationery. A fridge with drinks, but no food. Bremer wondered why Fink needed an apron. When he blinked, the harsh light from outside still lay over his pupils like a veil.

Timo let Fink show him where and how he'd been threatened with the knife. Bremer sketched, wrote, shook.

Brandenburg, he thought. Almost the only thing he and Timo had in common. Two Brandenburgers in Karlsruhe.

Look after him, the boss had said. *He's not here entirely of his own free will, if you get what I mean.*

No, I don't get what you mean, Bremer replied.

Whatever. Perhaps the two of you know the same girls from back then.

Bremer had a sudden urge to go home. Visit his parents and siblings, the girls from back then. Drift on the Breitlingsee in a rowing boat, like he did in his life before Nicky. In the evening he would row back to the shore, tie up the boat, April 1994, no jogger with short blonde hair tripping over him, cursing as she stumbled, yet still somehow smelling of spring.

"Did he touch anything?" Timo asked.

"Me!" Fink said.

"Anything else?"

Bremer wrote: *Door handle outside/inside. Shelf bracket below the magazines. Herr Fink's shirt collar, shoulder.*

"Why did he run away?"

"Because I told him he wouldn't be getting a cent, unless it was over my dead body!"

"Not advisable, Herr Fink, when someone's got a knife."

Bremer looked up and asked, "Why the apron, Herr Fink?" Silence descended on the room. He heard the hum of the fridge. Somewhere a clock ticked.

Eventually Fink raised his hands and showed them his palms. "Because I sweat so much."

Bremer wrote: *Apron – sweat.*

"That's some information," Timo said in a friendly tone.

Their Kripo colleagues, a man and a woman, came into the shop and took over. Timo became monosyllabic; he didn't like detectives being women.

Bremer went out onto the pavement and shooed away a few bystanders from the door and shop window. He caught sight of a cyclist the same age as him, around thirty, jeans, black coat, baseball cap. The man was standing beside a kiosk, straddling the crossbar, perusing a magazine. Bremer was sure he'd seen him before, some-where else a few minutes earlier.

Our streets, our people.

Timo came out. "Falafel?"

"Yes," he said.

This was something else they had in common. A falafel wrap, every lunchtime when they were on duty together.

They headed south from Werderstrasse, waiting at the next junction as a Turkish family hurried across the road – father, mother, three young daughters, everything a bit chaotic, the mother hectic, one of the children stopping in the middle of the road.

"In fifty years we'll have a Muslim chancellor," Timo said. "Bets on?"

Bremer turned the corner. "No."

"No what?"

"I don't want to bet."

Out of the corner of his eye he could see Timo shrug. "I don't care, and my children can move to New Zealand if they don't like it. I've heard there're hardly any Muslims in New Zealand."

"That's all happened very fast with the children. On Friday you didn't even have a girlfriend."

"Purely hypochondriacally, I mean."

Bremer smiled; he liked Timo's word play. Swapping similar sounding words, sometimes funny, sometimes not. Last month Timo's neighbour died. He bought a bunch of flowers for the widower and said he'd come to offer his indolence.

Did he really say "indolence"? Nicky had asked.

He was trying to cheer him up.

Strange chap, your colleague.

Bremer parked close to the Lebanese takeaway.

"Same as usual?" Timo said.

Bremer nodded and watched him wander off. Over the past couple of months Timo had adopted a slow, menacing walk like cops from

American TV series. Small-town officers in New Mexico or Texas who have to look intimidating if they want to make it to retirement age. Why Timo felt the need to be intimidating, Bremer had no idea. Testosterone, maybe. Or the sense that as a Brandenburger he didn't get enough respect around here. Bremer felt this too sometimes.

"Strange" is the wrong word.

Oh really? What's the right word then?

I don't know. "Unpredictable" perhaps.

Unpredictable and friendly, unpleasant and funny, Bremer thought, focusing his gaze on Timo's back to stop thinking about Nicky. In his head, however, she kept talking, even now a few weeks later on 29 April, 2004, just before half past eight in the evening: *I don't want you to call. Or write.*

OK.

I don't want any contact for the time being.

No contact, he thought. From one day to the next disappearing so completely from his life, as if she'd never existed.

His mouth was dry and goose pimples were creeping up his arms. He undid the seat belt and got out of the car, unfastening the top button of his shirt. Sunlight assailed his eyes from every angle, dazzling reflections from car roofs, windows. All of a sudden he felt tears on his cheeks. He forced himself to think about the lake and the rowing boat, alone on the water, no jogger, just the girls from back then, and today merely being the day after then.

His breathing calmed. Everything's familiar, everything's the same, he thought, at least that: the squeaking tram brakes at the Augartenstrasse stop, the smell of frying oil. Timo going into the Lebanese takeaway at midday, as he so often did. The cyclist back again, looking over at him, his bike leaning against a streetlamp, the magazine the only thing missing.

All normal, he thought. Nothing had changed. Almost nothing.

Timo was now at the counter, a rough hulk of a man in a black leather jacket with POLIZEI written on the back in white. His thumbs in his waistband, his upper body moving faintly, rocking back and forth. They needed to talk, Bremer thought. It wasn't their job to intimidate people. They were supposed to make them feel safe, not scared.

He was just about to turn away and get back into the car when a man, who hadn't been visible before, came up behind Timo and put a hand to his head, and Bremer wondered why he was doing this, why Timo had suddenly disappeared from view, then realised that the man was holding a pistol with a silencer which now pointed down at the floor where Timo must be lying. Bremer opened his mouth and tried to call for help, but no sound came. He tried to move, do something, but in vain. He was trapped in a leaden state of shock that had begun on 29 April, 2004, at 8.25 in the evening, and which still robbed him of his breath and every ounce of his strehgth. Confused, he registered that the man with the pistol was no longer standing where he had been, but was now outside the takeaway, looking in his direction, and to his left the cyclist was hurrying towards the police car, towards him, armed with a pistol too.

When Bremer heard muffled shots, the fear of death chased through his limbs and finally he was able to move, to drop to one knee. But it was too late; he couldn't even get a hand to his gun. He saw the driver's window shatter, then went crashing into the bodywork, no longer hearing or feeling anything. In a strangely crackling silence he lay on his back, the silver flash of the patrol car in the corner of his eye, and above him the evening sky, waves rocking the boat, now it was time to row back to shore, he thought. When he tied up the boat he noticed that something was missing. He looked along the footpath, there was nobody there, no jogger stumbling, falling with a supressed curse, rolling over and bringing the aroma of spring into his life. Spring was now gone for ever, he thought, before he lost consciousness.

TWO YEARS LATER

I

1

A Sunday evening on the balcony, night already creeping across Annaplatz. In the distance she heard piano music, in her head she saw a film, memories laden with melancholy. Not a moment when you want visitors.

The doorbell rang again.

Louise Bonì took the blanket off her legs and got up. The candle, which had burned halfway, flickered with her movement. A birthday candle, fat and with a blue rim, virtually no smell. Occasionally it crackled and spat into the evening, which suited the occasion.

The birthday of a dead person.

Squeezing past the little table she peered over the window boxes, which had been empty since anyone could remember, and down to the entrance. To begin with she couldn't make out anything in the dark, then a silhouette moved slowly into the light of the streetlamp. Leather jacket, shoulder-length hair, a man's face she hadn't seen in months – half a year to be precise.

She pressed the button to open the door. Kilian came up quietly and quickly.

"Hi," he said softly.

"I do have a phone," she said.

He pushed her into the apartment and closed the door. She realised he hadn't come to celebrate the birthday with her. His eyes appeared exhausted and twitchy, his skin rough. He looked gaunt. Not the surfer boy of six months ago, when she'd envied his youthfulness and sense of adventure.

15

She followed him into the kitchen. No light, he indicated.

"OK," she said, feeling tense.

He stood right beside her, talking under his breath. A few weeks ago, a man, probably from Freiburg, had ordered some illegal weapons, two pistols with silencers: a Makarov and a Tokarev. They'd been picked up yesterday.

"Slowly, slowly," Louise said. "Start at the beginning."

"It's a long story."

"Keep it short – I want to go back onto my balcony."

Kilian rubbed the sides of his nose with two fingers. "You know I've changed sections?"

She nodded. From surveillance to organised crime, an act of youthful despair. He'd made mistakes in investigations half a year earlier. Over the winter she'd occasionally wondered why she never bumped into him at police HQ, in the cafeteria, on the stairs, not even at the Freiburg Kripo Christmas party. Now she understood. He'd gone undercover in December and was now on secondment to the regional Criminal Investigation Bureau.

"Who are you after?"

"Russians up in Baden-Baden."

"Do they have names? There are loads of Russians in Baden-Baden."

"Forget it," he said. "We'll nab them in a couple of weeks. Until then you're not to even *think* about Russians in Baden-Baden." He smoothed back his straggly hair. "But that's not what this is about."

"So the weapons aren't connected to your case?"

"No."

"How do you know?"

"From my informer."

"Does he know the buyer?"

"No."

"How does he know he's from Freiburg?"

"Because of the number plate. He wrote it down. Or part of it, at least."

"Does he know what the buyer is planning to do with the pistols?"

"No." Kilian turned his head and the light from the hallway fell on his face. For a moment she fancied she could see something in his expression other than exhaustion: fear.

Kilian and fear – this was new too.

"Maybe just someone who collects weapons."

"No," he repeated. A man had ordered the guns by phone and someone else had picked them up. Two pistol buffs? Unlikely. The weapons were needed for something else. And why would you need illegally acquired pistols with silencers?

Louise said nothing. She sensed her thoughts and body getting into gear. Her soul was dragging behind, still sitting on the balcony, remembering a bear of a man who was no longer around. His death last October had silenced the corridors of Freiburg police HQ, and the heart of Kripo had been beating more slowly ever since. In fact it wasn't beating at all anymore, and she wasn't the only one who felt this; lots of her colleagues did too. A large proportion of the organism's energy and strength had emanated from this man who'd always been there, and now was there no longer. Whether you bowed to him or opposed him, the result was the same: the willingness to give it your all.

"Will you deal with it?"

She sighed. "Have you got anything else?"

"No."

"That's not going to be enough for me." She raised her hands, at a loss. "I need to talk to your informant."

Kilian gave the hint of a smile. "Alright then, let's go."

"To Baden-Baden?"

He nodded and put a hand on her arm. For a moment she sensed the intimacy from before, but the fear and exhaustion in his eyes remained. He said they had to be very circumspect, they couldn't put the informer in danger. If he were exposed, his life wouldn't be worth a damn and the entire operation would be wrecked, which would be a disaster for all concerned. "Five minutes, not a second longer. And nobody's to find out you've spoken to him, not the Russians nor our lot."

"OK."

He took his hand away. "Have you got anything to drink?"

"Water."

"That'll do."

He took the glass she'd filled from the tap. His hand was shaking slightly.

When he put it down she came over and gave him a hug. His body felt cold, bony and strangely timid. "You look awful," she said. "You smell awful. Your hair . . . my God."

She heard him breathing; his hands were clenched behind her back. After a while he mumbled, "Only a few more weeks."

"Or months or years."

"So be it, then."

"Want a shower?"

"No time."

In the hallway she turned towards the balcony. The candle had gone out, maybe a draught when she'd opened the door to her apartment. The quirks of fate, she thought. That Kilian should turn up on Rolf Bermann's fiftieth birthday. Six months ago he was on the investigation team and she'd last seen him at Bermann's funeral.

When she reached for her bag Kilian said, "No gun, no police ID. Absolutely no ID."

"Naked, then?" she said, putting the bag back.

"As God created you."

She laughed. "God created me with a police ID, Kilian."

Spas, thermal springs, casino, festival theatre, parks and, of course, Russians since the nineteenth century. Not much more than that came to mind when Louise thought about Baden-Baden. Of the towns in Baden with more than fifty thousand inhabitants, it was one of the few she didn't know. She'd never been here before, not even driven through it.

And a remarkable crime statistic: not a single homicide last year, 2005 – the only district in Baden-Württemberg to record zero. In Freiburg, five times bigger, the corresponding figure was ten.

They'd driven via the A5 but didn't come off until the Rastatt exit, to be on the safe side, then doubled back to approach Baden-Baden from the north. Kilian took labyrinthine detours to end up in one of the posh parts of town and for the last ten minutes they'd been waiting, parked in a quiet little street, beneath the dense foliage of a tree. Behind hedges Louise could see the odd light, but most houses were in darkness – the ladies and gentlemen of the district were already asleep.

"Tell me about the informer," she said.

"Later. I want you to be impartial."

"Tell me about yourself instead."

"Can't do that. Right now I don't exist."

"Not even privately?"

"Especially not privately." He shrugged. "Well, I suppose the holiday wasn't bad."

"Girlfriend?"

"Gone, I think," he said, giving her a fleeting smile. "What about you? Ben?"

"In Potsdam, I think."

"You're not together anymore?"

"He comes down sometimes. We're together then."

Just before midnight a text message pinged.

"We've got to be quick," Kilian said.

*

They walked as quietly as they could between hedges down a narrow, cobbled path that lay in the cold glow of a few streetlamps. After a hundred metres they turned off and headed up a dark slope between lighter gables. Muffled voices from somewhere, Kilian immediately stopped, put an arm around her shoulders and Louise clasped his waist. They kept wandering in silence; she felt his pounding heart and tensed muscles. They took another turning, then Kilian stopped at a head-high garden gate set back in a hedge and hugged her hesitantly.

Ben, Louise thought, closing her eyes. You can come down more often.

But it didn't work. She only loved him when he was here. When he was away she didn't miss him. What she was missing was the great love, the partner for the second half of her life. As if youthful dreams returned when you were in your mid-forties. A bit of hope.

When she heard the hinges of the gate squeak softly she realised they weren't alone. Kilian pulled her into a garden, past a woman dressed in dark clothes who rapidly shut the gate again.

The woman led them along the hedge and away from an elaborately decorated villa beyond trees and shrubs. She stopped by the rear wall of a garden shed and turned around. She could be in her mid-thirties and her face was so bright that even without any light Louise could clearly make out her features.

"Irina," Kilian whispered. "The informer."

As Louise nodded in surprise she felt Irina's hand in hers. A note: the registration number.

"The two last numbers are missing," Irina whispered. "A white Polo or Golf, very clean, how do you say it . . . well looked after." Her breath smelled of alcohol – red wine, perhaps – and espresso. Her voice was breathy; she appeared to have a cold. A classically beautiful woman, 1950s Hollywood, only Russian-style, everything a bit more powerful, more proud, confident.

But frightened, too.

"Ask your questions!"

"The buyer . . ." Louise began.

"Slim, as tall as Alex, no older than thirty-two."

She was about to ask who Alex was but caught herself in time. It must be Kilian. "German?"

"From here. Baden-Württemberg."

"Did he speak in dialect?"

Irina nodded. "Keep asking. Quick!"

"What does he look like?"

Irina put her hands to the sides of her head. "Light, short hair, almost bald, but not completely. Simple man, bit nervous. A . . . courier, not a boss."

"When and where did he pick up the weapons?"

"Yesterday evening, perhaps eleven thirty, in my husband's restaurant in old town: Iwan and Pauline. Already closed, I was doing till, my husband already gone, then he came." A bodyguard had taken the buyer to her husband's head of security, Niko. Few words were exchanged. An envelope full of money was placed on the table, followed by a tightly sealed shoebox containing the pistols that Niko had put in there earlier: a Makarov and a Tokarev, as per the order. The buyer didn't open the box; he just took it and left.

"Ordered by phone?"

"Yes. Beginning April."

"And you don't know who ordered them?"

Irina shook her head; her hands signalled regret. All she knew was that Niko at least knew the caller and must have vouched for him. Otherwise her husband would never have let the deal take place; it wasn't at all lucrative for them. But Niko didn't know the "courier" who'd come to pick up the guns.

Having wandered to the corner of the shed, Kilian now came back and said, "You've got to go back in."

Irina returned his glance, then looked at Louise. "Quick!"

"If Niko knows the caller, surely it means—"

"Not Russian. Not business partner. Niko said to my husband: 'A German acquaintance. You don't know him.'"

The muffled laughter of two men drifted over from the villa. Then a faint buzzing: an electric blind.

"Irina," Kilian urged, his hand on her right arm. Irina placed her left hand on his and took a step back.

"Can you find out who the caller is?"

"How? I cannot ask!"

Before Louise could thank her, Irina had turned away and was heading back to the house.

"Come on," Kilian whispered.

"Do you know Niko?"

Without responding he pushed her towards the gate. His hand remained at her back as if he were trying to ensure she didn't stop.

"So?" she said when they were on the footpath.

A disgruntled sideways glance, then he put a finger to his lips and pulled her along.

When they were back inside the car he said, "He's not called Niko. Just like Irina isn't Irina."

"A 'German acquaintance', Kilian. That must narrow it down."

"Forget it."

"And after you've arrested them?"

"If Niko's still alive then you can interrogate him."

They left Baden-Baden via a different labyrinthine detour and Louise felt she knew a little more about this small town. Now Baden-Baden had a face, a beautiful, pale face full of gentleness and fear.

"Irina and Alex," she said when they were on the motorway.

Kilian didn't react.

"Are you in love with her?"

His eyes flashed at Boni. "Promise me you won't try to contact her. That you won't come here on your own. If you need anything, text me."

"Yes, yes, I promise. Well, are you?"

His focus back on the road, Kilian didn't reply. Awkward and aloof – he'd never been like that in the past. His worry for Irina couldn't explain this alone. Of course, it was also down to the debilitating investigations, working undercover against organised crime, and for months on end. But most of all, Louise thought, it was down to Kilian himself; in his enthusiasm for the job he hadn't been sufficiently equipped to deal with his own mistakes. Six months earlier, a witness whose house he was watching had tried to take her life. The light had been on in her bathroom for three hours, and Kilian did nothing. And why should he have? Who hadn't forgotten to turn off the bathroom light once in a while? The man they were looking for at the time had pulled the witness out of red bathwater, and Kilian said, "I fucked up." And because he was a daredevil he then rushed into the dirtiest job Kripo could offer, to make up for his mistake.

When they were back in Freiburg Louise said, "Let me out in Stühlinger, at Babeuf."

"Didn't you want to go back to your balcony?"

"The bosses are at Babeuf."

"You're taking it seriously then?"

"No idea . . . Yes."

"Good," Kilian said, sounding satisfied.

They were in Egonstrasse and stopped outside Babeuf. Above the door hung a sign saying PRIVATE PARTY. Through the windows, amongst clouds of smoke, were a few faces she knew, a few familiar ones – they seemed to be having a good time. Louise was pleased she hadn't joined in.

"Is it someone's birthday?"

"Rolf's."

"Rolf? Which section?"

"Rolf Bermann."

Kilian gave her a look of astonishment.

"He'd've been fifty today."

He looked away and said, "The candle on the balcony?"

Louise didn't respond. None of his business, she thought. The old Kilian, yes, but not Kilian now; she wasn't going to talk to him about things like this.

"Could you keep my name out of it?"

"We'll see," she said. "Graeve will ask."

"OK. So long as it's just him." When she opened the car door he stroked her hand. "People die. It happens."

"There are people who *shouldn't* die – don't you know that, Kilian?" She got out and bent to look at him with a tired smile. "Yes, I think you do."

Two drunk bosses stinking of cigarette smoke, not something you saw every day, certainly not the distinguished Reinhard Graeve with tie askew and rolled-up sleeves. The other was Leif Enders, who Boni hadn't known long enough to be either surprised or not. He'd arrived in the southwest from Aachen only a week earlier, to succeed Bermann as section head. The bigwigs spent four months looking without really trying, until Louise told Graeve, "There'll never be another Bermann, why don't you just have D11 shut down?"

A week later she heard Enders' name for the first time.

They were standing outside Babeuf, Enders with a beer and a cigarette, while Graeve – tall, slim and visibly peeved – rolled down his sleeves. "Quite a lot of unknowns," he said in a low voice.

Louise nodded impatiently. "That's what it's like."

"A fellow officer with no name. An informant with no name. An organisation with no name. I'm just saying."

"They're not so much trouble when you're sober."

He gave a sour laugh.

"Alcohol, dangerous territory," she said to Enders.

"I know, I've read your file, Frau Bonì." He had a nice voice, warm, slightly hoarse.

"Here in the south we use first names."

"Leif." He blew out smoke. "I don't care what's in it, your file."

"We'll see."

Enders grinned, he jerked his hands and spilled some beer. Louise and Graeve made a swift retreat; Enders kept drinking to avoid any more hazards. There was a pause in the conversation while Graeve was preoccupied with the buttons on his sleeves and Enders with his beer. Louise stared at him, his features, his eyes. Something about this face wasn't right. Something was missing.

The moustache. The head of D11 without a tache – absolutely inconceivable. And he drank differently from Bermann, oblivious to the world, with slightly too much relish.

They huddled together again. "The officer and informant, are they reliable?" Enders asked.

"As far as I can tell."

"What if you're being used?"

Louise shrugged. "I'm not going to rule out the possibility, but I don't think so."

"Where do we go from here, then?" Graeve asked. He was having difficulty doing up his buttons because his jacket was wedged awkwardly between his elbow and ribs. "Half the force is busy with the World Cup. The Dutch are going to be staying in Hinterzarten."

"I only need Natalie for now." Louise took his jacket, laid it over her arm and smoothed it with her hand like a housewife from a 1950s film.

"You have my blessing," Enders said.

Graeve, the Kripo head, was slower, maybe drunker. She sensed he wasn't able to deal with the situation – work matters on an evening like this that had probably got a bit out of hand. His greatest strength was his rationality, which, like the moon's halo, shone in every direction and took account of absolutely everything. At the moment it wasn't up to much; he knew this and it unsettled him. "What is it that you're worried about, Louise? An assassination? A murder?"

"There's no point speculating, boss, not in your state."

"Might be connected to the World Cup," Enders said. "The intelligence services are already warning of attacks."

"We ought to notify Stuttgart, then."

Louise sighed. "Let's start by looking into the owner of the car."

"I want the name of the officer," Graeve said, smoothing down his tie. "You can tell me tomorrow."

"OK. But only you, nobody else." Again she looked at Enders, who reacted calmly, briefly closing his eyes and shrugging. "Nothing against you," she said.

"I won't know the officer, so what would I do with their name?"

"Right," Graeve said, taking his jacket from her arm and slipping it on. "Taxi?" He felt for his mobile.

Louise nodded.

"See you, then," Enders said, heading back into Babeuf.

Graeve ordered the taxi, then asked Boni, "What do you think of him?"

"He's going to have a tough time."

"Give him a chance, will you?"

She couldn't help grinning. A boss who understood her insinuations.

Half past two on Monday morning. The night lay heavily over Annaplatz. Louise glanced at the extinguished candle and went back inside. She began to get undressed, the phone clamped between her ear and shoulder, listening to it ring. She tried again but Ben didn't answer.

2

Natalie, twenty-three-year-old IT expert and aspiring inspector, a happy, hard-working girl who loved life and men, but at eight o'clock every Sunday morning was in a meadow next to the Rhine, patiently shooting arrow after arrow from a simple longbow into straw targets. Louise had gone along once last summer to watch. At nine o'clock she'd fallen asleep in the sun. Natalie had woken her at eleven, a look of utter satisfaction on her face that Louise would never be able to feel.

"Three," Natalie said, putting some printouts on the desk.

Louise took them, got up and grabbed her coat from the back of the chair. Three white Polos or Golfs, fewer than she'd feared. One woman's name, two men's names. One of the men was eighty-four. "Doesn't quite match the description."

"Maybe the informer was mistaken," Natalie said.

"Play around with it a bit. Swap the numbers around, that sort of thing."

"Until we end up with a male owner around thirty years old?" Natalie opened the door and said, "Oh!" Leif Enders was standing there, about to knock. She left and Enders came in. He looked hung-over from the neck up and ten years older than he really was – late forties. But his shirt was pristine white with no creases.

"How many have you got?"

"Three."

"Let's go."

Louise hesitated. "Let's?"

"You and me."

"Here in the south we have a hierarchy. Someone is head of the section – that's you – and the others drive around – meaning me."

"The hierarchies are flattening out," Enders said.

They went down the corridor, its white walls gleaming in the artificial light. In the first few weeks after Bermann's death Louise expected to see him turn the corner every time she wandered through the office. Rolf Bermann was a gloomy face in the neon light, a powerful voice behind half-open office doors, a moustache that twitched menacingly. Not someone who was just not here anymore.

"I'm not a fan of all this team nonsense," she said.

Enders smiled. "Do you want to go on a training course?"

"In team nonsense?"

"Improving social skills, conflict management, dealing with bosses."

She laughed. "Is my reputation that bad?"

"You spread fear and terror." In the car park Enders gave her his keys and pointed to a silver Daimler. "You drive – residual alcohol."

They got in, Louise started the engine, wound down the window and said, "If you ever stink of booze again I won't travel in the same car as you."

Marie Heim, resident of Merzhausen, not at home. "Marie and Nina Heim" read the nameplate above the bell. Nina's the baby, the caretaker said and gave them the name of a travel agency in the centre. They drove back into town. In the company car park they found a white Polo, although Louise thought it looked neglected rather than clean and looked after. After Enders had taken some photos they went in. Although they hadn't agreed on an approach, Louise sensed he wouldn't stick his oar in. He didn't want to control her, didn't want to make his mark; he just wanted to be there, for whatever reason.

Marie Heim was thin and looked pale and completely exhausted. She sat in front of her computer with one hand on the tummy of the baby sleeping next to her chair in a carrier. When Louise introduced herself and Enders, Marie got up quickly and stood bent so as not to have to take her hand away from Nina. A breath of wind would have made her sway.

Louise asked her questions, probed. On the evening in question Marie said she'd driven the Polo to her brother's in Lahr.

"Sweet," Enders said, pointing at the baby.

"Yes," Louise said. "Very sweet."

Marie Heim nodded, aghast.

Outside Enders called the Lahr station and had officers sent to her brother's house.

They waited in the sunshine.

"Fear and terror, did you say?"

"Admiration too, on occasion." He laughed.

During all those years Bermann had reacted to her a bit like this. In terrified admiration.

Enders' telephone rang. Confirmation from Lahr.

"Now there are only two," he said.

Friedrich Krüger, the eighty-four-year-old, lived in a small, smoke-filled two-bedroom flat in the Haslach Estate, nine two-storey blocks in south Freiburg, built in 1962 by the American Economic Cooperation Administration with Marshall Plan funds and long since in need of refurbishment. Louise thought Krüger's ground-floor flat was strikingly neat and tidy, as if he'd set all of his strength against the gradual decline of his surroundings. But he hadn't been able to improve the material substance – the windows let in draughts, the whiff of mould hung in the air, and voices and noises from other flats could be clearly heard.

Krüger had grumpily shown them into the sitting toom. The over-head light was on; outside a sprawling bush in front of one of the two windows let in virtually no light. The furnishings were those of an unassuming, indifferent old person: functional, vaguely coordinated, from different periods. On the walls were faded reproductions of landscape paintings, while shelves housed many photos indicating a different time and a woman who probably no longer existed.

"*Where* am I supposed to have been?" Krüger sounded angry; his cheeks were red. He was tallish, his hair slicked back, light-blue shirt, beige cardigan.

Enders held up his hands to placate the old man. "It was just a question, not an allegation."

"Baden-Baden," Bonì said. "Saturday night around eleven, half eleven."

"And what exactly are you implying I did?"

Enders sighed. "Nothing, Herr Krüger."

Staring into the distance, Krüger took a packet of cigarettes from the breast pocket of his shirt, lit one and made them wait. The fingertips on his right hand were stained brownish-yellow, and there were yellow patches on his white hair and face too, whether from smoking or not. "I play skat on Saturday evenings."

"With friends?" Louise asked.

"You don't play skat on your own."

"Here?"

"Of course not here," Krüger said, pointing a finger at here. "Do you really think I'd invite friends to this shabby estate that the reds are allowing to fall into disrepair so that they can pull the whole lot down and sell off the land at a price?"

"It's a nice flat you've got though," Enders said.

"Did you drive there?"

"How else would I get to Zähringen? Walk?"

"We need a name and a phone number."

Enders made a vague hand movement. "Clean and nicely laid out, probably not too expensive—"

"Every penny we spend on living here is one too many."

"Herr Krüger," Boni said.

"These stoves – cost me a fortune!" He pointed his finger again, ash fell onto the carpet without Krüger realising. "If you leave me in peace I'll give you a name and a phone number, but it's under protest. It's an *outrage* that you're going to pester my friends!"

"Who's J. Krüger?" Enders asked.

"My son."

"Does he live above you?"

"As you were able to see from the nameplate, yes. With his wife and my grandson."

"Is your car in the garage?" Louise said.

"I can't afford a garage." Krüger went into the hall. Louise heard him make a call, telling a "Herbert" that the police were going to be calling him and apologising for the bother.

Soon afterwards the door to the flat closed behind them.

By the side of the road was a white Golf, as well looked after as the flat.

When they were back in the car Enders called the number. Herbert confirmed what Herr Krüger had said: a game of skat in Zähringen on Saturday until midnight.

They drove slowly along the yellow buildings of the estate that were set at an angle to the road. The balconies were dark honeycombs, one of the awnings had half of its material missing and render was crumbling from the bottoms of the walls. The garage doors were made of wood and the area in front of them wasn't tarmacked. Weeds and bushes grew everywhere. Lots of parched grassy areas, and on one of them a group of black boys were playing football. Like all Freiburg officers, Boni came here occasionally as the police academy was on the other side of the road. Bermann's second home, where he used to work out in the gym whenever he had a free moment, and take the little rooms by the hour for rendezvous with his blondes.

Ben had once taught at the academy.

Ben who hadn't rung back. Who had gone away in a very different manner from Bermann, but away all the same.

"Krüger's staying on our list," Enders said.

"Absolutely," Louise replied.

Twenty minutes later they were in the hallway of an expensive period apartment in Herdern, talking to the wife of the owner of the third car, who was in Stuttgart on business. At the weekend he'd been on business in Wuppertal and wouldn't be back until Thursday because he had to go on to Heidelberg and Munich.

"What does he do?" Enders asked.

"He's a salesman." The wife, a plump, pretty woman, red in the face from cooking, cocked her head. "Insurance policies."

"Who would be able to confirm he was in Wuppertal on Saturday evening?"

"Quite a few people, I'm sure."

"Do you have an address? A contact?"

"For a woman, you mean? No."

While Enders jotted down the husband's mobile number, Louise peered through open doors into bright rooms with tall ceilings. The dining room was set for two: white placemats, champagne flutes, flowers.

Having noticed Boni's gaze, the woman smiled. She had a contact too.

On the stairs Louise said, "We can cross him off our list."

"They're cheating on each other. Maybe he plans to shoot her. Or she him."

"With two pistols?"

They laughed.

"What now?" Enders asked when they were back out on the street.

"Herbert in Zähringen."

"Do you doubt Krüger's alibi?"

"His car was in Baden-Baden on Saturday night. With or without him."

When they were back in the car Enders' phone rang. A brief conversation, then he said, "Shit, I forgot," and put his mobile away.

"Correct," Louise said. "Every Monday at noon. The section heads, their deputies and the boss."

"A tip-off would've been nice."

"If the bus comes soon you'll make it in time."

Enders laughed, rubbed his eyes and shook his head.

She pulled over by the bus stop and he got out. "Bye, then."

"Get back in," she said, smiling. "It's on the way."

Herbert, surname Nickel, was two years older than Friedrich Krüger and in a wheelchair. A slim, simple man who spoke softly in short sentences, and whenever he didn't say enough his wife filled in for him.

The three of them were sitting at the kitchen table, each with a glass of water.

"More like a quarter to twelve," Nickel's wife said.

"Do you play too?"

"Oh no, no."

"Ewald does," Nickel said, pointing at the kitchen wall. "Ewald next door."

"But he went away yesterday. He's still young and likes to travel."

"Ewald, Fritz and me," Nickel said. "Almost every Saturday for the past fifteen years, from seven till midnight."

"At eight o'clock I bring them a few sandwiches and beers."

Louise took a sip. "Did Friedrich Krüger come by car?"

"He always comes by car."

"He does live a long way away," Nickel's wife explained.

"Does he drive himself?"

"He always says he'll keep driving until they lay him in his grave."

She smiled.

"Did you see him arrive by car on Saturday evening?"

"No, no I didn't," Nickel replied.

"But he spent the evening here?"

"Yes." His hands lay lifeless in his lap. The man as a whole looked lifeless apart from his face and head. Catching Boni gazing at him, he misinterpreted her look. "War wound."

"More a postwar wound," his wife said. "An accident in the camp at Ulyanovsk. 1947. Don't ask."

"No," Nickel said. "Don't ask."

"They left him lying injured for three days."

Nickel's hands started moving. "Maybe you'd like to talk to Ewald too? I've got a mobile number."

"No," Louise said, getting to her feet. "Thanks."

Rather than go straight back to the car she walked a little in the shade of tall trees. She felt calm, a hint of serenity – this was new. However painful she found Bermann's death, without him the time of struggles was over. She didn't have to prove anything to anyone anymore, convince anyone. She did what she had to and nobody was going to stop her, not Graeve, not Enders; both trusted her judgment.

Apart from that she was now the bedrock of D11.

Crossing the road, she stopped and held her face to the sun as she waited for the phone to connect. "Found another one?"

"No," Natalie said. "Just the three."

"Check the taxi firms. Saturday evening, half six there, back shortly after midnight." She gave Krüger's address in Haslach and Herbert Nickel's in Zähringen to Natalie, then waited, her eyes half closed, feeling the warmth creep into her cheeks, her bones. Louise thought of Irina, the woman in the dark in Baden-Baden, who was so brave. She thought of Kilian, who she couldn't help worrying about because he thought he had to atone for his carelessness. How heavily the past weighed if you allowed it to.

But who knew that better than she did?

Let go, she thought. It's worth it.

In her mind she pictured Friedrich Krüger, whose flat was dominated by the past. Maybe there wasn't much else for old people without partners. Lost in the present, the future dismal. And so they dragged along everything that was in the past – photographs, dead people, memories, furniture, better worlds. Memories.

Did guns fit the picture?

A Makarov, a Tokarev, both with silencers, both from Russia. According to Irina the caller had specifically asked for these two models. Boni didn't think he was a collector. Whoever wanted to use the pistols had experience with them and had ordered them for that very reason.

Did Friedrich Krüger have experience with a Makarov and a Tokarev?

She thought of Enders' question. Was she being used? She couldn't imagine that Kilian was manipulating her. On the other hand he *had* changed. Who knew what had happened to him since he'd fallen into the abyss? Or what Irina had in mind? She had to talk to him again.

Natalie called back.

Friedrich Krüger had taken a taxi to his game of skat.

3

This time Krüger didn't let her into the flat, but made her wait outside the door. His pupils were unmoving black stones, his voice sharp, a man full of hatred for women, police officers, the world and maybe for himself too. "Do you really have nothing better to do? No wonder this country is going to the dogs."

"Why the taxi, Herr Krüger?"

"None of your business!"

"If you don't talk to me here then you'll have to in an interrogation room at police HQ, with a lawyer if you like."

Leaning towards her, he hissed, "I have arrhythmia from time to time, happy now?"

"Like last Saturday?"

He gave the hint of a nod.

"Why didn't you cancel?"

"I haven't missed an evening in fifteen years. When it's over, it doesn't matter where I am."

"Why didn't you mention the taxi earlier?"

"Because it's not important, for God's sake!"

"Could anyone else have used your car?"

"Who would have done that?"

"Your son? His wife?"

"My son's got his own car."

"I'm assuming he has a key to your flat?"

"Of course."

"Is he at home?"

"Are you going to harass more people? Waste more time?"

"Where is he, Herr Krüger?"

"At his gardening business," Krüger said, shutting the door.

A polystyrene box of curry on her lap, Boni sat on a bench in Wiehre, opposite Julius Krüger Garden Centre, and watched. A gravelled area served as a car park, beyond which stood a long, narrow building with a flat roof and side walls of glass. A few vehicles were parked there, including two green delivery vans inscribed KRÜGER – FOR HOUSE AND GARDEN, surrounded by colourful flowers. The garden centre wasn't far from Annaplatz; she'd been here a few times in summer to buy a random selection of plants because she thought the apartment of a normal woman in a normal relationship and thus a normal future ought to have plants.

If there's one thing you're not, it's normal, Ben had said.

That's going to change now, she replied.

Bermann's death had got in the way.

She couldn't deal with death.

Leif Enders called. "He took a taxi, then?"

"Of course," she said, her mouth full. "The car was in Baden-Baden, wasn't it?"

"Where are you?"

She gave the address.

"Stay there, I'm on my way."

Opposite her, one of the delivery vans left the car park, a woman in green at the wheel. A short-legged brown dog came scurrying out of the garden centre, barked at the van or the woman, then ran back in.

Ten minutes later Enders arrived in the back of a patrol car. He told her that Natalie had called the insurance salesman and got a number in Wuppertal, a woman . . . a "client". He did indeed have an alibi, as did the car. Louise nodded apathetically; she'd already crossed the insurance salesman off the list. "Has she run a check on Julius?"

"Not even a parking ticket. She's still looking."

"What about the father?"

"He's eighty-four, he was playing skat, Louise."

"You're too gullible. How do you get to be section head if you're so gullible?"

"Not a problem in Freiburg."

They laughed.

Louise called Natalie and asked her to check if the father had links to the Russians, the Stasi or the East German army. The internet told her that Tokarevs and Makarovs were both used by soldiers in the GDR. "And check the traffic control camera footage."

They crossed the road. "How does that work – moving from North-Rhein Westphalia to head up a section here in the south?" Each German state had its own police force; changing from one to another was unusual and quite complicated.

"They couldn't find anyone."

"Are you being serious? Nobody wanted to come to Freiburg?"

"Nobody who wanted to succeed Rolf Bermann. You come to sunny Freiburg and find yourself standing in a huge shadow."

"Doesn't seem to have put you off."

"That's right," Enders said.

They crossed the car park and went into the Garden Centre. Enders spoke to a young cashier, who pointed at a thin, medium-height man in a green apron standing by a table near the entrance, absorbed in pinching out leaves and arranging white cut flowers. When he looked up Louise noticed a faint similarity with the father, his eyes just as fixed and piercing. But then Julius Krüger snapped out of it, turned to them with a suave smile, and the similarity evaporated.

He knew who they were and why they were here; his father had notified him. "I have to apologise for him," he said quietly. "Sometimes he can be a bit . . . short with people." He'd thrust his hands into his apron pocket, the thumbs still outside, his back was slightly rounded – a shy, introverted man who came across as even more inconspicuous beside the virile Leif Enders.

The dog, a terrier, came trotting over, jumped up at Julius' leg and was given something from his pocket. As he watched it go, Julius seemed to withdraw into himself. Absent-mindedly he said, "No doubt you're here because of the car. My father's car?"

"Yes," Boni said.

He looked at Enders. "But how come his car ended up in Basel if he—"

"Not Basel," she interrupted him. "Baden-Baden."

Julius shot her a glance, then looked back at Enders, as if the latter were his natural ally even though he still hadn't said a word. "I can't explain that."

"You didn't use it?" Louise asked.

"I haven't driven it recently, not for weeks, I'd say. Months, even."

"Saturday evening?"

"No. We had people over on Saturday evening. Friends from Staufen." Julius' eyes and hands wandered to the flowers, and Louise caught the fleeting shadow of an unpleasant memory. But as she'd done quite a good job of setting her memory to suppression mode, she didn't recall the name of the flowers or the circumstances.

"You were there the whole time?"

"Absolutely."

"Who took the dog out?" Enders asked.

Julius looked up and fixed his eyes on him. "Me. I always go out at night. You never know who might be hanging around."

"How long were you out for?"

"Not long, fifteen minutes. Maybe only ten."

"Not long because of your friends from Staufen?" Louise said.

"More acquaintances than friends."

"So you *weren't* there the whole time."

"If you say so . . . I was out for ten minutes. But you can't get to Baden-Baden in ten minutes, can you?" He grinned, and Louise caught herself being rather taken by this grin. There was something boyish about it, innocent, but at the same time bold. A quiet, shy boy who once a year summoned up the courage to tell a joke in the playground.

"Not without losing your licence, that's for sure," Enders said.

Julius gave a subdued laugh.

"Look at me," Louise said, and he obeyed, looking at her mouth – clearly he couldn't do the eyes. "Did someone else drive your father's car, by any chance?"

"Who would that have been?" His voice had faintly softened.

"Another friend?"

"Acquaintances, in truth they're more like acquaintances . . . I don't know. I didn't look to see if the car was there." Julius turned away, tenderly stroking the leaves on the flower stems.

"Chrysanthemums," Louise said, unable to suppress a sigh. A memory of the ex-husband she'd booted out, a husband who was not only fond of submissive lovers, but flowers too, especially chrysanthemums. Around the turn of the millennium he'd dragged Louise along to the "Chrysanthema" in Lahr three years in a row, to decorate her like a trophy with colourful flowers and turn their long-defiled apartment into a fake, fraught idyll.

"The Japanese emperor's flowers," Julius said.

"That's hard to believe."

He nodded. "The imperial seal is a golden chrysanthemum flower."

"The chrysanthemum throne," Enders chipped in.

"The things you two know . . ." Boni said.

"Sun and immortality," Julius said. "Pure, simple and perfect."

"We need the names of your friends from Staufen, Herr Krüger."

"Acquaintances," Enders corrected her gently.

*

Good cop, bad cop, Louise thought on the way back to the car. Silly, but why not? All she found disconcerting was that their individual roles seemed to have been fixed without any prior agreement.

Each doing what they did best.

They drove off. In the rear-view mirror Louise saw the terrier barking at them from the path. Enders said he used to have contact with lots of Russians back in Berlin. He'd make a few calls. Perhaps someone had heard something. Louise nodded, surprised to realise that she was content. They thought along similar lines, she and the new boss. Irina and the Russians in Baden-Baden, two Russian pistols, a Russian prisoner-of-war – too much Russia not to follow the trail.

"What do you think?" Enders said. "Julius like Caesar?"

She shrugged. "Leber was called Julius too."

"Leber?"

"In the resistance against the Nazis."

He turned towards her, and out of the corner of her eye she saw bright teeth and laugh lines. "The things you know."

"Bedtime stories my mother told me."

"Instead of Winnie-the-Pooh you had Julius Leber and . . . what's his name . . . Stauffenberg?"

"Him too, but mainly women. Hanna Solf, Elisabeth von Thaden, and so on."

"Never heard of them."

"Anne Frank, Sophie Scholl."

"Yes, of course . . . Inspiring stories, why not?"

"Until the end."

"Read *Winnie-the-Pooh*, nobody dies."

"I'd be missing something," Louise said.

4

Natalie had news. Photographs, a name.

They were standing around her desk – Louise, Enders, Natalie – focusing on black-and-white printouts of four photos, stills from traffic cameras. The date stamp was the same on each: Saturday. All four showed Friedrich Krüger's white Golf, clearly identifiable from the number plate. Julius Krüger was behind the wheel in two of the pictures; a different man in the other two.

"Ricky Janisch," Natalie said, placing a police photograph on the table. "No previous, but a provisional arrest two years ago for assault. There wasn't enough evidence for a conviction."

Louise turned the photo around. Janisch was in his early thirties, pale, gaunt face, stubbly fair hair. Pointy chin, open mouth revealing crooked teeth, and eyes slanting slightly towards the bridge of his nose. She thought of Irina's description: a courier, not a boss.

She took a photo with her phone and sent it to Kilian with the words: *Is this the courier?*

Then she turned back to the images and ran through the chronology once more.

21.32: Krüger drives along Basler Strasse.

21.33: Krüger at the lights at the corner of Eschholzstrasse. A dog's head is visible behind him.

21.40: Ricky Janisch turns onto the B31a from Eschholzstrasse, heading for the motorway – alone.

21.47: Janisch a few kilometres further west on the B31a, still alone.

Julius must have brought Ricky Janisch his father's car, having said he was taking the dog for a walk.

"Any more photos of Janisch and the car?"

"I'm working on it," Natalie said.

"The A5, Baden-Baden. 'Iwan and Pauline' in the old town. Basler Strasse a few hours later. He must have brought the car back at some point."

Nodding, Natalie made notes.

"What else do we know about Janisch?" Enders asked.

"He's thirty-one, was born in Lörrach and has been living in Freiburg for two years. Mats Benedikt will be here in a minute, he can tell you more."

"Mats Benedikt?"

"A colleague from D13," Louise explained, slightly surprised. Assault wasn't enough to get the department for national security involved. There must be more to this.

"Organised crime?" Enders said.

"No, that's D23. D13 is national security. Natalie, what's national security got to do with Janisch?"

Her phone vibrated. Kilian's answer: *I'll be in touch.*

There was a knock at the door, Mats Benedikt came in, nodded to the group and shook Enders' hand. As ever, his soft brown eyes looked focused behind his glasses.

"Ricky Janisch," Louise said.

Mats Benedikt handed out sheets of paper. "A member of the 'Southwest Brigade'. Two dozen right-wing extremists from the Breisgau area, including a few women. Prepared to use violence, but they hold themselves back, don't draw attention to themselves, at least most of the time."

They looked at the information on Janisch, the assault in August 2004, while Mats Benedikt gave a summary. "A comrade from the Brigade wanted to leave. They beat him up, hit him with metal bars, breaking his arms and legs. But as they were wearing masks he wasn't able to identify them with absolute certainty." He did think he recognised Janisch's voice, which was why Janisch was arrested. But the magistrate released him the following day after other members of the Brigade confirmed his alibi.

"For those of us a little slow on the uptake," Louise said, "Ricky Janisch, the guy in the photos, is he a neo-Nazi?"

"One hundred per cent," Benedikt said.

D11 was a hive of activity. Graeve was called, informed, then he left. Marianne Andrele, the public prosecutor, swept through the corridors and offices, with Freiburg's chief of police, Hubert Vormweg, in tow. Neo-Nazis planning an attack in "green" left-wing Freiburg? Before or during the World Cup? It was hard to think of anything worse.

An eight-strong investigation team was assembled around Bonì, Leif Enders and Natalie, including Mats Benedikt. Surveillance squads were briefed – for now the Krügers and Ricky Janisch were to be kept under observation only, and not confronted with the photographs yet. A colleague was to be sent to Dortmund, where two Turks had been shot dead in early April, probably further murders by the Česká killer. He would go on to Nuremberg, headquarters of the "Bosphorus" task force leading the investigation into these racist killings. Enders disappeared into the hurricane of commotion. Natalie sat at her computer, searching the internet for clues as to potential victims. Every half an hour she gave Louise names, dates and threats. Non-white footballers. Homosexuals. Politicians with migrant backgrounds. Greens. Feminists. Former neo-Nazis. No, Louise kept saying, maybe, no, no idea, what do I know?

The afternoon passed and Bonì waited without knowing what she was waiting for.

Enders popped in and remarked, "You southerners are a bit hysterical."

44

"Not me. I'm calmness personified."

"The calm before the storm."

She smiled. "Go and have a beer, Leif."

"I've got to go upstairs. Conference call with the regional police authority."

"What are you going to tell them? We don't have anything."

"They're going to tell *us* something."

Enders left, Natalie arrived and put some pieces of paper in front of her. Names, faces, clues.

"Stop," Boni said.

"Stop what?"

Louise pointed at the printouts. The needle in a haystack. Everything else was more important now. Especially the Krügers and Janisch. Once they knew everything about those three and what connected them, the haystack would shrink and the needle would begin to shine.

"Another half an hour," Natalie said. "Then I'm going."

"Yes," Louise said. She put the names, faces and clues onto the pile of "potential victims".

She waited, still unaware what she was waiting for.

Shortly after six o'clock Natalie came back, already in her coat and scarf, with a fresh spray of perfume, her dark-blonde plait undone and hair brushed. "It's getting gruesome," she said, putting another sheet of paper on the desk.

Boni pulled the printout towards her. A newspaper article, in the centre of which was a faintly blurred photograph of a pale Friedrich Krüger wearing a grim expression. The headline: AUSCHWITZ KILLER IN FREIBURG?

She read on.

Krüger joined the SS in 1940 as an eighteen-year-old. From mid-1943 to the end of 1944 he served as a guard in Auschwitz. In the summer of 2002 he was arrested, suspected of having been involved in the murder of some of those deported there. On health grounds he was released from custody the following day. His case never came to trial; the public prosecutor abandoned proceedings due to a lack of evidence and witnesses. Krüger himself had denied the charges.

Nazis and neo-Nazis, Louise thought, leaning back and putting her hands in her lap. "Is there any connection between Janisch and the Krügers besides the car? Activities in common? Friends in common? *Comrades?*"

"I haven't found anything online."

"Keep searching."

"Please, no more today."

"Are you meeting someone?"

Natalie nodded and swept her hair from her forehead.

"Tell me more."

"No." She smiled her girl's smile and cocked her head, looking enchantingly sweet. "You're work."

"And seventeen paygrades above you. Tell me more!"

They laughed.

Work, Louise thought once Natalie had closed the door behind her. Work, and anything else?

No. She was work and vice-versa, nothing else. She'd never been able to do it any other way, nor had she wanted to. Wherever she went, work came with her. It was in her, it was what she saw, thought and felt.

From the very beginning, since 1983. The year when her first brother Germain hurtled to his death in a car on an icy French motorway.

Were the two things connected. Had she become a policewoman because of Germain's death?

She dismissed the thought, shut down her computer and got her coat. In the corridor Enders was tapping something into his phone. His white shirt was creased, as was his face. There were sweat patches in his armpits.

"What's Stuttgart saying?"

"We shouldn't focus on the neo-Nazis too soon, we should consider other possibilities too."

"I'd like nothing more. Shall we go for a drink? On me."

He shook his head. "I've got to see the chief upstairs, then I'm meeting a friend for a beer."

"You've got friends here already? After only a week?"

He gave a faint smile, then wiped his phone screen on his sleeve. "A schoolfriend from Aachen, Wolfgang. He's been living here for a few years."

Louise put on her coat. Death and lies, she thought. Nobody was going to pull the wool over her eyes. "Rubbish."

"What do you mean, rubbish?"

"Wolfgang from Aachen, don't make me laugh."

With a grin, Enders pointed a finger upwards.

Outside, in the gentle rain, she realised what she'd been waiting for all afternoon: Rolf Bermann to turn up and give orders she could disobey.

How simple things were sometimes.

Kilian came at four in the morning. In a T-shirt and shorts she stood facing him in the dark kitchen, unable to hide her grumpiness – he'd dragged her out of a deep sleep. "Things need to change," she said. "This is getting on my nerves."

He smiled joylessly. "Stop asking questions, then." He looked even worse than he had on Sunday evening, utterly shattered, his eyes black hollows. He was blinking with tiredness and stank of alcohol.

"You need to get some sleep, Kilian."

"Maybe tomorrow."

"Have a lie-down on the sofa. Just a couple of hours. I'll wake you at six."

He shook his head. "I've got stuff to do." He moved his lips to her ear. "She says it's him."

"Sure?" Louise whispered back.

"Ninety per cent, the photo isn't completely sharp."

"Ricky Janisch, a Freiburg neo-Nazi."

They were silent for a moment, then Kilian said, "But that doesn't necessarily mean anything at this stage, does it? Maybe he needs money. Does a bit of this, a bit of that. Weapons, drugs, girls for some client."

"It can mean everything. Amongst your Russians are there any neo—"

"Yes," he said, interrupting her. "But that's irrelevant."

"How can you be so sure?"

Because, Kilian replied, they'd been onto the Russians for months, bugging them, observing them. If there were a connection, they'd know about it. "Leave the Russians alone, OK? If they get wind of anything we'll have a big problem on our hands."

She nodded wearily. Suggestions, pleas from all sides. Not the Russians, Kilian was saying. Not just the neo-Nazis, Stuttgart was saying. She thought of Leif Enders who wanted to contact Russian sources. She had to make him swear to be careful.

"Do you know who he's got in his sights? Janisch?"

"No. If you hear anything from the Russian neo-Nazis . . ."

"Sure." Kilian made to leave. In the hall he said he'd be away for the next few days, possibly uncontactable. Then he left. Louise gazed at the dark stairwell and heard only the occasional scraping of his shoes, and finally a click as the front door closed behind him.

She went back to bed but couldn't sleep, because she was thinking of Ben who hadn't been in touch. Ben Liebermann, this is hanging by a thread, can't you see that? In a long-distance relationship you have to be close to each other, otherwise the distance becomes too great and you can't find the way back.

A few months earlier they'd still been chatting about the future. Since Potsdam there hadn't been a future anymore, just a past and the occasional bit of present.

She got up and dressed. Half past four, the first signs of light in the east, rainy light, the perfect moment to break rank and go her own way.

5

Zähringen, Alban-Stolz-Strasse, tower blocks. Louise parked between the railway line and the estate. "I'm here," she said into her phone. "The red Peugeot outside number 21."

Two minutes later a shadow appeared by the passenger door, one of the two surveillance officers. Gerd was in his mid-fifties, short and round, spent the nights in dark streets as he edged towards retirement and didn't like being disturbed. He dropped onto the seat beside her and closed the door almost silently. With a sigh, he said, "For heaven's sake, Boni." His breath smelled of coffee, beer, onions and cigarette smoke. "It's five in the morning. What are you doing here?"

She gave him a friendly smile. "Which flat?"

"Number 23, seventh floor, far right."

Boni leaned forwards but couldn't see much of the building, only the rectangles of balconies and loggias that were painted white. "Tell me more."

"There's nothing to say," Gerd said.

"Then tell me what there isn't to say."

She heard him giggle. Janisch, he said, had come home around 4.30 p.m. At seven he'd gone to a nearby pizzeria to meet a friend who they hadn't yet managed to identify. They went on to a pub and around half past eleven he walked home, clearly having had a few.

"Did he give the friend anything? A box? Anything else?"

"No."

"Have you got photos?"

"In the car."

She gave him her e-mail address and Gerd promised to "send the photos over".

"Is the friend a neo-Nazi too?"

"More like a lefty. Black hoodie, baseball cap, trainers. Antifa."

"That's how the Autonomous Nationalists dress," she said.

"The who?"

She told him about the "Free Fellowships", small groups of independent neo-Nazis who'd been gaining in popularity since the end of the nineties, especially in cities. The Autonomous Nationalists emerged from these in the early 2000s, and they'd been in Baden-Württemberg since 2005. There were no skinheads and they weren't in tightly organised squads, but they were extremely violent. Having adopted the appearance and initiatives of radical Antifa, they came across as young and cool. Imitating their opponents prevented them from being identified so easily by the enemy; they no longer stuck out.

"No, no," Gerd said, rubbing his eyes as he spoke. "A radical leftist. That's the problem here, Boni: Antifa. The far right don't dare come to Freiburg. The moment a fascist shows their face in public, their name, picture and address are on the internet. Are you trying to tell me there's now two neo-Nazis in the same restaurant in *Freiburg*? No, you're seeing ghosts. Our problem is Antifa, not the far right."

Louise simply nodded; she didn't want a discussion, not with Gerd who no longer had anyone at home to discuss these things with, who sometimes couldn't be stopped. His wife had left him some time ago, supposedly to shack up with a colleague from the Criminal Investigation Bureau – it must have been a Kripo officer. The children had moved out long ago, leaving only a budgie. In summer Bermann had seen Gerd sitting on a bench in the Seepark, a cage with the chirping budgie beside him.

"You're seeing ghosts," he repeated softly.

Yes, she thought, occasionally that's true. Demons sometimes too.

They lurked in the supermarket, in bottles of amber-coloured liquid, crying out, "Drink, drink, drink!" They still lay in wait, three years since her last mouthful. "When does Janisch start work?"

"Half six, according to DHL. Sorting and loading. He sets off in the van around eight, half eight."

"Up in Hochdorf?"

Gerd nodded, then tapped his finger on the windscreen. "Light."

She leaned forwards again. The window of Janisch's flat was lit up. Seconds later the light went on in the room next door. Frosted glass: the bathroom.

"You should go," Gerd said. "To be on the safe side."

Boni gave a brief shake of the head. "I'll watch him now. You go home."

Gerd frowned. "This is *our* job, Boni, and we're good at it. I've been with Surveillance for five years and Marek for nine. You focus on Antifa, they're planning something, I'd put money on it. Sending some neo-Nazi muppet to Baden-Baden to get weapons, then in June they'll look to bump off some FIFA official or someone like that. That's why you should be focusing on them, not on that guy up there," he said, pointing to the building. "We've got our eye on him."

"I'm staying," she said.

"Oh well, it's your responsibility. Let's drive in convoy." With a faint grunt he climbed out of the car as quietly as he'd got in, each movement controlled and without any unnecessary noise, despite the tummy. Once out he became a shadow again, blending with objects, walls, the night, only detectable from the glow of a cigarette that flared briefly.

Five minutes later the photographs arrived, a selection, thirteen in total. Janisch entering and leaving the building. Janisch in the drizzle outside the tower blocks, dark jacket, chunky shoes, probably boots, meant to look soldierly, masculine, but the overall impression contradicted this – he walked with a slight stoop, hands in his jacket pockets, and had spindly legs.

Janisch in the pizzeria, his friend already waiting, the two of them high-fiving. The other man as per Gerd's description, plus colourful tattoos on his arms, goatee, and black gloves sticking out of his back trouser pocket. They ate, chatted, laughed and drank beer.

Janisch and his friend in an empty pub on the corner, just one blurred photo; clearly the risk of being seen taking the picture had been too great. In the last photo, which showed the two men parting company outside the pub, Louise recognised on the friend's lapel a sticker with a black rim and two black flags on a white background. An Antifa logo originally. But one of the Antifa flags was red. Two black flags inside a black circle: a symbol of the Autonomous Nationalists.

She put her phone down and leaned back.

Janisch with the "Southwest Brigade", the friend an AN sympathiser at least, Friedrich Krüger in the SS – too many right-wing extremists to be a coincidence.

6

A long, boring morning. Ricky Janisch drove around western Freiburg, delivering package after package in the rain, his coat red with yellow shoulders and sleeves, yellow baseball cap turned back to front. The odd cigarette break, three coffee breaks with take-away cups behind the wheel, sometimes tapping on his phone, once taking a call. Nothing else happened.

Gerd texted to say she was behaving as obtrusively as a hippo-potamus. *Your fault if he notices something.*

She didn't reply but dropped back slightly. The surveillance officer's silver car momentarily disappeared into the mist. Further ahead a yellow dot shot away, then braked hard. The rear doors flew open, a heavily laden Janisch leaped onto the street and into the entrance of a building.

Enders called. "Is there any point in this?"

"I don't know yet." She heard him breathe, clear his throat; his beautiful voice remained silent. So this was Enders' way of waiting for an explanation. "It was just an idea. A gut feeling."

"Let me get this right. At half past four in the morning your gut feeling says: Two surveillance officers aren't enough, I'll go and do it myself, sod the office, the paperwork and everything else – there'll be a point to it in the end?"

"Yes," she said, taken aback. "You've summarised it well."

He laughed. "Let me know next time."

The rain had become heavier; the drops were loud as they hit the roof and windscreen. "The informer confirmed that Janisch is the courier," Louise said.

"About that," Enders said. "Stuttgart wants names. I suspect this is coming from the Ministry of the Interior. They want to know who the officer and the informant are. Graeve's been stalling, but I don't know how much longer that's going to work."

Louise felt anger well inside her, but also a touch of fear. Things were threatening to get out of hand. "He won't tell them, he knows he can't do that."

"They'll put the pressure on, first him, then you."

"We'll stick it out." The yellow van drove on, the silver car behind, and she followed mechanically. She was troubled by an unpleasant thought and before she could hold herself back, she said, "What about you?"

"But I don't know anything."

"That's not what I mean."

After a long pause he said coolly, "Are you seriously doubting my loyalty?"

"Your loyalty to who?"

"Graeve and you. My colleagues here."

"I'm just asking the question. They'll put pressure on you too."

"Kiss my arse!" He'd already hung up when, startled, she began to laugh. A phrase from her skirmishes with Rolf Bermann, although it had been *her* phrase, and Bermann's perennial response: *Not in a million years.*

At midday Janisch took a lunch break. The transporter van was parked by the side of the road in a sleepy residential area; the surveillance officers had reversed into a space thirty metres away. Louise drove past them and Janisch too. In the rear-view mirror she saw him sitting in the driver's cab, arms resting on the wheel, holding a huge sandwich in both hands. His head hovered over his lunch, black leads dangling from his ears.

Just before the next junction she found a parking spot.

Are you out of your mind? Gerd texted her.

Bonì got out and hurried beneath an umbrella into a side street. Opposite was a bakery with tall tables by the fogged-up window. She was met by a steamy warmth.

Louise hurriedly ate a focaccia. She didn't see the yellow van.

Her phone rang: Natalie.

A dozen further potential victims, of which two were Natalie's "favourites". "A left-wing activist from Berlin, black bloc, 1 May, that sort of thing. There's going to be an Antifa gathering here tomorrow."

Louise wiped her mouth with the back of her hand and stifled her impatience. "How's that going to help, Natalie?"

"Graeve said Cords wants me to keep going."

"Cords" was the affectionate rather than disrespectful nickname of Hubert Vormweg, chief of Freiburg police. He was a mild-mannered Swabian and old 68er, who was hardly ever *not* dressed in corduroy, owning suits in every conceivable shade of brown. Even his ties were cord. "Anyway," Louise said, "how was your date?"

Natalie laughed. "The other one is a gay Green politician from Bremen with a Turkish background. Next week he's giving a speech at—"

"Spare me the details, would you?" Louise interrupted, her mouth full. "Anything else on Janisch's drinking buddy?"

"No, not yet."

A flash of yellow appeared in her field of vision: the DHL van trundling towards the junction. Under the protection of her umbrella she hurried back to her car, upon which two more long hours ensued, the high points of which were Gerd and Marek being relieved by female officers in a black Polo and a text from Gerd that read: *See you tomorrow then, Bonì.*

Ricky Janisch delivered package after package.

At around half past two he seemed to be finished. But rather than driving back to Hochdorf in the north of the city, he headed for Merzhausen in the south.

Then he left Freiburg.

After passing through Au, Janisch followed the Hexental valley towards Wittnau. "What now," one of the surveillance officers, Birte, radioed in her deep, harsh voice that became more brittle each year – she was a mother of three and often shouted at home, *otherwise they don't do as they're told.*

"Stay on him," Bonì said.

Her mobile rang.

"No other delivery depot," Natalie said. "Only Hochdorf. There's no reason for him to be to the south of Freiburg, it's not his area."

"Relatives?"

"Only in Lörrach, as far as I can make out."

"Where are the Krügers?"

Natalie had spoken to the surveillance officers there. Friedrich Krüger was at home, cleaning windows. His car was parked outside. Julius was in the garden centre, drinking a coffee and talking to his dog. Which meant it was unlikely he would be meeting Janisch to the south of Freiburg. "By the way," Natalie said, clearing her throat. Graeve had been to see her again. In half an hour two teams of interrogators would be heading out to question Friedrich Krüger at home and Julius in the garden centre. They would confront them with the photos and Ricky Janisch. Get some steam up.

"What?"

"Stuttgart's suggestion, Cords' order."

"Are they bypassing me?"

"It's not hard to bypass you, you're not here."

"Put me onto Enders."

"He's with Cords."

"The boss, then."

"They're all with Cords. Neo-Nazis in Baden-Württemberg – that's given them the willies."

"Is Stuttgart sending people?"

"Not yet, Enders says. So long as Cords and Graeve toe the line."

Janisch had gone past Wittnau and was slowing down as he approached a junction a hundred metres from Bollschweil. Louise put her phone down and, like her colleagues, fell back.

Birte's hoarse voice over the radio. "He's turning off. K4956 towards St Ulrich."

"Yes, I see that. Keep going and wait in Bollschweil."

Janisch left Hexentalstrasse in the direction of the Black Forest, and soon disappeared amongst the hills and woods into Tal der Möhlin. Boni took the precaution of staying behind Birte's black Polo. In Bollschweil she turned the car, sped back and turned off. Racing down the narrow road at 100 k.p.h., it was luck that she spotted the yellow van through the mist. A fleeting shimmer of yellow in the woods to her left – Janisch had driven onto a gravel road that led nowhere.

Louise braked hard, turned again and parked on the grass verge. In the knee-high grass at the junction with the gravel road stood a wooden post with a homemade sign. A blue arrow pointed into the woods, below which were two words, also blue: DOG COURSE.

She called Natalie. "No name, no address."

As she heard Natalie tapping away at her keyboard, Louise hurried down the gravel path, trying to avoid the many puddles and at the same time keeping the DHL van in her sights. In the thickening fog it was in danger of vanishing altogether.

"Got it," Natalie said. "A hundred metres further on there's a clearing and a cabin on the edge of the forest. There's a few obstacles in the clearing."

"Have you got a name?"

"Give me a sec."

The rhythmical tapping again as she scurried after the van, with Natalie muttering "Oh come on" and "It can't be that hard". Louise stopped abruptly when the van came to a halt. Finding cover behind trees she watched Janisch, a package under his arm, follow a path that led to the clearing. At the edge of it she could make out the wooden cabin with wire-mesh dog pounds to the side. Part of the clearing was sectioned off by a simple post and rail fence, behind which lay the course. Several dogs started barking, more casually than aggressively; some fell silent again while others started up.

"Walczak," Natalie said. "Thomas Walczak."

"Check the database. I'll call back." Boni put her phone away and hurried across the soft forest floor towards the van while Janisch approached the cabin. She still couldn't see anyone apart from him. The package didn't appear particularly heavy. It was larger than a shoe box; two pistols plus silencers and ammunition would easily fit inside. But would Janisch be delivering the guns only today? Three days had passed since Baden-Baden.

Louise heard a shout she couldn't place; perhaps it was Janisch. It was promptly answered by a deeper male voice. Janisch changed direction and disappeared from her field of vision between the cabin and the first dog pound.

She was reaching for the handle to the driver's door of the van when he appeared again without the package. Louise saw the outline of another man behind him, maybe Walczak – taller and broader than Janisch. She thought she could make out bare arms, a light-coloured fur gilet, facial features hidden by a beard. Carrying the package, he walked slowly towards the cabin.

Boni began to make her way back, stooping as she hurried from tree to tree, always casting an eye to the clearing. When the man reached the cabin he stopped by the door and turned towards her. Although it was impossible, she thought she felt his eyes on her, over a distance of fifty metres through the rain, fog and dense forest. Goose bumps appeared on her arms and she held her breath.

While Janisch got into the van and the unknown man entered the hut, a thought flashed through her head: never get too close to that man.

They intercepted Janisch at the junction of the gravel road and the K4956. Birte's Polo blocked the way, its silent blue light flashing; Boni came from the side. She yanked open the driver's door, the other hand on her holster, said what she had to say – illegal dealing in firearms, the necessary caution.

Janisch stared at her in consternation. His face was narrower and more pointed than in Gerd's photos. His hands stayed on the wheel as if he were clutching its stability. "What?" he eventually muttered, his eyes darting about. He'd begun to think.

"Come on, out," Louise said, waving her hand. She grabbed his wrist, pulled him out of the van and held him tight when he tried to sink to the ground. The DHL cap fell from his head. He floundered as he stood back up, slightly hunched, fear and anger gleaming in his eyes.

Birte had got out of the car, a short, wiry woman with a brisk step and unwavering movements. She put handcuffs on Janisch and searched him for weapons. The contents of his pockets were laid out on the bonnet of the Polo: keys, two mobiles, a penknife, a wallet bursting with coins, cards and receipts, a brown rectangular envelope, chewing gum, more change and finally a pair of SAP gloves with quartz sand padding on the knuckles and backs. Birte chucked them onto her bonnet with a scornful laugh.

Boni put on some disposable gloves and picked up the envelope, which had already been opened. She peered inside. A bundle of banknotes, fifties and hundreds, four or five thousand euros in total. Too much for a Tokarev and a Makarov with silencers and ammunition.

She held the envelope in front of Janisch's nose. "What's this for?"

"No idea where you got that." Like the expression on his face, his voice was a mixture of submissiveness and aggression. It was high-pitched and monotone, the vocal cords quavering with tension, a Baden accent.

Louise picked up the cap and put it on his head. Then she nodded to Birte, who shoved him into the Polo.

The blue light rapidly disappeared into the fog that seemed to be getting denser as the day went on. Louise glanced back at the forest; no noises or movement from Walczak's direction. Then she went over to the DHL van and got in. She knew full well that forensics would accuse her of destroying evidence, but right now it was more important that Walczak didn't see the vehicle.

She drove it around the next bend towards St Ulrich, then walked back. The goose bumps reappeared, the sight of Walczak by the cabin door, the bearded face, the voice in her head: never get too close to that man.

7

Twenty minutes later Enders' car came shooting out of the fog too quickly and he missed the turning. Louise heard the brakes, the three-point turn. When she got in she caught his gaze. She knew that something needed to be cleared up, but it would have to wait. "Have we got a search warrant?"

"Not yet." Enders turned onto the gravel path and said coldly, "If you doubt me, you'll have to change sections."

She nodded and he nodded back. It was cleared up.

Rain had set in. Stones crunched on the forest floor. Enders drove quickly; they didn't want to give Walczak much time in case he heard them coming.

"What do we know about him?"

"Very little so far."

Thomas Walczak, forty-five, born in Frankfurt, trained as a carpenter, sent twice to a youth detention centre for assault. Joined the army after his apprenticeship, signing up for a few years. In his late twenties he was sentenced to five years' imprisonment for grievous bodily harm; since his release he'd kept a low profile and shut himself away here at some point. No landline, no mobile number, no hits from search engines. The property was leased and belonged to Bollschweil council.

"Has national security got Walczak on its database?"

"No. Nor has the Criminal Investigation Bureau. If he is a member of the far right, there's nothing on file."

The forest opened up for a few metres and the clearing emerged from the fog. Enders stopped and they got out quickly. Dogs started barking and shadows moved in the faintly visible pounds. To the left was the cabin, a dark shape in the whitish grey. They approached it, two metres apart, their footsteps all but silent on the wet ground.

"One more thing," Louise said. "He has a particular look."

"What do you mean by that?"

"Feral. Brutal."

Enders nodded but didn't look at her.

There was a dim light in the one small window at the front of the cabin. When they were ten metres away the door opened and the man in the fur gilet stepped out. He stood motionless as he faced them. Beneath the gilet he wore a T-shirt, his muscular arms covered in tattoos. His beard was unkempt, his hair not especially long and shapeless. Dark slacks, old and ripped, filthy boots, their side zips open.

They stopped three metres away from him.

"Enders and Bonì, Freiburg Kripo," Louise said. "Are you Thomas Walczak?"

He gave a vague nod but ignored their badges. "It's *Waltsak*, not *Walchak*."

"We've just got a few questions, Herr Walczak," Enders said.

Walczak looked at him apathetically.

"Ricky Janisch," Louise said.

"Never heard of him."

"The man who was here half an hour ago."

"There was nobody here. Just a delivery guy."

"Yes," Louise said. Her gaze wandered to the tattoos which, close-up, looked amateurish. Some of the motifs couldn't be made out as the lines were wobbly, poorly drawn. Stick-like figures, mostly women with large bums and breasts, a man with an erection, a few animals that bore a vague resemblance to dogs. It almost looked as if Walczak had tattooed them himself.

"What did he bring you?"

"A package."

"What was in it?"

"Medicines for the dogs."

"Could we see?"

Walczak frowned grimly, turned and went inside the cabin, and came back with the unopened package Louise had seen Janisch carrying. Two dogs accompanied him, a collie and a young Alsatian. He uttered a barely audible command and they sat right beside him. Tails wagged, the collie yawned.

Walczak took a black clasp knife out of his gilet pocket and opened it, a tactical combat knife, slightly curved with a pyramid-shaped tip. Bonì instinctively reached for her holster; out of the corner of her eye she saw Enders do the same.

Walczak noticed this but didn't react. He quickly slit open the packing tape and lifted one of the flaps, revealing green polystyrene chips protecting boxes of medicines and small bottles.

"Please put the knife away," Enders said.

Walczak obeyed.

Raising her free hand, Louise said, "May I?"

He gave her the package and she rummaged through the polystyrene: little boxes, glass. She read some of the labels. No pistols, no silencers, no ammunition, but she hadn't been expecting to find them. Janisch hadn't come to bring guns, but to collect his fee.

"Don't you want to know what we're looking for?" Enders said.

"No," Walczak replied.

She handed the package back to him. His eyes were fixed on her, no let up, just her and him and her, she thought, nobody else, nothing else. She sensed that he'd categorised her as "dangerous", and also sensed a sinister alertness and aggression on his part. But he was controlled and wasn't going to allow himself to be provoked.

Not in the presence of Leif Enders.

"Did you give Janisch anything? The delivery man?" she asked.

"A signature."

"An envelope?"

"No."

"He was carrying an envelope containing several thousand euros. Are your fingerprints on it, Herr Walczak?"

"That would be weird, wouldn't it?"

"What's the money for?"

"Don't ask me, ask him."

The Alsatian stood up, whimpered as it sniffed at Walczak's trouser leg, then sat again. The collie lay down and rested its head on its front paws.

"Are they yours?" Enders said.

"Yes."

"The others too? The ones in the pounds?"

Walczak nodded.

"How many do you have?"

"Nineteen."

"Do you breed dogs?"

"No."

"Where are they from?"

"Animal shelters."

"Keeping nineteen dogs fed, bet that costs a bit."

Walczak nodded at the clearing. "People come asking me to train their dogs."

"And that's enough?"

"Usually."

The dogs in their cages, the clearing, the cabin, Louise thought, this was Walczak's world, nothing else, nobody else. The occasional delivery man, a customer, a neighbour. Kripo officers.

Enders continued with his questions, caught up in the thicket of routine from which he was unable to find a way out. He might be missing something crucial, she thought.

She had no idea what that might be.

But maybe they already knew. Youth detention centre, assault. Nineteen dogs from the animal shelter.

"Are you registered as unemployed?"

"No."

"Not on benefits?"

"I don't need money from the state."

"Why not?"

"I like being a free agent."

And so it went on, routine questions that Walczak answered curtly but politely, sometimes with the hint of a smile. He didn't regard Enders as a threat, Louise thought; he wasn't going to be cornered by routine questions.

Finally Enders gave up and thanked him stiffly.

"Any time," Walczak said.

They made their way back to the car. Not a sound behind them, as if Walczak hadn't moved and was watching them go.

"We can kiss goodbye to the search warrant," Enders said.

Louise nodded. Voluntary isolation and a visit from a delivery man who wasn't responsible for the area weren't enough.

As she walked, Boni turned around. She could just about make out the dark cabin and a shimmer of light, although not Walczak anymore. But she sensed he was still standing there, following them with his gaze.

"You were right," Enders said, his eyes narrowed and frowning. She could see that Walczak had got to him. He couldn't gauge the man, couldn't understand him, couldn't understand anything.

Their eyes met.

"Who have they got it in for, Louise? Janisch, Walczak. The buyer."

"And the Krügers."

"Do you think the Krügers know the score too?"

"Them and others."

"Shit," Enders said.

In the car she said, "What's the deal with Stuttgart?"

"No idea."

"You've got to reassure Cords and Stuttgart."

"Cords?"

"The chief."

"Won't work. He's been rung up by the ministry in Stuttgart and a federal public prosecutor."

"But nothing's happened yet," Louise said, confused. But she guessed what was worrying the big cheeses. A right-wing terrorist attack before or during the World Cup would be a disaster. It couldn't happen under any circumstances.

"And no press," Enders said.

"Of course."

He stopped; they'd reached the K4956.

"Who's with the Krügers?"

"Nobody. So long as my section's responsible, I'm the one sending officers out, not Stuttgart."

She looked at him with a slight feeling of embarrassment in the back of her neck. "I guess that answers my earlier question."

"Is that your way of apologising?"

She got out with a curt laugh. "Not something I'm familiar with, Leif."

On the short walk to her car she rang Natalie. She needed more on Walczak. Get one or two people to do some ringing around. Childhood and teenage years, women. Maybe some officers, prison guards or lawyers remember something. If, like Janisch, he was on the far right there must be clues. Talk to cellmates, neighbours, youth welfare offices.

"His parents," Natalie said.

"Yes."

Bonì drove off. Enders let her pass, then he followed close behind as if he wanted to make sure he didn't lose her in the darkness. It felt good to see him in her rear-view mirror, to picture that thoughtful face, those serious eyes whose look gave the impression they'd known each other for years. This allowed her not to think of Walczak for a while; he only re-entered her head when the Freiburg traffic separated her from Enders.

Walczak, who must suspect that she would come back.

Alone.

8

She didn't have Ricky Janisch taken to one of the interrogation rooms, but to a drying-out cell in the basement – ten square metres, harsh neon light, tiled walls, their voices accompanied by a booming echo. Enders wasn't exactly thrilled but he played along. The aim was to stoke Janisch's fear and insecurity.

But he wasn't afraid anymore. The anger had gone too. He sat there almost relaxed, balancing the chair on its back legs, his eyes half closed.

Louise left it to Enders to ask the questions, reap nothing.

The fingerprints on the banknotes. You opened the envelope and counted the money.

No I didn't.

The pistols. Someone saw you in Iwan and Pauline's.

Couldn't've been me, never heard of the place.

What are the pistols for?

What pistols?

Louise was standing next to Enders by the wall, arms crossed, looking down at Janisch who appeared to grow calmer by the minute. By contrast Enders couldn't hide his frustration.

She watched him struggling.

"Two possibilities. First, you got hold of the weapons for someone and then delivered them. Second, *you* bought them. Either way, you're in on it."

"I don't know what you're talking about."

"How do you know Julius Krüger?"

Janisch sighed. "That's it. I'm not saying another word without my lawyer."

"That was ten words without your lawyer."

Janisch puckered his lips faintly, a smile, almost scornful.

"I need a cigarette," Enders said, moving away from the wall.

Louise followed Enders out of the room and locked the door. They went up the stairs and outside. "I can't take him seriously, that's the problem," Enders said, putting his head back and exhaling smoke. A twitchy column rose upwards. She watched it disperse with slow, almost meditative movements. How could you take Janisch seriously? An opportunist and a show-off, trying to pass as a hard man and only attacking when his opponent was inferior, but then he was remorseless. He'd probably become a right-wing extremist because he saw himself as manly in the self-proclaimed war on minorities.

Another question bothered her more. Why was Janisch so sure that nothing would happen to him? He didn't know what they had on him. Or rather, what they *didn't* have on him. For example, that Irina wouldn't testify she'd seen him in Iwan and Pauline's. Or that the stills from the traffic cameras proved nothing more than what they showed: Janisch in Krüger's car on Eschholzstrasse, Janisch in Krüger's car on the B31a.

"He knows the magistrate's going to let him go tomorrow," Enders said.

"He's not clever enough for that."

"Maybe he is."

"Doesn't matter," she said. "Janisch is just the courier. We'll keep him under surveillance for a few days, see what happens. See what his comrades in the Brigade do. The Krügers, Walczak."

"Have we got that much time?"

This was the problem. Two guns in circulation that might be earmarked for an attack – but they had no idea where and against whom.

"Would be a bad start to a new job," Enders said.

His mobile rang, he listened and muttered, "OK." Mats Benedikt, who he'd sent with a forensics team and search warrant to Janisch's flat. They'd now done a preliminary search. No pistols or other weapons, but lots of rubbish – the neglected flat of an unattached neo-Nazi. Pamphlets, brochures, music, films and posters from the Fascist armoury, a sort of shrine to Rudolf Hess, then pizza boxes, full and empty beer cans, porn videos, crockery encrusted with food.

"I'll drive over later and take a look," Louise said.

"Weren't we going to see the Krügers later?"

"After that."

"After that work's finished for the day."

"Let's not go through this again please."

"I'm just saying, I can't come. I've got something on."

"Wolfgang from Aachen?"

"That sort of thing." Enders smiled, but it looked fake.

Another ring – her phone this time. Janisch's lawyer had entered the building. They gave him a few minutes with his client, then went back down to the basement.

Outside the cell Louise said, "I've got an idea."

"I thought you might," Enders said.

The lawyer, Christoph Rothe, examined the facts of the case and the images from the traffic cameras without saying a word. He was a polite older gentleman, wearing a dark jumper over a light-blue shirt, pleated trousers, no jacket. His light-grey hair began halfway up his head, swept backwards in a slight tangle. More than once Louise felt the urge to run her hand through it and make his head look neater. Although Rothe had never been seen as a right-wing extremist himself, he'd represented a couple of dozen neo-Nazis in various Baden-Württemberg courts over the years. A polite elderly gentleman with radical clients.

Eventually he laid his hands on the table, crossed his fingers – narrow pianist's fingers, nails carelessly trimmed, a simple gold ring. On the side of his middle finger she noticed a callus, a man from the age of pens. He smiled. "Let's wait and see what the magistrate says tomorrow."

Clearly fed up, Enders said nothing.

"Yes," Louise replied.

"Is that it, then?"

"That's it."

They got up, Rothe with a stiff back, Janisch beaming, unable to believe his luck. "Just one more sleep," he said, baring his crooked teeth.

They left the room. Louise phoned for some officers to escort Janisch back to his cell.

"Nice trick," Rothe said, pointing at where they'd just been.

"The interrogation rooms are getting a lick of paint," she said.

Rothe shook hands, a friendly but stern smile on his lips, then he walked away with a slight stoop, shuffling a little. When he was out of earshot Louise said to Janisch, "Shall we give you a lift?"

"A lift? Where?"

"Home. It's raining."

She watched the penny drop. First there was fear in his eyes, followed by anger. Janisch took a small step towards her. "*Now?*"

"Calm down," Enders growled.

"When forensics is finished with your flat."

"You can't let me go! Only the magistrate can do that!"

"And the public prosecutor," Enders corrected him. Two constables arrived and handcuffed Janisch.

"Two hours," Louise said. "Then my colleagues will take you home. With blue lights if you want. Maybe your comrades will come over for a glass of fizz."

She walked with Enders to the lift; the doors muffled Janisch's curses. Enders rubbed the back of his neck. He looked doubtful, tired. "Do you think the Brigade lot will find out he's already been released?"

"Them or someone else."

"Alright, I'll have a word with . . . the public prosecutor."

"Andrele."

"Andrele. And Surveillance."

"They have to keep an eye on him. We don't want anything happening to him."

"It wouldn't be that much of a pity," Enders said.

"No," Louise countered. "We're not like that. We're the good guys. If we were like that we wouldn't be good guys anymore."

He just looked at her.

"A lesson from Bermann," she said.

On the third floor they came across Graeve who had a grim expression. "Custody review hearing tomorrow at ten, then he can be released." She thought of the unanswered question from earlier: why had Janisch been so sure that nothing would happen to him? What connections did he have?

"Have you got a minute?" Enders asked.

Graeve was almost gone, but he stopped. "A minute, no longer."

"In my office, if you don't mind."

"Say it here."

Enders smiled calmly; he looked alert again. "Janisch is my section."

"He's getting out, end of story."

"Is that what HQ wants?"

"Stuttgart," Louise said.

Graeve shrugged and narrowed his eyes. "Must be down to the gloomy weather."

"He's practically out, Boss."

As Graeve listened his face brightened. At least they still had some autonomy; they weren't merely acting on Stuttgart's instructions. The interference from above must really rankle with Graeve, seeing how idealistic and full of integrity he was. Fair. The problem was that he expected the same from those around him. But you couldn't expect idealism or integrity from interior ministries and federal public prosecutors, let alone fairness. They were solely concerned with politics. Graeve wasn't naïve; he knew that. He was running into walls with his eyes open.

A friendly nod, then he walked off. At that moment Enders' secretary came into the corridor. Vormweg was expecting him. Raising his index finger, Enders said, "You're not going on your own."

Bonì sighed. "I don't know what your problem is, all of you."

"Find a colleague. Mats, anyone."

She went into her office and looked for a colleague but couldn't find one, only a pile of documents from Natalie and some information from forensics: a check had been run on the fingerprints on the envelope – Janisch, Walczak and two other people.

Bonì went to the bathroom and looked for a colleague but couldn't find one.

She went outside, got into her car, but couldn't find anyone.

9

Far off to the west the bank of cloud had opened and the evening sun lay heavily behind a grey veil, an almost obscene sight pumped full of dark red like an inflamed mole. In Haslach the car glided through amorphous patches of light. In front of the garages by Krüger's building some black boys were playing football. The Golf was parked in the same place by the side of the road.

As Bonì got out, Walczak suddenly came to mind. She saw him standing in the fog in his small, insular world, looking as if he were waiting for her. He was a good example of why she was increasingly likely to go solo these days. Witnesses and suspects reacted differently to her than they did to her colleagues, especially if she was on her own. She elicited something, spoke to the dark, hidden sides of people. Provoked them even when she didn't mean to.

Good cop, dark cop.

Viewed kindly, she thought, that could be seen as a skill too.

Friedrich Krüger wasn't at home. As the windows in the flat above were lit up, she rang the bell marked "J. Krüger".

"Hello?" A boy's voice.

"Bonì, Freiburg Kripo. I'd like to talk to your father."

A long pause.

Then Julius in a monotone: "Come up."

In the small hallway the first thing that caught her eye was a slim, metre-high wooden cross on the wall opposite. The martyred Jesus, simple, almost childish in style, perhaps a replica of a Romanesque original. Kitchen noises could be heard through a closed door, a drawer being opened. The smell of lentil soup and homemade bread hung in the air like a distant memory.

"We were about to eat," Julius said, staring at her mouth; he couldn't look her in the eye even here.

"Five minutes. I need you and your father."

She followed him across the hallway to the cross, past a beige wall hanging with red writing, an aphorism in old German, in which she was able to make out "Baptism" and "Faith". A spear and helmet as decoration, and below the last verse it said "Ignatius of Antioch". Then the cross, slim and modest, despite its height.

The dining table was set in the small sitting room. On a chair sat Friedrich Krüger, his arms crossed, giving her a hostile stare. He was in the same clothes as yesterday: light-blue shirt and beige cardigan. Beside his plate was an open Bible.

The dog was asleep beneath the window bench. No plants or flowers in the entire room.

"You're the eleventh plague," Krüger said.

"I'm all the plagues in one," she replied.

"That isn't my son."

"No, that's not me," Julius confirmed.

Louise raised her eyebrows, surprised by the impudence with which both men denied the obvious. She looked into the father's hard eyes. "That's your car."

"And? My car's outside, anyone can break into it."

"*Was* it broken into?"

"Even though he looks a bit like me," Julius mumbled. The back of his neck was red, his head hunched between his shoulders.

Outside there was a dull thud. Cheering, some shouting. The footballers.

"Have you been to see the Africans?" old Krüger asked, not taking his eyes off her for a second.

She returned his gaze and waited.

"The Turks? The Russians? The Gypsies?" He splayed his yellowed fingers and balled them into fists. "No. You've only been to see respectable people. You're harassing *us*." His voice was louder, blood shot to his cheeks. Outrage like yesterday.

The terrier woke up, raised its head and gave a quiet whimper.

"I admit, there is a certain likeness, but it's not me," Julius said, still looking at the photograph.

"What about the dog?" Louise tapped the head of the terrier. "That's your dog."

"Not necessarily."

"Unbelievable," she said.

"Louise Bonì, what's that?" Krüger asked. "French? Is that why you haven't been to see the Africans? Solidarity amongst foreigners?"

"The photo must've been taken on another day," Julius said.

She pointed at the date stamp. "22 April. Saturday."

"You don't like the respectable people, the Germans, do you?" Krüger got to his feet, came around the table and shuffled past her. For a moment she heard his strained breathing and had the smell of him in her nostrils, a lonely old man, musty clothes. He left the sitting room.

Julius brushed her with his gaze. "On Saturday evening I just took the dog out."

"No," Louise said. "You drove the car to Eschholzstrasse and gave it to this man," she said, pulling out two more photographs and putting them in front of him: Janisch in Krüger's Golf, Janisch having his picture taken after arrest.

Julius shook his head.

"Yes," she said.

"No. I don't know that man."

His father came back, a cigarette between his lips. "Who's that supposed to be?"

"Ricky Janisch. Member of the 'Southwest Brigade', a National Socialist sympathiser. Is that the connection, Herr Krüger? You were with the SS."

"And because of that you think you can get away with everything?" He sat down with a venomous smile, in a fog of smoke.

Energetic footsteps approached from the hallway. A skinny woman in an apron came into the sitting room, her face damp, cheeks pale. "Perhaps you could come back tomorrow," she said. "Dinner's ready."

Louise held the photos up. "Do you know this man, Frau Krüger? Ricky Janisch?"

Screwing up her eyes, Julius' wife took a look. "No."

"Do you know Thomas Walczak?"

She gave an indifferent shrug and left the room. In the hallway she called her son, Lothar.

Boni looked at Julius, then his father. "What about you?"

No reply.

Nodding, she said, "Don't forget, Herr Krüger, I'm the ten plagues. Get yourselves a lawyer."

Krüger's eyes, half closed, were fixed on her. His body moved back and forth to the rhythm of his breathing.

She took the photographs from the table and turned to Julius. "I need the names and addresses of your friends in Staufen."

At that moment Lothar came into the room, a quiet sixteen-year-old with acne and restless eyes, tall like the grandfather and anxious like the son.

She offered him her hand. "Hello."

He nodded. It wasn't a firm handshake, his fingers cold and soft, but he held her gaze.

"But they're only *acquaintances*," Julius whispered.

*

Outside it had become dark, the bank of cloud had closed up and it was drizzling. In front of the garages the young footballers, now including some white boys, were running around laughing, having forgotten everything around them. She got into the car. Maybe it had been a mistake to mention Walczak, she thought. She'd tried provoking the Krügers, tried to signal she was onto them, knew names, suspected connections. People who felt threatened made mistakes.

She doubted Krüger would ever feel threatened.

Unlike Julius.

And maybe Lothar.

10

Merzhausen still lay in Freiburg's evening glow, then the light came to an end. Au, Wittnau, the dark countryside. Fog lay on the hillsides of the Black Forest to the east.

Enders called. His voice was close, no noise around him as if he were in a soundproofed room. "Well?"

"I couldn't find anyone to go with."

"Yes," he said.

"There just aren't enough officers. Bloody staff shortages."

"Yes."

"That's how it is."

"Yes," he said for the third time. He sounded detached and disappointed. As if he'd already given up the struggle against her.

So soon, Leif.

Bermann had resisted for years and lost in the end. But they'd learned to respect one another. Trust one another.

She needed resistance, something to rub up against. Simply letting herself go with the flow of events didn't work. You've got to understand that, Leif.

"Tell me, Louise, how was it?"

"They're lying, denying everything. And they're religious." She told him about her visit as she drove through Sölden. Jesus on the cross, the Ignatius saying, the Bible on the table. The denials from father and son, Julius' indifferent, cool wife, the boy.

"We'll bring them into HQ tomorrow," Enders said. "Have Julius photographed for identification etc."

"We ought to impound the Golf."

"Why?"

"Fingerprints, traces of a break-in."

"They're not under suspicion of murder, Louise."

"They're obstructing the investigation."

"We can't even prove the Golf was in Baden-Baden," Enders said. "Let's wait and see what emerges tomorrow."

Boni put her foot on the brake and turned onto the K4956 towards St Ulrich, which was in darkness. She continued more slowly. As Enders was silent she thought briefly of the different types of lies. It was particularly dependent, she decided, on *who* was doing the lying.

At least when she was involved.

"Did you make a mental note of the saying? Ignatius's?"

"'Let your baptism be your weapons / faith your helmet / love your spear / endurance your armour / let your works be your affirmation.'" She cursed to herself. The fog and Ignatius had made her miss the turning to Walczak's clearing. She stopped by the side of the road and waited.

"Warlike," Enders said. "Helmet, armour, spear."

"Sounds like crusaders."

She heard him laugh.

"Hard to imagine with Julius."

"With the old man, though."

Enders cleared his throat. "What now?"

"What do you mean?"

"Whereabouts are you?"

"Don't ask," she said.

Having stopped where the gravel track began, in the glow of the courtesy light she wrote questions to Kilian on her mobile, made up of abbreviations, allusions and names in case anyone else read them. Were there any more right-wing extremists amongst the Russians, did Irina know a Friedrich or a Julius Krüger, was Niko acting on his own, could she have a photo, might the Russians have someone on some sort of hitlist? *Sorry, it's important, thanks.*

Then she reached for the documents Natalie had prepared for her. Two or three pages on Walczak, as well as a newspaper article from the same day with the picture of an elderly man from Rwanda, the name highlighted in yellow: Ludwig Kabangu. Stuck to the paper a Post-it with Natalie's writing: *The perfect neo-Nazi victim!!! NN forums spewing bile!!!* "Perfect" was double underlined and some words in the text were also highlighted in yellow.

She put the article to one side and read the information on Walczak.

A childhood on the run.

Aged six picked up by hikers in the Taunus. Aged seven removed by police from a train heading to France. Aged nine caught stealing in Munich. Time and again he was taken back home. An underage vagabond, aggressive, lashing out, hardly saying a word. When he was ten a patrol car found him by the side of the road in the Nordend area of Frankfurt, beaten black and blue. At the youth welfare office they finally understood. It couldn't be proven that the parents had done anything as the boy wouldn't speak. But they didn't protest either, and so he was put in a home.

And he began to beat up other children.

More homes followed. More children were beaten up. Then youth workers and teachers too.

When he was fourteen his parents reported him to the police. They said he'd "stalked" and "threatened" the father on several occasions. He was given a restraining order. A teenager banned from getting near his own parents.

Two more homes, more residents and youth workers beaten up. His first spell in a youth detention centre. Then his second.

When he was nineteen he did a carpentry apprenticeship in Berlin.

Three years later his parents caught him prowling around outside their house in Frankfurt. They called the police, but the officers couldn't find him. As nothing had happened the parents didn't bother pressing charges.

He joined the army, signing up for six years. Less than two months after his discharge he came to blows with an acquaintance in Berlin and beat him to within a whisker of his life. Five years inside. After his release in 1996 the trail went cold.

In 1999 he turned up again, leasing the land with the clearing. The owner was Bollschweil council. *Nothing linking W to the far right,* Natalie had noted. *More tomorrow! Have a nice evening! N.*

Louise put the printouts to one side. Her eyes caught the wooden sign, its blue writing invisible in the darkness: DOG COURSE. In front of her the fog, the outlines of the nearest trees; five metres further on the gravel track disappeared into the greyish-black.

She froze.

In the past, she thought, these were the moments when she would have reached into the glovebox and a few sips would have turned the procrastinator into the hunter. She didn't miss the sips, only the purposeful movements. Knowing what to do for a few seconds, a minute, to distract yourself. To overcome the unease. The only things in the glovebox now were the car's instruction manual and some condoms.

Boni picked up the newspaper article on Ludwig Kabangu, Natalie's perfect neo-Nazi victim. It was entitled THE BONE HUNTER, two columns and a portrait photo. A black man with a trimmed grey beard looking past the camera, demure smile, anxious eyes. The caption read: *Arrived yesterday in Freiburg: Ludwig Kabangu (65) from Rwanda.*

She skimmed the article, skipping from one yellow highlight to the next. *Rwanda . . . former German colony . . . German East Africa . . . staff surgeon . . . Freiburg . . . "racial eugenicists" . . . skull collection . . . reparations.*

A noise made her look up. Barking, two or three dogs. Sudden movement, a dark figure emerging from the fog, a man.

Beard, bare arms, fur gilet.

As Walczak approached her slowly more and more dogs appeared, perhaps a dozen. They raced to the car barking, some leaped onto the bonnet, then onto the roof, Walczak disappearing behind bodies. Two of the animals, an Alsatian and a boxer, had their front paws on the driver's door, barking at Louise, their jowls flapping. For a moment a collie crouched by the windscreen and placed a paw on the glass. When two dogs leaped back down from the roof onto the bonnet, it joined in their frenzy.

Walczak was now standing in front of the car, staring at her. Two possibilities, she thought: win his respect or lose it for ever.

Gingerly she opened the door. The Alsatian and boxer moved back and then pushed into the opening. But they didn't growl, they just looked excited. Friendly.

The same couldn't be said of Walczak. Never get too close to this man, she thought. Don't forget that.

She got out of the car, looked at him and said, "Evening stroll with the family?"

11

They stood by the fence in the clearing – Walczak inside the dog course, Louise outside, three metres apart – watching the dogs scamper around the enclosure, silhouettes moving back and forth, mostly invisible in the darkness. Her right hand was by her belt, close to the butt of the pistol. She could barely make out Walczak's face, even though three metres wasn't much. Further on stood the cabin, little more than a rectangle of wavering light – an oil lamp or a candle. In the damp air hung the smell of dogs, grass and forest.

"We arrested Janisch," she said. "Ricky Janisch." He turned his head towards her. "But he's already out again. He likes to talk."

"Must be on account of his job. Always on his own on the road." A boxer came running towards them, locked its jaws playfully around Walczak's bootleg, front legs on the ground. He let the animal toy with him for a while. Then a quiet command, a single word, and the dog leaped away.

"On Saturday evening he bought two pistols in Baden-Baden," Louise said. "A Tokarev and a Makarov."

"Sounds like a dangerous kind of delivery guy."

"At some point between Saturday and yesterday evening he dropped the weapons off with you. In return, this afternoon, you gave him an envelope with four thousand five hundred euros."

Walczak shook his head. "Why would I need pistols?"

"You passed the weapons on to someone else. Or you're going to."

"Bollocks."

"Who are the weapons for, Herr Walczak?"

"Ask the delivery man."

Bonì gave a mechanical nod. She was convinced her suspicion was right, that Walczak wasn't telling the truth, even though she couldn't sense it, unlike with the Krügers and Janisch. The only thing she could sense was his stifled aggression and an oppressive closeness that felt almost visceral. As if his hand were invisibly around her throat.

A tangle of dogs came tumbling into her field of vision. Howling, barking, then the animals leaped up and each went their own way.

"Always the same," Walczak said, pulling away from the fence and coming towards her, his tattooed muscles taut.

"What?"

"Once someone's done time you can pin everything on him."

She raised her hand. "That's close enough."

He stopped with a snort. One metre away, far too close. On her side of the fence Louise warily walked past him to where he'd been standing. She looked over at the cabin, where the light appeared to dim for a moment. Then it flickered wildly before settling again. As if someone had wandered past it.

A dog. A person.

She turned to smile at Walczak, but her heart was racing. Not a dog, she thought. That was a person in the cabin.

Walczak didn't appear to have noticed anything. He stared at her, motionless.

The clouds had opened up, the fog was white in the moonlight and now it was easier to see the dogs. In the distance bells rang out, Bollschweil perhaps, but in any event a different, safer world.

"Your fingerprints are on the envelope," she said. "Not on the banknotes, just the envelope. Yours, Janisch's and two other people's."

"Can't be."

"Whose are the other fingerprints?"

"You're asking the wrong man."

"Do you know Friedrich Krüger?"

He shook his head.

"Julius Krüger?"

"No."

"But you do know Janisch."

"From this afternoon."

"Has he ever brought you anything before?"

"No."

Louise nodded. "Because St Ulrich isn't his area. He makes deliveries in the west of Freiburg, not here."

"Not my problem." Walczak's head was slightly bowed, his eyes fixed on her, not letting go. Just her and him, she thought, nobody else, nothing else.

And someone in the cabin.

Boni suddenly realised that the distance between them had narrowed again. She hadn't noticed that he'd taken a step towards her, a hand on the fence. Now she could see the anger in his face, anger, curiosity and something else. Something undefinable.

"No closer," she said, wondering why he hadn't told her to leave. He was under no obligation to answer her questions; he could have sent her packing. But he hadn't. For some unfathomable reason he seemed to want to talk to her.

She was making progress. Getting ever closer to him in her own way.

"Eight homes in ten years," she said.

"I don't like it everywhere."

"Did you want to go back to your parents'?"

He raised his eyebrows but said nothing.

"You weren't allowed to. Restraining order."

"Go on."

She pointed at the clearing. "The dogs, all from the home."

Walczak laughed; it sounded supercilious and controlled.

"What I don't understand is why you beat up your youth workers. Other boys, yes, that happens, but youth workers and teachers?"

"Maybe they deserved it?"

"Why? Did they sexually assault you?"

"Wouldn't've dared."

"Other children?"

"You'll find out."

"Let's talk about your political views."

"Haven't got any."

"Problems with migrants?"

"None around here."

"You know what I mean."

"No."

"Do you vote?"

"I wouldn't know who to vote for."

"You said you don't need money from the state, you prefer to be a free agent."

He waited for her to continue.

"The youth welfare office takes you away from your parents. The homes, the youth workers, then the judges . . . You hate the state, that's why you don't want to take any benefits."

"So?"

She pulled out the gun, placed her hand against her leg, the barrel pointing to the ground. "Who's in the cabin?"

"Let's take a look."

Boni hesitated, taken aback. "We're going to take it nice and slow." She waved him along and followed a few metres behind to the small building that stood silently in the moonlight.

The dogs reacted to this change, sprinting quietly out of the fog to accompany them. At first it was just a few, then more. With her free hand Louise fished out her phone, dialled the emergency number and called for reinforcements. Walczak glanced over his shoulder and gave another of those derisive snorts she was now familiar with.

Halfway there, the dogs lost interest and dispersed.

Then they were at the cabin. Walczak stopped and looked at Louise. Furtive eyes, the hint of a smile on his lips.

Still no movement, no sound from inside.

"Go in," she said.

Without taking his eyes off her, he opened the wooden door and entered the cabin. With her loaded weapon Louise went behind him into the darkness, instinctively holding her breath when she was met by an intense cocktail of smells: dampness, dogs, cigarette smoke, food, rubbish, cheap perfume and alcohol. Her eyes darted across the furniture, walls, Walczak, then back to start again. To the left a kitchenette and a small plastic table with two chairs; by the rear wall a threadbare sofa and two armchairs of an indefinable age; to the right, mattresses with blankets and pillows; beside them in the corner a yellow cupboard patched up in several places. An oil lamp hung from the ceiling, its flame fluttering in the draught.

No second door.

Had she been mistaken? She looked at Walczak, who hadn't taken his eyes off her.

"Charlie," he said. "You've got a visitor."

"What the fuck?" a woman's voice responded, and from the sea of pillows rose a shock of blonde hair.

Charlotte Riedl, around fifty. "A neighbour, not that it's any of your business." She was a short, bony woman with a hoarse voice and a strong Bavarian accent, drunk, and a face that reflected an advanced stage of disillusionment. All the same she made an effort – golden eye shadow, perfectly curved painted-on eyebrows, her long hair dyed light blonde, multiple piercings in both ears.

She remained sitting, cigarette in hand, a pillow covering her bare breasts, while Bonì examined her ID card. Née Meier, but only forty-two, from Passau, resident at 70 St Ulrich.

"The campsite," Riedl said with her surprisingly deep voice, pointing behind with her thumb.

"There's a campsite here?"

"Not just any old campsite. 'Camping Riedl Erlebnispark am Schauinsland. Camping in paradise: pay for four nights, stay five.'" She gave a toxic smile. Thumbs and arms disappeared behind the pillow again.

Louise had spotted a small tattoo on the inside of her bicep. A number, 28, the day of Charlotte Riedl's birth. She gave her back the ID card. "Riedl, is that your husband?"

"Is that a trick question?" Her golden eyes narrowed, she frowned and shot a glance at Walczak, who was standing a few paces away in the semi-darkness.

"No," Louise replied thoughtfully.

Outside there was a muffled engine sound. Blue light flashed through the window, catching Walczak. His eyes were on her; again that feeling of oppressiveness, the invisible hand around her throat. She went over to the door and looked at him. "Are you here tomorrow?"

"I'm always here," he said.

Two patrol cars, officers from Freiburg South Louise vaguely recognised. She thanked them, sent them back to Freiburg and got into her car. Her mobile said 23.21. Nothing from Kilian. Nothing from Ben. Nothing from Rolf Bermann.

Boni drove off. She wasn't tired and she didn't fancy the silence of her apartment, where the memory of Ben Liebermann was gradually fading, whereas the memory of Rolf Bermann was still very much alive. She liked the idea of hanging around here a while longer, in the fog and in the forest.

A bit of relaxation after the fear of Walczak.

She picked up her phone and found 70 St Ulrich, Paulus Riedl, camping in paradise.

There was something else, too.

The number 28 was a symbol – the second and eighth letters of the alphabet, "B" and "H". The abbreviation for the neo-Nazi network that had been outlawed in Germany a few years earlier: "Blood and Honour".

12

Three gravel tracks that led in different directions after the entrance barrier, past predominantly empty parking places or patches of grass, then vanished into the darkness, half of the lanterns broken or not switched on. There was only the occasional camper van or tent, but nobody about apart from a boy peeing against a tree. The stench of latrines and disinfectant hung in the air.

This paradise was desolate.

Louise had parked in front of the barrier beside a small office on one side and a flagpole with the German flag on the other, and had wandered a few metres into the campsite. It was surrounded by forest; Walczak's clearing must be a few hundred metres to the west. That was the connection: Walczak. Janisch, the neo-Nazi, making a delivery to Walczak way outside his area. Charlie Riedl in Walczak's bed, with the number 28 tattooed on her arm.

The boy hurried away and disappeared behind a hedge.

"Oi!" a man's voice exclaimed behind her.

She turned around in shock. Beside the office stood a beefy man, around fifty, in tracksuit bottoms and sweatshirt, his arms crossed. His hair was dark and uncombed, his pale face bloated, rings under his eyes, a huge double chin.

Paulus Riedl – she'd found a photo of him online earlier.

Bonì walked up to him, not too quickly, returning his gaze.

"Let me guess," Riedl muttered.

"Correct, Freiburg Kripo."

"Has Charlie been up to something?"

"Charlie?"

"My worse half."

She smiled politely. "Nothing that would be in my jurisdiction."

Inside his office, paradise was no more appealing. A scratched reception counter with a Germany banner, squat office cabinets from the 1950s, a tiny, muted television set on a desk. Along the back wall was a pale-blue sofa, where Riedl must have been lying watching telly when she arrived. He'd pushed off a blanket and the pillow had fallen to the floor when he got up.

Riedl stood behind the counter, arms crossed, waiting.

"A patriot," she said.

He looked at the banner. "World Cup soon."

"Busy in June?"

A slow, contented nod that kept going. "Fifty-three bookings from Holland alone."

"Because of Hinterzarten?"

"Presume so." Reaching under the counter he put three more banners alongside the German one. There was a touch more energy in his eyes and voice now. "The team's arriving on 6 June. I'll drive over and watch them training. Maybe organise tours for all the Dutchmen here."

Louise pointed at the St George's Cross. "England?"

"Twenty-five bookings, based at Bühl. And Iran, two bookings. Friedrichshafen. Wonder whether they've got a mosque in Friedrichshafen?"

She tapped the red, white and blue tricolour. "As far as we're concerned the Dutch are the problem."

"They're not a problem. We're going to wipe the floor with them."

"I'm talking about a potential attack."

"Bloody anarchists. Football's football. Politics is politics. Why are you here?"

"For some television."

Riedl was resistant. First the CCTV cameras weren't switched on, then faulty, then some weren't switched on, some were faulty. Louise floated the possibility of a search warrant. Dozens of colleagues combing the campsite, a helicopter providing sufficient light, no sleep for Riedl and his guests that night. And – who knows? – the mayor might order the temporary closure of the campsite. Fifty-three cancellations to be sent to the Netherlands, twenty-five to England, and let's not forget the two Iranians. A ton of work, quite apart from the financial losses.

"Look, nobody can expect me to lose out and go bust," Riedl said, staring at the banners.

"No."

"I don't care if one of that lot's been up to something."

"That lot?"

"Not my responsibility."

"That depends."

He looked up. "Is that where we've got to? That I'm responsible if one of them gets up to mischief?" he said, jerking his thumb behind him in the direction of the campsite, the same gesture his wife had used, the hand staying up for a similar length of time.

"If you knew."

"I know nothing. I don't know them at all."

"Who?"

"The people who come here." He nodded, more to himself, which turned seamlessly into a shake of the head. "Not my responsibility."

"For what, Herr Riedl?" Louise asked gently.

"I don't know." He bent to take a laptop from beneath the counter and began to type. A printer awoke from standby mode.

The bookings register, Saturday midnight till this evening. Six pages, two for each day. Thirteen arrivals, ten departures.

"And the camera footage?"

Riedl typed again, then turned the laptop to face her. Split-screen, four different areas of the campsite, black-and-white images, Sunday, 00.01.

The footage was playing in real time.

"Fancy a fried egg for breakfast?" he offered with a crooked grin.

"I'd prefer to watch this sped up."

Fifteen minutes later, Sunday night, a perfectly normal day had gone by at a camping site. Louise yawned. Monday began. Riedl shuffled to the sofa, picked up the pillow and plonked himself down. He sat there apathetically, looking at the muted television set, the pillow on his belly, his hands on top of that. Louise couldn't help think of Charlie and the pillow in front of her breasts. Over many years of marriage the two of them had adopted similar gestures and postures, maybe similar affairs too.

Monday morning, five o'clock, Riedl's head had slumped to the side and he was snoring. Another uneventful day, at least at high speed. Occasionally Louise stopped the flood of pictures and looked at freeze-frame images. Guests leaving, guests arriving, she ticked off the names in the diary from the number plates she could make out reasonably well in the pictures. More children exploring the campsite, playing with balls. Paulus Riedl shuffling into view alone or with guests. Charlie Riedl, skimpy skirts, skimpy T-shirts, high heels. An elderly man taking a walk, wandering around and around, always the same route, the same time as on Sunday afternoon. Herr Breune, Riedl had said. Came every April with his wife for thirty years, and now he's been coming without her for nine. He buried her in '97.

Riedl woke up and looked at her in confusion until he seemed to remember.

Monday evening. A husband and wife quarrelling by a camper van. Something major – an embittered, silent, desperate argument in black and white. Later, individual groups of people on their way to the toilet and shower block. Around ten o'clock another camper van arrives, a "Sky Wave". Louise couldn't find an entry for it; must be a long-term guest.

She heard barking in the distance, several dogs: Walczak was out and about. Turning towards her, Riedl seemed to want to say something. But he just looked down at his hands. The barking stopped.

At around half past ten, Charlie appeared in the room, face flushed, lips swollen, hair tangled, T-shirt partly hanging out of her jeans. She smelled of sweat, alcohol and sex. "Oh," she said.

"Bonì, Freiburg Kripo," Louise said.

"Charlotte Riedl." She seemed to be thinking, her pupils darting around. "Kripo? Anything happened?"

"No."

"Good. Well . . . Gerti says hi."

"Thanks," Riedl said.

They listened to the clacking of Charlie's footsteps on the stairs above the office. Silence. Then the shower was turned on.

Riedl looked at his hands again; Louise continued to play the footage.

Monday night. The quarrelling couple going for a stroll, not even glancing at each other, not a word between them. One light going out after the next.

Then she found something.

Tuesday morning, 03.24.55. One of the screens showed two men in dark clothes, early thirties, trainers. The one in front was carrying a rucksack, had short dark hair, ears that stuck out slightly, and his bushy eyebrows sat strikingly close to his eyes. The other man's face was angular, cagy, and his head was shaven. They walked one behind the other on the strip of grass before vanishing from sight. None of the other cameras captured them.

At 03.53.12 they came back. The same camera. They must have left and reentered the campsite via the west, not the entrance.

Once again in slow motion. The shape of the rucksack had

changed. It looked fuller and heavier than half an hour earlier. A Tokarev and a Makarov plus silencers and ammunition weighed between three and four kilograms, Louise guessed. That was what the rucksack looked like, roughly – three or four kilograms heavier.

As the printer whirred she went over to Riedl, who'd nodded off again, and tapped him on the shoulder. His eyelids rose sluggishly, his expression one of confusion; comprehension was slow to return. He sighed. Not paradise, but Louise Bonì; merciless reality.

"It's getting serious now, Herr Riedl," she said.

Riedl stared at the printouts in his hands, blurred enlargements of the men's faces. He was sweating, his breathing shallow, almost silent, thinking hard about each word.

No, he didn't know the two men.

Louise suddenly understood. "But you've seen them before."

"Seen? In the past?"

"On Monday or Tuesday at your campsite."

He hesitated before answering. "Once or twice on Monday. I mean, you do bump into each other. Not on Tuesday, though, they left early."

"Was anyone with them?"

"Two women."

"I need names."

Numb, he returned her gaze. In his eyes was resignation and despondence. A man who'd given up trying to be happy long ago.

"You don't know the names." Louise tapped the bookings printout in her hand. No entry for the "Sky Wave" – not long-term guests. Riedl hadn't registered the arrivals. "Is that because the four of them are patriots, like you?"

The hint of a nod.

"A woman got out and went into the office. What happened then? What did she say?"

"That they were the comrades from Jena."

"So you knew they were coming? Had they booked in?"

"No. Last week, er, someone . . . rang up."

"Who?"

He looked at his hands, then leaned forwards and picked up the pillow. "Someone from the Heimat Guard. Andreas."

"What sort of Heimat Guard?"

"Baden Heimat Guard."

"There's a Baden Heimat Guard?"

Riedl nodded, more obviously this time.

"Are you a member?"

"No."

"Andreas what?"

A feeble shrug.

"Have you ever met him?"

"No. None of them."

"Anyone from the Southwest Brigade?"

"None of them either."

"Are you a member of a different group?"

"No."

"Do you know Ricky Janisch? DHL delivery man?"

"No."

"Friedrich Krüger, Julius Krüger from Freiburg?"

"No."

"But you do know Thomas Walczak."

He nodded. "We're neighbours."

"Is Walczak a patriot too?"

"No idea. Never talked to him about it."

"Who do you talk to about it?"

Riedl cleared his throat then shook his head, almost in supplication. No names, he mumbled, I'm not naming any names. Louise didn't probe further; this was something to work with for the time being.

Leaning against the edge of the desk, she arranged in her head what Riedl had said. "So you'll get the occasional call saying that comrades are coming from Jena, for example, keep a pitch free for them."

"Yes."

"You don't register them, don't ask for any money. Officially they were never here."

He nodded.

"Dammit," Louise said. "Describe the four of them for me."

Riedl tried, but clearly he found it a struggle. He didn't want to know exactly who was coming, didn't want to get mixed up in "something", avoided contact. Two couples, the women around thirty, the men a few years older. Nothing noticeable about them apart from the dialect, which to his ears sounded Saxon. The woman who'd come into the office had a tattoo on her right shoulder, a "black sun", a circle of runes, you know, like in the SS. Louise did not know. She went to the laptop, opened the browser and found the symbol. Three swastikas with short arms, one on top of the other to produce twelve "sunrays" or victory runes, at the ends of which another arm went off at right angles. Two circles connected the rays, one on the inside and the other on the outside.

"Dammit," she said again as a shiver ran down her neck. Janisch, the Krügers, the Southwest Brigade, a Baden Heimat Guard, comrades from Jena – a spider's web of neo-Nazis.

Walczak, who might be a member, but who might simply have handed over the weapons and Janisch's fee.

She went back to the desk.

Riedl didn't know why they'd come from Jena. He'd only exchanged a few words with them, about the weather, the Baden Rothaus beer, "Tannenzäpfle" – they knew it from Berlin, one of them said he liked the Black Forest girl, you know, the blonde on the label.

"Any indications? Do you know where they were heading from here?"

"No."

"Who's going to buy that, Herr Riedl? No state prosecutor, no judge." She leaned forwards. "You knew about their arrival. You let them camp here for nothing. You share their . . . mindset. Nobody's going to believe you don't know anything else."

"I need to think," Riedl said quietly.

"Do that." Louise moved away from the desk and stepped outside, her phone to her ear. The air was cool and damp, fog hung in the light of the lamps, though it appeared to be dissipating gradually. Again she heard a dog bark, more joining in. It was coming from the east. Walczak seemed to have wandered around the campsite with his dogs.

An officer from the crime squad answered in a bright, cheerful voice, full of energy and confidence at eleven o'clock at night. Louise gave her the Jena registration number: *If the car is found, identify the passengers, no arrests.*

She went back into the office. Riedl had fallen asleep again, his head slumped forwards, hands on the pillow, one clutching the index finger of the other. She woke him.

His eyes opened. Shaking his head he whispered, "But I heard something somewhere else."

Outside the night was clear; the fog had almost vanished and the layer of cloud had broken up. Louise saw individual stars in the sky above, while on invisible hilltops the red warning lights of windmills flashed. When she opened the car door she detected movement at the edge of the narrow tarmacked road that led from St Ulrich to Riedl's campsite. A dog, light fur, a collie. It disappeared between the trees without making a sound.

Boni sat in the car and put Riedl's laptop on the passenger seat. She turned slowly, passing the place where the dog had run into the forest. No other animals and no sign of Walczak either. Nonetheless she felt the fear in her chest, her lungs were tight, her breathing shallow. For the first time she was properly aware of what she'd suspected for a while: the moment might soon come when she couldn't hesitate for a second to make use of the gun.

Soon afterwards Louise turned onto the K4956 near St Ulrich. Grabbing the newspaper article that Natalie had marked up, she switched on the courtesy light and skimmed it for a second time as she drove.

Natalie was right. Ludwig Kabangu from Rwanda: the perfect victim.

This negro's coming from German East Africa, one of Paulus Riedl's comrades had said at the beginning of April, *to stir up trouble here. They've got the bones of some relative of his at the university, and he wants them back.*

Don't you worry about him, another had said. *We'll sort him out.*

II

13

Boni passed Annaplatz and stopped a few junctions further on outside an elegant Jugendstil building. With every kilometre of the drive the exhaustion had become more apparent. It had been another long, intense day, dozens of questions and barely any answers, plus her inexplicable fear. She resisted the urge to close her eyes for a minute. Right now it was essential that she carry on, she thought, to put together the pieces of the puzzle. Now they had to work fast and stay on the case. Whose job would that be if not hers? She knew more than anyone and she had nothing else in her life, nobody else. There was neither a family nor a partner waiting in her apartment, only a dead man and an absent one.

She opened the glovebox and reached for the bottle that wasn't there. Even the familiar movement felt good; three years of being on the wagon hadn't changed that one little bit.

Three years on the wagon . . .

She closed the glovebox in satisfaction and got out. Amongst all the setbacks in her life, all the failure, losses, emptiness, the dead and the missing, this was her one triumphal victory, and now and again it put everything else in the shade.

During the drive she'd had a brief phone call with Ilka Weber, the author of the newspaper article, and found out that Ludwig Kabangu was staying in a hotel close to the main station and would be here until Friday. Then she called her young, alert colleague from the crime squad again, who'd immediately made arrangements to ensure Kabangu got adequate protection for the next few hours while Louise discussed with Enders and Graeve how to proceed.

The door to Weber's top-floor apartment was marked simply "I. Weber". Behind it lay a vast hallway containing four or five double doors. Boni fancied she could hear the voices and sounds of all the people who must have once lived in this huge apartment. Now the only person here was Ilka Weber, a tall, plump fifty-year-old woman with long, undyed hair and oversized glasses. Her animated smile suggested she'd seen more convivial times.

Ilka Weber had shown Louise into a sort of anteroom to the sitting room, where they'd sat in the corners of a hard sofa, legs crossed. In Louise's hand was a glass of water, in Ilka's a cup of steaming tea, which she clutched tightly as if trying to fight a fundamental inner cold. In a soft voice she explained about Ludwig Kabangu, the bones, German East Africa, Rwanda being part of a German colony between 1885 and 1918, along with Burundi and Tanzania.

"Rwanda was a German colony?"

"Yes, easy to forget these days, isn't it?"

"More like I never knew," Louise said.

Ludwig Kabangu had come to Freiburg to take the bones of his grandfather's wife – "Grandfather Mabruk" – back to his home country. Kabangu was certain that in 1908 they'd been sent by a German staff surgeon by the name of Feldmann to the Freiburg Institute of Anthropology, and they were now supposedly being stored in a box in the university archive. The university insisted, however, that it could only respond to requests from the Rwandan embassy.

"Have you spoken to them?"

"I thought you'd read my article."

"Only skimmed it, I was in a hurry."

"With the head of the archive, Dr Arndt."

"Did he say that Kabangu wasn't going to get the bones back?"

"He said it was extremely unlikely there were any bones from German East Africa in the university archive."

"Is he right?"

"Maybe. Though that doesn't mean they shouldn't check."

"Sounds as if there's more than one . . . bone there."

Weber nodded. "In Freiburg University archive alone there are almost sixteen hundred, and in Germany as a whole many thousands."

"All from former colonies?"

"No, but some for sure."

"What do you actually mean by 'bones'? The skeleton?"

"In most cases we're talking about skulls."

"So the university here has got hundreds of skulls in its archive?"

"Long shelves of them in white boxes." Weber pushed her glasses up her nose and looked into her cup. Louise heard her breathing calmly and sensed she was enjoying this conversation, even though she seemed tired and slightly uptight. Apart from the noises they were making, it was silent in the apartment, not a sound to be heard in the two or four hundred square metres, not even the occasional creak from the floorboards.

"Why's the university playing so hard-to-get?"

"Bones from former colonies are a political issue," Weber replied. They were a tricky legacy for universities and museums because they were a reminder of the racist history of German anthropology. Besides, both financial resources and expertise were lacking for such an analysis. The government, meanwhile, was worried about reparation demands from the countries concerned, especially when it came to bones from German South-West Africa, which was now Namibia. Most of these, she continued, were the mortal remains of Hereros and Namas, slaughtered by their German colonial masters after 1904 – the first genocide of the twentieth century. The German government still hadn't apologised for the massacre, even though the UN defined it as genocide. German universities, museums and politicians were being similarly reticent, she said, about restitution claims.

"What do you mean by 'racist history'?"

"Back then, by measuring skulls from the colonies, they tried to prove that the 'white race' was more advanced." Weber had taken one hand off her cup. From 1900 to 1927 the doctor and anthropologist Eugen Fischer was in charge of the bone collection in Freiburg. He was one of the pioneers of National Socialist racial theory.

A long pause followed.

Nazis in the past, Nazis now, Bonì thought. The picture was becoming clearer.

Bonì left soon afterwards, leaving behind a needy Ilka Weber. Why don't you stay a bit longer? the eyes behind her glasses said. Let's keep talking, let's talk all night long, till the sun comes up and the apartment is saturated with our voices and sounds, so the memory will remain alive for a few days and nights . . .

The door closed almost silently behind Louise.

Outside, the darkness, while Walczak and the fear had returned too. Louise avoided Annaplatz, taking a roundabout route to the main station. She coasted slowly past Colombipark and turned into Poststrasse. *Brown Escort*, the officer from the crime squad had said, *Gerd Rehberg*, Gerd with the budgie.

The Escort was parked opposite the hotel. She parked in a driveway and hurried over.

Putting the window down, Gerd said, "Jesus, Bonì, now there's this African guy too."

"Is he here?"

Gerd nodded. "Fourth floor. Second window from the left."

The curtain was drawn, light shimmered through a gap. At that moment it went out.

"He's going to sleep," Gerd said.

"Is there anyone with him?"

"No."

Cigarette smoke billowed through the car window. Louise stepped to one side, then squatted with her back on the fender. Turning her head she could see half of Gerd's face and his left hand tapping ash from the cigarette. "Where's Marek?"

"Where should he be? Where I should be too. But I'm here because that's what you want."

As they didn't have enough surveillance officers for another all-night observation, Marek had stayed with Janisch and Gerd had driven to Kabangu's hotel. As back-up, a patrol car from Freiburg North cruised down Poststrasse every fifteen minutes.

Gerd stuck his head out of the window, gave her a half-hearted grin and nodded towards the hotel. "This guy here, is he meant to be the target?"

"Seems like it."

"What have Antifa got against an African?"

Louise sighed angrily. "Right-wing extremists, Gerd. Not only Janisch but others too. Two men from Jena who've probably been earmarked for the job."

"Jena, did you say?"

She nodded.

"You'd better be right."

"I'd rather I was wrong."

"That's actually my assumption, Boni," Gerd said in a friendly tone.

Louise took her phone and stood up. She hadn't asked Ilka Weber the most important question.

Weber answered immediately, as if she'd been sitting beside the telephone. She told Louise she'd first heard about Kabangu and his mission at the beginning of the previous week; the same was true of her editor. An association investigating Freiburg's role in German colonial history had held a press conference on Monday, during which they introduced Kabangu. Apparently the association had invited him about a week ago.

"Are you sure?"

"Yes."

Louise looked at Gerd, who was staring at her with small, weary eyes. A week ago, so mid-April. Riedl's neo-Nazi comrades had been talking about Kabangu's arrival already at the beginning of April.

Comrades whose names Riedl wouldn't share.

She'd tried, for several minutes. *I can't*, he'd whispered, almost in desperation. *No way.*

"Who could have known Kabangu was coming before you did?" she asked.

"The university," Weber said. Kabangu had written to the head of the archive in March, outlining his demand. "Say hi to Grandfather Mabruk," she said and hung up.

"Problems?" Gerd said, the next cigarette between his lips.

"You bet."

As she crossed the street to return to her car, Louise thought about Paulus Riedl. *I can't. No way.* The desperation in his voice, in his eyes, had nothing to do with her or the pressure she'd put on him, but with the past. For years this desperation had grown, destroyed his hopes, his life.

Charlie, she thought, was the cause of this despair. He'd been thinking of Charlie during their conversation. She was one of the "comrades".

And because, in spite of everything, he loved her, he was protecting her.

The remainder of the night was restless. She slept badly, dreaming of dogs, Walczak and Ben Liebermann, who haunted her days and nights as an ever more shadowy ghost. Later her dream was all about a dead person, who first was Bermann, then wasn't, and ultimately she couldn't place this person, who might belong to a remote past in a remote country, but who could equally be part of her present.

14

It was twenty past seven and they, Enders, Graeve and Bonì, were sitting at the end of a long table in the sunshine, somewhat apart from the few other colleagues in the canteen at this time of the morning. Having discussed the most important events of the previous evening, now they were silent. Enders was pensive and Graeve rattled, because at the bottom of the lake they were swimming in, the tendrils of a Baden neo-Nazi network were becoming visible.

When Louise had awoken at dawn she'd seen a text from Graeve: *Canteen, 7.00, just Enders, you and I.* On the drive there she'd wondered why he was splitting the investigation team, Enders and her on one side, Natalie, Mats Benedikt and the rest of the officers on the other. Now she understood. The pressure from Stuttgart was growing by the day. Graeve was attempting to control the flow of information.

"They want the names of my sources, don't they?"

He looked at her and nodded. The sun shone on his gaunt face, blue veins shimmered through his skin. There were rings beneath his eyes and he'd had a cursory shave; yesterday's stubble was still visible. It looked as if he'd slept as little as she had and he was losing his distance, which she didn't like. She needed a boss who stood above everything and radiated calm.

"They won't get them," she said.

"Of course not." Graeve turned to Enders, his eyebrows raised. Clearly he was waiting for a word of approval.

"What?" Enders said.

"Don't tell Stuttgart anything. No names, no information and no documents – not just as far as Boni's sources are concerned . . . nothing about Walczak and Riehmer etc. either."

"Isn't that obvious given the circumstances?"

"It should be at any rate."

"Riedl," Louise said. "Not Riehmer."

Enders gave a belligerent grin. "You're really mistrustful, you southerners. Yesterday Boni, now you. I'm not sure I'll ever get used to it."

"You'll survive."

Louise went to the counter and got herself another roll and some jam. By the time she came back the brief skirmish was over, Graeve was smiling, Enders nodding, looking relaxed. They watched her eat for a few minutes; they'd both had breakfast at home. As far as she knew, their home fridges were reliably refilled by someone. Someone who insisted on quality time and dinner together in the evenings. Both men wore their wedding rings every day; Graeve's seemed to have become part of his body, whereas Enders was always twisting and pushing his as if there was a problem with how it fitted.

"Kabangu," Graeve said, splaying his fingers as if he'd noticed Boni looking at him. "We can't give him protection around the clock. We're not a security firm."

"We have to," she said. "Until he goes back."

"Then he needs to go back *today*. Talk to him."

"What if he doesn't want to?"

"Talk to him. Let's move on. Riehmer."

"The man's name is Riedl, boss. *Riedl*. It isn't that difficult."

"Why do I keep saying Riehmer?"

"Too little sleep, too many worries?"

"I had an instructor called Riehmer," Enders said.

"Eventually you're going to collapse, and nobody wants that," Louise said, chewing.

Suppressing a smile, Graeve sighed, stood up awkwardly – stiff hips, stiff back – and went to the counter.

She looked at Enders and thought: the morning of truth. "At some point you're going to have to come out with it."

"About Riehmer, you mean?"

"Wolfgang from Aachen and that rubbish. And why do you want to drive around with me all the time?"

Graeve returned to the table with a thermos jug and poured them all more coffee.

"Old Riehmer," Enders said cheerfully. "The only real communist in the North-Rhine Westphalian police. A tough cookie, Stalin-worshipper. God, we really respected him. I'm your Gulag, he used to say. If you collapse and stay on the ground, you'll get extra shifts. If you vomit on my shoes and keep running, you'll get the day off."

"Nice. Now we know too," Graeve said with a fleeting smile. "Now: Riedl. What are we going to do with him? How do we get the names of his neo-Nazi chums? We've got to make him talk."

"It's going to be hard," Louise said. "His wife is mixed up in it."

They put together a to-do list. Warn Kabangu and get him to leave the country. Then interrogate Riedl, Walczak and Janisch, if possible at the same time. Maybe squeeze in the anxious son Lothar somewhere, Louise thought. Maybe if she observed him for a bit, on the way home from school, with friends, she might get some ideas.

"Let's round them all up," Enders said.

She shook her head. "Not Riedl for the time being. Nor Walczak. The Krügers – fine."

"Not the Krügers either," Graeve said. "We haven't got anything incriminating on them."

"I see it differently, boss."

"Because you, how shall I put it, assess the facts . . . creatively." Rubbing the bridge of his nose, he continued talking. "I should also tell you that the ministry has implied we ought to keep our distance

113

from Janisch. It seems as if our Verfassungsschutz colleagues are keen to recruit him as an informer. As far as I can make out, domestic intelligence have been on him for a year. They want to infiltrate the Southwest Brigade and Janisch appears to be the only possible candidate."

"Who's supposed to believe that?" Louise said.

Graeve laughed; for a moment he looked almost liberated.

"Is he under observation?" Enders asked.

"No idea."

"If so, the Baden-Baden lot know," Louise said. "We're certainly not going to leave him in peace. He's got hold of illegal firearms."

"Can we prove that?" Graeve asked.

"Not yet." As she spread jam, plum this time, on the other half of her roll, she tried to compose a thought. The word "informer" echoed in her head and made her feel uneasy. "Have they already contacted Janisch?"

This elicited a stiff smile from Graeve. "They're not giving me any details."

Louise nodded gratefully, and then the thought came to her. If Janisch were an informer for the Baden-Württemberg Verfassungsschutz, this would explain why he'd been so surprised when they arrested him yesterday, and why he had been so certain during questioning that nothing would happen to him.

And why Stuttgart was turning the screw.

They fell silent. Enders' question hung ominously in the air, and with it the consequences. Did the Verfassungsschutz actually know about Baden-Baden? About a planned attack? Irina?

"Best not to think about it at all," she said.

15

Ludwig Kabangu, sixty-five, medium height, slim, his hair grey and short like his beard, red shirt, jeans. A quiet man who moved with noticeable circumspection, and gave off an aura of melancholy and loneliness.

He'd been picked up by a woman of around the same age and now the two of them were walking up to the Colombischlössle. Trenchcoat from Burberry, patterned blouse buttoned at the neck, a discreet necklace – a distinguished woman who looked slightly stiff but friendly. A professor or academic, a representative from the university perhaps, or the media, a TV arts presenter or journalist working on the review section of a national newspaper. She was pointing at the building, apparently explaining something to him.

They were speaking French. Louise, who was walking ten metres behind them, picked up the occasional word. Kabangu didn't say much; the woman was doing the talking. The manor house built on the site of the former St Louis fortress, English neo-Gothic style, a museum of prehistory and ancient history with Palaeolithic sculptures of women and "other wonderful exhibits, shall we go in?"

"No, thank you," Kabangu said. "Perhaps tomorrow."

Her mobile vibrated. Birte, who'd replaced Gerd at seven o'clock and was wandering through the park on another path, taking photographs. "Done," she said.

"Send them over."

Two images of the woman, including a close-up. Louise forwarded them to Natalie, who in turn was going to e-mail them to the Federal

Criminal Police Office. This was purely a routine matter; the woman didn't look like there would be more on her than a handful of parking tickets and perhaps an affair in thirty years of marriage.

"My colleagues have arrived down below, I'm off," Birte said, as hoarse as ever, the occasional consonant catching in her strained throat.

Louise glanced towards Eisenbahnstrasse. A patrol car had stopped outside one of the hotels, support for the worst-case scenario. They had to improvise for the next few hours until they'd had the chance to talk to Kabangu. "OK, thanks."

"Let me know if you need me again."

"I do need you again."

Birte wandering along the pavement, on her way home. She had to get two of her children to school, after which her next assignment would be waiting.

Louise was still holding her phone when a text arrived from Natalie: *Have you looked at Gerd's photos?*

As she followed Kabangu and the woman, now on their way to the eastern exit of the park, she typed: *Yes, why?*

Gerd had sent three images before going home, his haul from an uneventful night: the dimly lit hotel from the front, from one side and from the other. A lot of black, a lot of night and a single sentence: *You're mistaken, Boni. I'll bet you anything.*

Natalie texted back one of the photos, or rather an enlarged detail from one of them. Louise could see a wall and a garage entrance, all of it in almost total darkness. A red circle marked a point on the entrance. Shielding the screen from the light she was able to make out a small patch of white and a few outlines inside the red circle. The face of a man with low eyebrows and ears that stuck out slightly.

Boni started walking again, quicker this time.

Natalie rang and said agitatedly, "Can you see it?"

"Yes."

"The line of sight is right. He's watching the hotel."

"Looks like it."

Having crossed Rotteckring, Kabangu and the woman were now heading for the old town. A hundred metres to the right was the patrol car, moving slowly in their direction.

More cars, more pedestrians. Cyclists. Nobody who looked suspect.

Everyone was suspect, she thought.

"Do you think I'm making too much of this?" Natalie said.

"No."

She'd immediately recognised the man in the garage entrance, having seen other photographs of him from a different night. Monday night, camping in paradise: the man with the rucksack.

The two men in the Sky Wave were indeed on Kabangu's trail.

The old and new town halls, the fountain with the monk statue, then ambling over to Kartoffelmarkt, Haus zum Waldfisch, the Raubrunnen. The woman talked, Kabangu listened and Louise followed nervously.

She'd notified Enders, who'd organised more patrol cars, said he'd be there himself in half an hour and insisted she speak to Kabangu *at once* to urge him to leave. And to tell him that it would be best if he spent the remaining time before his departure at police HQ.

Louise was torn. Wasn't it better to wait until she could speak with Kabangu alone and undisturbed? Hopefully he was safe during the daytime and in the city centre; they'd be much more likely to attempt something when it was dark, on the way back from a restaurant in the evening, or in the middle of the night in the hotel.

Apart from that she didn't want to scare anyone off. Kabangu's departure wouldn't close the case; the neo-Nazi structures would still be intact. If they were going to have a chance of securing evidence and carrying out arrests, they mustn't be visible too soon.

Far too risky! Enders had said, cursing as he hung up.

Münsterplatz, the blood-red Historical Merchants' Hall, other buildings. Kabangu and the woman were walking past the rows of houses at an almost maddeningly slow pace. Finally they turned their attention to the Minster; she seemed to be asking him whether he wished to climb the tower, and it looked as if he said no. Turning southwards, they wandered amongst pedestrians through the narrow alleys that connected the streets of the old town. Louise stayed on their tail, five metres behind.

In Salzstrasse Kabangu unexpectedly put one foot into the runnel of water that ran along the street, immediately followed by the other. Only then did he roll up his trouser legs a few centimetres. He stood there, looking at his feet, as the woman laughed.

When Kabangu looked up he was smiling.

Gerd called. "Isn't Janisch meant to be working today?"

"What?"

"Because he's still in his flat."

"Janisch is still in his flat?"

"Correct, Boni."

Her thoughts came thick and fast. According to Marek, Janisch had spent the evening at home without any visitors, as far as they could tell. Had he called in sick?

A few metres away, Kabangu stepped out of the runnel, his shoes and trouser bottoms soaked. Laughing, he threw his head back and balled his fists. All of a sudden his joy appeared aggressive, full of bitterness and anger.

"Boni?" Gerd said.

"Go in."

"Into the flat? Are you crazy? Without a SWAT team?"

"Find the caretaker and tell him he has to invent an excuse to get into Janisch's flat."

A tram arrived; Kabangu and the woman vanished from view. From nowhere Leif Enders appeared, grabbed her arm and pulled her in the opposite direction from the tram. Then the tram had gone and they ran to the museum clad with construction hoardings. Kabangu and the woman were now halfway across Augustinerplatz, a fair distance away from them. Dozens of people swarmed around them, far too close to be able to protect Kabangu.

"I'm going to hang up now, Boni," Gerd said.

"Go in with the caretaker, for Christ's sake!" she urged him, cutting the connection as she walked alongside Enders down to Gerberau. Kabangu and the woman headed for Fischerau, then stopped. The woman pointed at the canal with the crocodile sculpture and Kabangu nodded, his hands on the railing. A man – tall, thin, shoulder-length hair – came rushing towards Kabangu, knocking into him. Kabangu teetered and instinctively took a step to the side to avoid falling. The man raised a hand as if in apology. Kabangu spun around, annoyed, then gave a dismissive wave of his hand and reassured the woman who'd put a concerned hand on his arm.

"I'll sort this out," Enders said breathlessly, moving away from Louise.

The phone: Gerd again. "You can't be serious, Boni."

"I don't believe it—"

"What do you mean?"

"Call Graeve. Let him decide."

"Now you're talking, Boni."

She put her phone away and followed Kabangu and the woman into Fischerau, keeping an eye on her colleague at the same time. His phone to his ear, Enders had set off in pursuit of the man, taking him back to Augustinerplatz. Uniformed officers came towards them and Louise just glimpsed them apprehending the man before the houses alongside the canal blocked her sight.

Ahead of her, Kabangu and the woman crossed the small bridge to the Altstadt-Café and sat at one of the little tables in the sun, which had banished for good the rain, clouds and fog of the past few days.

A few minutes later they had cups in front of them, the woman talked and Kabangu listened, a peaceful tableau, while Louise, unnerved and exhausted, leaned against a wall in the shadows.

Enders strolled over to her, shaking his head. A frantic but harmless passer-by. They were taking him in nonetheless; Mats Benedikt would check him out more thoroughly. He pointed to the café. "Let's go inside and talk."

"Not now, Leif, it'll have to wait. I need some quiet time."

He nodded. "No problem. It's been going on for a while now, so a few more hours or days won't make any difference."

"Will I want to hear it?"

"I don't think so."

"Louise," Enders said.

She gave a start.

Bonì had sunk into a half-asleep, half-awake state, her head on his shoulder, ten minutes rest a few paces away on a wooden bench belonging to a little shop. Still shady on their side of Fischerau, whereas Kabangu and the woman sat in the sun on the other side of the narrow canal. A waiter was at their table, taking money from Kabangu.

"You or me?" Enders said.

"Not yet."

"Me, then."

Kabangu and the woman had got up. On the other side of the bridge they parted with kisses on cheeks. The woman went off towards Augustinerplatz; Kabangu headed in the other direction, passing Enders and Louise just as her phone rang.

Gerd.

"Bloody hell, Bonì, how did you know yet again?"

"What?"

"That Janisch has passed away."

"Janisch is *dead*?"

Having got up, Enders sat down again, a gloomy look on his face, his eyes darting between Louise and Kabangu. Louise too felt the adrenaline shooting through her veins; her heart had started racing.

Janisch, Gerd said, had "gone to sleep peacefully. I suspect it was the excitement." He was lying in bed, no signs of foul play or suicide, by the look of things a compassionate heart attack in the middle of the night – he fell asleep and didn't wake up. Gerd was still standing beside the body, talking nineteen to the dozen, that's what you'd wish for, isn't it, Bonì, what more could you ask for, no carp in your trousers, no mess on the floor, that's how you'd want to die when you have to, and eventually you do have to.

Louise stood up and hurried alongside Enders after Kabangu. Enders asked her questions under his breath while Gerd continued speaking, looking at the body again, lovely that he left us so peacefully, murder virtually ruled out, and I mean, we were there, Marek and me, outside his door, and Marek also thinks there must've been something up with his heart or his head or lungs. At any rate there weren't any suspects in the building. We'd have noticed them if there were.

"For Christ's sake, Gerd!"

"He had something wrong with his heart, Bonì."

Grabbing her arm, Enders said, "I'm going to drive over there."

"Enders is coming," Louise said.

"It's the only explanation, because there wasn't anyone in there. Enders?"

"Bermann's successor."

"Oh, him."

"And you talk to Kabangu!" Enders said. "Now!"

She flapped her free hand at him. "Have you called forensics, Gerd?"

"Not yet."

"Do it."

"Nobody touched that guy last night, Boni. Not even a fly."

Without responding she cut him off. Kabangu had reached Kaiser-Joseph-Strasse and was turning right. She ran to the junction, catching up with him and stayed as close on his heels as possible, avoiding pedestrians, cyclists, trams, while keeping a watchful eye on everything and everyone.

The further they went down Rathausstrasse, the quieter it got. Kabangu stood for a long time at a pedestrian crossing, missing a green light – a scrawny, slightly stooped man, lost in thought.

In Eisenbahnstrasse Louise crossed the street shortly after him. She noticed a man standing on the slope in Colombipark, looking down at them. Bald, narrow sunglasses, black hoodie, the pockets bulging with his hands, black jeans. When he turned away, an array of piercings in his ear glinted in the sunlight. He went over to a bench and picked up a can of beer. Then he crossed the grass in the other direction. On the back of his hoodie was a word in white letters, Gothic script; from that distance Louise couldn't make it out.

There was practically nobody in Poststrasse. A patrol car overtook her, followed sedately by a cyclist.

A group of arrivals were at the hotel reception, half a dozen elderly women.

"Four fourteen," she heard Kabangu say, slightly gruffly.

A monstrosity of a key in his hand, he walked past the lift to the stairs and went up them, stooped, one hand on the banister. Louise followed him silently, thinking of Janisch. Where was the mistake, how could they have lost him with two surveillance officers outside? Janisch, who'd been so important, the link between the Krügers, Walczak and the Riedls.

Janisch, who might have been an informer.

Second floor, a text from Natalie. It was the photo of a man Louise didn't recognise: pale, bloated face, acne, early thirties.

Her phone vibrated. "I can't talk," she whispered.

"You don't have to," Natalie said, continuing. Jena Kripo had called back. The Sky Wave had been rented since Saturday and was expected back this coming Sunday. It had been hired by Matthias Seibert, resident in Jena. He wasn't answering his phone, wasn't at home and his neighbours had confirmed to the Jena officers that he'd gone on a trip in a campervan. "But he didn't," Natalie said. Seibert was the person in the photo she'd texted and looked nothing like the two men caught on Paulus Riedl's CCTV on Monday night. He might have arranged the hire of the van, but he wasn't using it himself.

Third floor. Kabangu stopped, as did Louise. She heard him trying to regulate his breathing.

Matthias Seibert, the Jena officer had said. He's known to us. Although Seibert was "on the right of the political spectrum" he was "one of the harmless ones". In the past he organised concerts for neo-Nazi bands under the Blood & Honour banner, now he did the same under his own name. He was believed to be a member of the Thuringian Heimat Guard, occasionally spotted at far-right demos or hanging around with officials from the National Democratic Party. Other than that he hadn't been on the police's radar. Uncompleted apprenticeship in data-processing management with Carl Zeiss. Part-time job as a sales assistant in an electronics store, no previous convictions, if you want to know more ask the Verfassungsschutz, they're well integrated into the scene.

"Do we want to know more?"

"We do," Louise whispered.

They'd reached the fourth floor. Kabangu unlocked the door to his room and went in. Louise followed slowly along the deserted corridor. She thought of the night-time face on Gerd's photograph and the man with the sunglasses just now in Colombipark. If Kabangu really was being recced, she wondered why she hadn't noticed anyone suspect earlier – on the way from the hotel to the Colombischlössle,

123

across to the old town. Even in the café by the canal there had been no-one remotely suspicious-looking for an entire hour.

She knocked at the door. "Monsieur Kabangu?"

Perhaps, she thought, because one of those doing the recceing had been with Kabangu the whole time.

Someone who looked totally unsuspicious.

16

"But I *can't* leave," Ludwig Kabangu said in his rapid, harsh French. He'd given Louise the armchair by the small coffee table, while he sat on the edge of the bed. He wafted his arms in the air, palms pointing upwards almost in supplication. Over the past few minutes, beads of sweat had formed on his brow and his red shirt had dark patches under the arms. Louise was sweating too; an electric heater made it feel increasingly warm in the room.

"I promised my wife I'd bring home the mortal remains of her grandfather. Many years ago she said to me: Every morning and every evening I think about Grandfather Mabruk. He's not well, he complains inside my head. He's utterly homesick. He's missing the smells of home, the smell of the soil, the forests, the food, cooked cassava. He's missing the sounds of home, the lowing of the cattle, the wind in the trees. He's so homesick that it hurts, my wife told me, and that's why he can't find any peace in a foreign land. How could you find peace in a foreign land? I'm missing the peace of home, Grandfather Mabruk told my wife. So I promised her I'd bring him home." Leaning forwards, Kabangu moved his left hand to the left. "But you don't know where he is!" my wife said. His right hand moved right. "I said: I'll find out. And I did find out. Grandfather Mabruk is here, in your city, in Freiburg." He laid his hands on his knees. "I can't leave without him."

"Maybe," Louise said, "I didn't express myself clearly enough."

"Oh yes, you did," he said, smiling impatiently. "Somebody wants to kill me."

"It's a possibility, at least." She stood up and went to the window. "May I?"

"Do you not like the smell of my room?"

"Only the heat in here, Monsieur."

Boni tilted open the window, turned and leaned against the windowsill. No, she didn't like the smell of the room either. Kabangu had been smoking, African cigarettes perhaps, at any rate an unfamiliar, harsh, tarry smell that disagreed with her.

He pursed his lips. "A group of right-wing extremists, that sounds most . . . unusual. I would go as far as to say: unlikely."

"Really?"

"Those people don't know me. They're not losing anything or suffering because of me. In truth, maybe there are other people who want me to leave?"

"That's irrelevant."

"Not for the university, I fear."

"For *me* it's irrelevant, Monsieur Kabangu, and I'm not interested in anything else."

Her phone rang again. Excusing herself, Louise took the call. "Can you talk?" Enders said.

"I can in German." She smiled and held up two fingers: two minutes. Kabangu nodded. "He's eccentric, mistrustful and is refusing to leave."

"Tell him you've got a body, cause of death undetermined."

"OK. What about you? Found anything?"

"Nothing," Enders said. He was standing beside Janisch's bed looking at the body. The bare torso was half covered by a duvet, his arms stretched out over the top of it, his features for the most part relaxed. "As if he'd died peacefully."

"A guy like him doesn't die peacefully."

"And not at this time." Gerd's voice was audible in the background; she heard "kitchen" and, at the end, "heart attack". "There are remnants of vomit," Enders told her. Then, in a virtual whisper, "Who do I have to call to ensure a post-mortem's carried out ASAP?"

She heard new undertones in his beautiful, hoarse voice, a sudden mistrust, clearly aimed at Gerd, as if now anything was possible in this case.

"Marianne Andrele, the public prosecutor."

She put the phone back in her coat pocket and returned to the chair. She wished Bermann were still here; she needed him after all. Bermann, who had so many failings but not the worst failing of a police officer: he could not be corrupted or intimidated.

"Please," she said eventually, "go home. We've got a dead body."

"So have I," Kabangu countered.

"When Grandfather Mabruk knew I was going to bring him home he started speaking to me too. It's high time you got going, he kept telling me. First I have to find out where to look for you, I replied. I'm in a beautiful city with lots of little rivers, he said. So I went to a library, looked in the books for a city with little rivers and found too many. Make an effort, Grandfather Mabruk said, I'm missing home so much, it's really painful! So I tried harder, but I couldn't find this city. Help me, I said, which country is it in? I don't know, but I sense it's a brother nation. Yes, the country is our big brother and we're his little brother. Tanzania? I asked. No, you fool! he exclaimed. Yes, he insulted me! Can you imagine?"

Kabangu laughed, a happy yet mechanical laugh. "He was very impatient. Grandfather Mabruk, my wife often said, was a loving but very impatient man. He was like that when he was alive, and is even more so now that he's dead and can't find peace. Peace, she often said, was incredibly important to him. She said many more things about him, she knew lots of things." Kabangu rubbed his hands on his trouser legs; they were shivering almost imperceptibly. His eyes were half closed and around his mouth was a faint smile.

"Is your wife no longer alive?"

He confirmed this with a nod and Louise thought his wife must have died some time ago. Loneliness had had plenty of time to eat into him. Loneliness and imagination.

As he said nothing more, she asked, "So how did you find the city in the end?"

"By remembering my *own* grandfather and why I'm called Ludwig and why all my siblings and cousins have German first names."

Kabangu's grandfather had worked in a German military household at the beginning of the twentieth century, for fourteen years until the outbreak of the First World War. With his "master" he'd gone to war as a member of the colonial force and had fought against the British–Indian and Portuguese armies over German East Africa. His "master" died before the German surrender; Kabangu's grandfather returned unharmed. He passed down to his children a "deep friendship with Germany", as Kabangu put it, and took the job of naming the grandchildren himself: Ludwig, Friedrich, Oskar, Rudolf, Adolf, Theodor, Magdalene, Karoline and Wilhelmine. "Germany," Kabangu said, "is Rwanda's 'brother nation' that Grandfather Mabruk spoke about, do you understand?"

Louise nodded even though she wasn't sure. "So was Mabruk a friend of Germany too?"

"Aren't we all? He threw his arms in the air and smiled. "He wanted to go home nonetheless, and who can blame him? How are you supposed to find peace in a foreign land, even when that foreign land is called Germany?"

Louise stifled a yawn; she was too exhausted to deal with this heat and Kabangu's laborious explanation. All the same she asked him to continue. While he was talking to her he wasn't going out into the street, and as long as he wasn't on the street he was safe.

"Armed with this knowledge I returned to the library and tried even harder. Soon I realised that there were large collections of bones of Africans in Germany. Many of these come from German South-West

Africa and some from German East Africa. Grandfather Mabruk guided me in my search. He took my hand that chose the books and my eyes that scanned the words. And so we came across a German military doctor, Dr Feldmann, who in 1908 sent 'anatomical preparations of negroes' to the Anthropological Institute in Freiburg. We learned that Dr Feldmann had stayed near to Rwanda, namely by Lake Victoria to the east, and Lake Tanganyika to the south. But we couldn't discover whether Dr Feldmann also travelled to Rwanda, to the village in the border area where Grandfather Mabruk was buried in 1907.

"So we got on the coach and travelled there. Grandfather Mabruk was very sad when he saw the village and his pain became terribly acute. Bring me home, he whispered, bring me home at last! I asked the residents of the village and discovered the following from an elderly lady. She'd heard from her father and grandfather that a long time ago a German expedition with doctors and scientists had come to the village to combat sleeping sickness. The Germans rounded up the sick and took them to a secret place. Some returned healthy, some returned blind, some returned dead. The villagers protested and their ancestors likewise protested; they were so upset when one morning their graves were found in a real mess, the lady said.

"When the expedition left, the graves were tidied again, but without looking inside them. Had anyone done so they would have seen that they were empty. For the Germans had taken the bones with them for scientific examination. This must have been in late 1907, for the lady said it was the same year that the German prince visited the Rwandan king."

"The German prince?"

"Adolf Friedrich, Duke of Mecklenburg."

Louise smiled without knowing why. Reaching down beside her she opened the door to the minibar, where she found a lot of beer, a lot of wine and a lot of chocolate, but nothing to help combat the heat or tiredness. She left the door open to allow her left leg at least to get some cool air. "No water?"

"I drank it yesterday afternoon. But look here," Kabangu said, pointing beside the desk.

Leaning forwards Louise saw five 1.5-litre bottles of water out of their packaging. On the desk stood two glasses. Kabangu drank some too, and for a while they said nothing.

"Was Feldmann on that expedition?"

He shook his head. "We weren't that lucky. Grandfather Mabruk and I left the village, went back to the library, kept searching and eventually found a very detailed report in a 1908 medical yearbook about sleeping sickness in the German colony, written by one of the doctor's colleagues, Dr Robert Koch. Koch himself had gone to German East Africa to experiment with medicines. The report mentions the expedition. The names and outcomes of all those who underwent treatment are detailed, as well as the villages they came from, including Grandfather Mabruk's. For scientific examination, it says, bones were sent from particular villages to Dr Feldmann who was stationed in Shirati by Lake Victoria. This was the proof we'd been looking for. Grandfather Mabruk was part of the 'anatomical preparations of negroes', which Dr Feldmann had sent to Freiburg!"

"How did he react?"

"He was beside himself with joy. I'm in Freiburg, he cried, dancing and shedding tears of happiness."

In a woozy moment of exhaustion Louise thought it was possible that Grandfather Mabruk actually was in Freiburg, even here in Kabangu's room. The dead didn't disappear, they stayed. They went wherever you did, she thought, and perhaps the only difference between Kabangu's dead person and hers was that hers didn't speak. They were silent and this meant that, although ever present, they were also absent in a painful way.

Say something, Rolf, she thought. Germain. Talk to me.

"Who was that woman this morning?"

Kabangu frowned. "You've been *watching* me?"

"To protect you."

"You're allowed to do that here?"

"Preventative observation, paragraphs 3 and 5 of Baden-Württemberg police law, on instruction from my boss's boss. What's her name?"

"But I don't want to be under observation!"

Louise nodded. "That's by the by. What's her name?"

"Maria." Visibly cross, Kabangu told her that they'd met after his arrival in Basel, on the way from the airport to the station. Louise probed further: How did this come about? Who first spoke to who? Who suggested the meeting in Freiburg? *Meetings*, Kabangu corrected her. They'd already met yesterday and the day before that, so today was the third time. In Basel he helped Maria with her heavy suitcase, and as she spoke French she helped him get to Freiburg. That afternoon they were planning to go to the university archive together. He had another appointment with the head of the archive.

"What's Maria's surname?"

"Schmidt."

"Does she live in Freiburg?"

"Yes." Resting his hands on his knees, Kabangu said, "Is she one of those right-wing extremists? Is *that* what they look like, the people who are trying to kill me?"

"Prove to me they don't."

"There's only one thing I want to do," he whispered, his voice now deep and exasperated.

Louise nodded.

Mabruk.

But was this really about bringing Mabruk home? she thought. Wasn't it in some intangible sense more about Kabangu himself?

*

A hand on her arm; she opened her eyes and found herself staring at Kabangu's face. He was standing right beside her, stooped, in a fresh grey shirt. "Your telephone," he said kindly.

She reached for it and saw "Kilian" on the screen. But when she answered there was nobody there.

A text message arrived. *Takeaway, usual, 30 mins?*

OK, she wrote back.

"Have I been asleep?"

"Yes."

Kabangu stepped back as Louise got up. She glanced at her phone again: half past twelve. She'd been asleep on the armchair for an entire hour. "Maria Schmidt, yes? With 'dt'?"

"I don't know." He touched her arm again. "I don't want to be watched anymore."

"Protected, Monsieur Kabangu."

"Alright, then. I don't want to be protected anymore." He came from a country, he said, where the state had wielded arbitrary power for a long time, as it had in Côte d'Ivoire where he'd spent several years. Being under police surveillance in Germany frightened him, especially given his ongoing dispute with a German institution, the university. "I hope you understand."

"No," Louise said on her way to the door, past Grandfather Mabruk and other dead people. "I want to protect you and I'm *going* to protect you. I don't need another dead body, Monsieur, I couldn't cope with another corpse. You have a good time with yours, with Grandfather Mabruk. You travel, chat and spend your days with him, but I have no fun with my dead. They torture me, they hound me into my dreams and they're always silent. No, I don't understand, and not looking out for you is inconceivable."

"That's different," he replied. "Look out for yourself. I've no objections to that."

17

Kilian didn't turn up.

She had got to the takeaway in the north of Freiburg on time and was now sitting at a wooden table by the window with a curry sausage. She ate and waited. The dead had stayed outside. Not fans of the music in here, they preferred to spend their time outside in the sun.

So she thought of the living.

Of Ludwig Kabangu, who talked at greater length than was good for his credibility. Of Julius Krüger, who'd been tasked by someone to drive his father's car on a specific day at a specific time to a specific place. Thomas Walczak, who was passing on weapons and money, and therefore knew more of the people involved than the others – Janisch, the two men from Jena, the person who'd given him the money for Janisch. Of Paulus and Charlotte Riedl, who knew someone who knew about Ludwig Kabangu.

Of Janisch, who was dead.

They had to get into gear, finally. Show they meant business. Arrest Julius Krüger, Walczak and the Riedls. Maybe that would mitigate the danger for Kabangu. Four of those involved in custody; surely the others would sit tight rather than launch an attack.

She called Enders.

"No public prosecutor is going to allow that. Intimidation is not a legitimate reason for arrest."

"Try, at least," she said. "Where are you?"

Enders had arranged for the removal of Janisch's corpse and

had gone straight from his flat back to HQ. Graeve wanted to speak to him – Stuttgart was fuming. "What about Kabangu? How did he react?"

"He's not going anywhere."

"Shit."

She told him the short version of the long story. Enders kept quiet before cursing again. He sounded increasingly nervous; the pressure from above was taking its toll. Maybe it was just that they were less and less in control of the situation: Janisch dead, Kabangu intransigent, the evidence sketchy.

"Are you still with him?"

"No," she said. A patrol car was outside the hotel and Birte was going to be taking over for an hour at half past one. Then it would be her turn again, but Enders didn't need to know that.

They finished the call.

At one o'clock she bought some chips, ate them and waited again. No Kilian.

Her tiredness returned, her exhaustion. Not the sort of exhaustion you get over with a few weeks' holiday. More a kind of psychological and emotional exhaustion.

What a life she led, she thought. Far, far away from all social junctures. No friends, no relationship with a future, no family. Her contact with her mother, father and second brother had thinned out to a few telephone calls per year.

A club would be a good start. Table tennis or skat or Zen meditation. A child.

A child at forty-six, that would be something. The look on Rolf Bermann's face would have been reason enough to have a child at forty-six.

Ben, she thought, come to Freiburg, they had a future now. She laughed softly.

A phone rang. The owner of the takeaway had an argument with a supplier.

Natalie sent a text. *Appointment at the university archive, 2 pm, Dr Arndt.*

Another ten minutes passed.

She got up, leaving her coat on the back of the chair as a sign for Kilian, and went to the loo. She sat there thinking seriously about a child at forty-six.

The lock snapped and she saw the bolt turn. Then the cubicle door opened and Kilian stood before her.

"At least turn around," she said.

What Kilian had to say in a whisper and at great haste was worth a bit of shame.

Irina, who wasn't called Irina, had confirmed that Niko, who wasn't called Niko, was involved in the Russian neo-Nazi scene. In addition he had contact with far-right extremists in the US, for example the former leader of the American Ku Klux Klan, "Mike". A Holocaust denier, he was often in Europe, staying in Moscow and Vienna. Irina's husband approved of these contacts but made sure that people like Mike, who was under surveillance by the authorities, stayed away from his organisation. In response to Louise's questions, Irina had remembered a brief conversation from a few weeks ago. Her husband Niko had jokingly pointed out that "the American" owed him something if he got weapons for his "hooded friend". She interpreted the conversation to mean that Mike had given Niko a guarantee about the buyer of the pistols.

"Hooded friend?" Louise asked.

Kilian nodded, frantically sweeping back his hair. His eyelids were fluttering.

"Is the buyer a member of the Ku Klux Klan?"

He shrugged. "Your case, not mine."

Was the German Ku Klux Klan involved in a contract killing?

She knew next to nothing about the German offshoot of the

Klan, only that there were a few chapters and bizarre websites of white Christian fanatics. Until now she had thought of these groups as bizarre too, but not dangerous. The odd burning cross at night over the past few years, vague contacts with the far right . . . In western Germany, at least, the Klan seemed to be more folkloric than an actual problem.

"No more questions now, Louise. Too dangerous."

"OK." She sat on the closed toilet seat and stared at Kilian, who hadn't for a second let go of the handle of the cubicle door, perhaps out of nervousness, perhaps to have something to hold on to. He looked ill and at physical breaking point, a spectral man unable to find peace.

"Who knows about me?"

"Only Graeve."

"Have you told him about Daria?"

"Daria?"

Kilian rubbed his eyes and didn't respond.

"No, not a word," Louise said. "How are things looking your end?"

"It's all quiet. *Too* quiet."

"Are you going to get through this?"

Intimating a smile, he nodded again. "I've got to go."

She laid a hand on his arm. "Wait. Janisch, the courier, might have been an informer."

"Criminal Investigation Bureau?"

"Domestic intelligence." She told him about the calls and about "Birte" from Stuttgart. The Verfassungsschutz, regional police directorate and the Ministry of the Interior were involved, putting pressure on Cords and Freiburg Kripo for reasons unknown. Put simply, things were happening that were out of their hands.

Kilian's eyes were half closed, his pupils were wandering. He seemed to be thinking feverishly without coming to any conclusion.

She told him about Janisch's death.

He just looked at her, silent, lips pursed, and she guessed what was going on inside his head: he was wishing he'd never told her about the guns. She couldn't blame him. The more uncontrollable the situation, the more dangerous it became for Irina.

Daria.

Without another word he opened the door and vanished.

18

Enders had come over the river and was waiting in the sunshine outside the archive, an attractive, two-storey villa, perhaps late nineteenth century. "I need a few minutes' peace," he said.

"You've come to the wrong person, then," Louise said.

He moved right next to her and for a moment she was surprised by a typical Bermann combination of smells: scrambled eggs with bacon, a lunchtime beer and espresso. Only the cigarettes didn't fit; Bermann hated smoking. "Ku Klux Klan, eh?" he said softly. "This is getting better and better."

"Mats might know something about them."

"I spoke to him earlier and he doesn't know much. There's no information at all on a Baden Klan group, but up until a few years ago there was a chapter in Schwäbisch Hall under the parent organisation 'European White Knights of the Ku Klux Klan'. It was dissolved in 2002 or 2003 and, according to Mats, it was a rallying point for neo-Nazis from a variety of German states, for 'Blood & Honour' activists and suchlike. Apparently a few of its members were Verfassungsschutz informers."

"Maybe the chapter's still active."

"Or active again," Enders said.

They went through the passageway to the inner courtyard and climbed some steps to the entrance. "Be ruthless, OK?" Louise said.

He smiled. "I need some more action anyway."

*

Peter Arndt, head of the archive, sat like a statue at a plain desk, his hands clasped in front of him. He was a friendly, smallish man in his early fifties with intelligent, alert eyes, which made him appear full of knowledge and ideas. Louise bet he was someone who could make sense of practically everything because he'd heard of, or read about, practically everything, even about people who wanted to bring home their dead from foreign lands, and others who couldn't get rid of theirs – she might ask him if she got the chance. He was surrounded on three sides by surprisingly modern shelves with sliding doors of satinised glass. Hundreds of books behind them which could only be guessed at, silent shadows as if everything they contained remained impenetrable or buried; perhaps it was simply to protect them from dust and light. On the fourth side sat Enders and Bonì, the villa's windows behind them.

"Ludwig Kabangu," she said.

Arndt nodded.

She sensed that Enders wanted to pick it up from here, but there wasn't enough time for detours and diplomacy. So she placed a hand on his arm and said, focused, "The background, Herr Arndt . . . At the beginning of April an unknown person, possibly a member of a Baden-Württemberg chapter of the Ku Klux Klan, ordered two pistols from a criminal organisation. A Freiburg neo-Nazi, member of the Southwest Brigade, picked up the guns last Saturday and that same night might have handed them over to a middleman living near Bollschweil. Late on Monday night this middleman gave the pistols to two men from Jena, probably neo-Nazis too, travelling with two women in a rented campervan. We fear that they've been contracted to kill Ludwig Kabangu, sometime in the next day or so. Our question to you is: How can the man who ordered the pistols have known in early April that Kabangu would be coming to Freiburg three weeks later?"

Arndt had turned pale. His hands had separated and his fingernails were rubbing the tip of his thumb. "Neo-Nazis?"

"Not that we're accusing you or your colleagues of anything, Dr Arndt," Enders said.

Arndt looked at them; seconds passed.

"A kingdom for your thoughts," Louise said.

"My thoughts? I don't listen to gossip."

She smiled. "A luxury we can't afford."

Arndt seemed to have grasped the seriousness of the situation. In a calm voice he began to talk, choosing his words carefully, as if he wanted to avoid adding any rumours to the gossip he didn't listen to.

An academic colleague by the name of Erik Willig, a historian, married, rather quiet, always friendly, shouldered responsibility. He'd never done anything wrong, apart from on one occasion when he'd said something to a PhD student from Berlin that wasn't like him at all. When the student ranted on about parallel communities in Neukölln and the incompatibility of Islam and democracy, Willig said – not verbatim, but something along these lines – *You ought to come along some time, there's a small circle here of socially conservative intellectuals, professors, journalists, writers, doctors, even a judge and public prosecutor, who all think like you, and we're always happy to welcome interested parties.*

By chance a research assistant had overheard the brief chat and a few weeks later told her successor about it, who a month after that came to see Arndt. To give an idea of this group's ideological orientation, the first assistant said, Willig had mentioned the Institute for National Policy and the Weikersheim Trust, both of which – as her successor commented angrily – were right-wing.

Although it was on his mind for a while, Arndt said, he hadn't made much of an effort to follow up on the allegation because the PhD student had already moved back to Berlin, the first research assistant had disappeared back into the mass of undergraduates, while her successor had turned up the following day, just as angry, accusing a fellow student of "sexual harassment". Instead he casually asked Willig if he'd heard of the Weikersheim Group, as an acquaintance of his had been invited to one of their events. Rather than correct the name or ask any questions, Willig had just said no.

"You call *that* gossip?" Louise asked.

Arndt didn't reply; he merely rubbed the sides of his head.

"That's more than gossip."

"Maybe, yes."

"What sort of organisation are they?" Enders asked. "The Institute and the Trust?"

"As far as I'm concerned they're—"

"I know what you're thinking," Arndt interrupted Louise. "On the other hand, surely we have to be able to put up with this . . . that some people think differently. Harbour radical, undemocratic ideas."

"So long as they just think that way," Enders said in a friendly tone.

Arndt made a gesture of agreement.

"I'm sorry," Louise said, "but I'm not going to put up with it."

"We need names," Enders said. "The PhD student, the first research assistant."

Arndt nodded frantically, grabbed a notepad and started writing. "I'll sort it out." Looking again at Enders, he explained that the Institute for National Policy and the Weikersheim Trust could be considered New Right organisations, Christian–Conservative think tanks, networks undertaking lobbying and educational work along their ideological lines.

"You've done your homework," Louise said.

"I assume that Erik Willig knew about Kabangu's e-mail?" Enders asked.

"We have a team meeting every Monday morning where we discuss matters that go beyond day-to-day concerns. A restitution claim from a former colony falls into that category."

"Did Willig have anything to say about it?"

"All he said was, 'We don't have any.'"

"Bones from former colonies?"

"From German East Africa."

"Is that true?"

Arndt sighed. "It's very, very unlikely."

"But not out of the question."

"No, not entirely."

"You do have the remains of one person, at the very least."

Arndt gave a sombre grin. "Grandfather Mabruk?"

"Do you sense his presence?" She raised a hand as if Mabruk were in the room.

"No, Frau Bonì, I do not, and I hope you don't either."

"Who is that?" Enders asked.

"The grandfather of Herr Kabangu's dead wife."

"Yes," Louise said, "I do sense his presence. He's my bad conscience, my memory, my nightmare. He's the voice of my dead and the emptiness they've left behind. Yes, I sense him . . . Fairly clearly." Pointing to her head, she added, "Here."

"We're all a bit tired and overwrought," Enders said.

She smiled. "Where can we find Willig?"

Arndt got up, shooting her a slightly tense glance as he made for the door. "Where Grandfather Mabruk supposedly is."

Arndt briskly led them out of the building and north across Werthmannstrasse to Platz der Alten Synagoge a few minutes away. He held open for them the door of the university building, then went down some steps, holding on to the banister. Louise followed more slowly, behind Enders, her legs and head reluctant to enter the harsh neon light and the room that housed the dead. Down here was where the university kept the Alexander Ecker Collection, the bones of 1,599 bodies, the oldest from the first half of the nineteenth century, the most recent from the early twentieth.

She listened to the discussion between Arndt and Enders. Please, Arndt said, so far all this is mere assumption, hypothesis and speculation. But highly plausible, Enders countered. Think about it: a black man from a former colony claims that back in the day the Germans illegally opened graves and stole bones, and comes to Freiburg to demand restitution from the university – surely that makes him the perfect target for neo-Nazis. Arndt raised his hands as if to continue the conversation when Enders' mobile rang. "Hi Natalie?" he said.

With the phone to his ear he turned to Louise. She saw bafflement and fury creep into his expression. "I'll be there in ten."

The Ministry of the Interior had removed Janisch's body from Freiburg forensic department; the post-mortem would be carried out in Heidelberg.

Birte had driven off and two colleagues were now keeping watch on Kabangu, spending their lunch break outside the hotel that he hadn't yet left.

Thirty minutes gained.

Louise stood at the entrance to the basement; Arndt had hurried away to look for Erik Willig. She restlessly ran her eyes over shelves on which hundreds of white boxes stood side by side in the neon light, full of bones, skulls, teeth and whatever else. The remains of people from different continents and eras.

From a scientific viewpoint the collection was extremely useful, Ilka Weber had said. The objects allowed us to understand why and how racist anthropologists like Alexander Ecker and his successor Eugen Fischer had undertaken their research and collected bones. She underlined, however, that this didn't justify the circumstances in which the bones had found their way to Freiburg, nor the university's policy of looking for specific remains only at the request of governments. For some people, the idea that their dead forefathers

143

had become objects of scientific investigation was intolerable, and possibly illegal too.

Louise moved away from the door and wandered down the nearest row of shelves. The dead, including her own, were silent. Say something, Rolf, she thought. Germain. It would be fun. Only ever having my own head for company and not talking doesn't make it easier. I can't really speak to the living. Say something, Grandfather Mabruk.

And suddenly, amongst all the silent white boxes, she understood. She knew why she'd become a police officer: to get on top of death.

That was why she'd become the job and the job had become her. To come face to face with death, understand it, prevent it. To be quicker than death. To undo Germain's death. That was why she put up with death after death: to prevent the one death that had left her reeling.

How bizarre. And sentimental.

"Frau Bonì?"

She followed Arndt, returning to the living who, in their own way, were dealing with the dead too.

Erik Willig, a tall man in his early forties, stood beside a small table in the last row of shelves and looked at her. The first thing she noticed were his angular features: the narrow face that looked as if it had been carved from light-coloured stone, the nose barely the width of a finger, the ears more pointy than oval and his wedding ring wafer-thin.

"Your little group," she said without preamble. "What's it all about?"

Willig cocked his head. "What group?" His voice, at any rate, sounded pleasant, calm and friendly.

"Do you meet once a month and get worked up about the asylum seekers on Hammerschmiedstrasse?"

He turned to Arndt with the hint of a frown. A man taken by surprise, being accused unfairly. Arndt didn't step in.

"Do you sing Heimat songs from the colonial era?"

"You must have got me mixed—"

"And when you're bored with your little group you order the murder of a black man who's got too big for his boots?"

Willig bent over the table, tidied a few documents into a pile and put them in a briefcase, followed by his laptop. His hands weren't shaking, he wasn't driven to making any rash comments; he looked calm, totally unruffled. Louise sensed that she wouldn't get anything out of this man; he would only ever say "No". "No, I don't know people like that", "No, I don't think like that".

But it wasn't her intention to get anything out of him.

"Have you told anybody about Ludwig Kabangu?"

He looked up. "Is that what this is about? Giving back the bones? No, I've not told anyone. Why?"

"Your wife? Your intellectual friends?"

"By no-one I mean no-one, Frau Bonì." Willig took a summer jacket from the back of the chair, reached for the briefcase and said that he assumed he wasn't being accused of any criminal offence and so he was now going to go for a late lunch with a colleague. With a friendly goodbye he left the archive, almost with a spring in his step. His self-assurance was palpable, he felt untouchable.

"Couldn't you have done that a bit . . . differently?" Arndt said. "Been a bit more diplomatic? Subtle?"

"Not if I'm trying to prevent a murder," Louise said. "And now I want to get out of this basement."

Outside, on the way to the car, Gerd called. "It's all fine, Bonì, I'm here," he said.

"*Where* are you?"

"With your African guy. It's my turn to keep an eye on him again, not that anything's going to happen."

Phone to her ear, she got into the car, switched on the engine and thought: Gerd, who'd actually been off duty for a few hours, who ought to be sleeping but couldn't sleep because he felt responsible for Janisch's death.

Another person plagued by the dead.

"Speak of the devil," Gerd said. Kabangu had left the hotel and was heading south. She heard Gerd get out, the noise expertly muffled – a real professional who could function even when tired. And who would function now, after what had happened to Janisch.

"I'll relieve you in an hour."

"No hurry, Boni, I've got my eyes peeled. I'll be here till half past six."

With an inward sigh she drove off; Gerd's eyes had been "peeled" on Ricky Janisch too.

19

L othar Krüger and a girl, obviously his girlfriend as they were holding hands. A tuft of red hair in a shock of blonde, shaved at the back of her neck and a plait above. A piercing at the corner of her lips, black T-shirt, thin legs in ripped jeans, fifteen years old at most, a head shorter than him. Punk, either on the far left or far right – only insiders could tell.

They were standing in the sun opposite the school, a moped beside them. They were whispering and giggling. Louise took a few photographs through the driver's window and sent them to Natalie. Then she got out and wandered over to them, through huddles of noisy schoolchildren.

Lothar noticed her first. He said something; the girl turned her head and stared at Louise. He must have already talked about her; the girl seemed to be in the picture. She nodded, her eyes full of curiosity at first, then utter scorn.

Louise stopped less than three metres away and waited.

The two of them calmly took their coats from the seat of the moped, put on their helmets and got on, the girl behind. On the back of her jacket were the words: *Fight Racism. Support the Preservation of Peoples and Cultures.*

Lothar turned and wheeled the moped onto the road with his feet. Both were looking at Louise as they slowly drove past.

They certainly weren't afraid.

*

Gerd called again. Kabangu had met the woman and gone into the university archive with her. "A dried-up old maid type, if you know what I mean."

"I do know what you mean."

"Pretty negligible risk, I'd say."

Louise drove onto the forecourt of police HQ. "I'm not so sure, Gerd."

"Then it's best I don't say any more, Bonì, to be on the safe side."

She got out, hurried up the stairs and went into Natalie's office. Natalie looked as fresh as a spring day, full of zest and confidence.

"Some new info," Natalie said.

The Sky Wave from Jena had recently been reported missing in Aachen, by Matthias "Matze" Seibert himself. He'd hired the camper van in Jena, where he'd presumably handed it over to the men and women from Riedl's campsite. Now he'd turned up at a police station near the Dutch and Belgian borders, around four to five hundred kilometres from Jena, claiming that the vehicle had been stolen outside a restaurant in Aachen city centre.

"They know everything," Louise said.

"But how?"

Bonì shrugged. "The web is working."

"Maybe there's . . . we've got a . . ." Nathalie broke off.

"No, it's much simpler than that. The Krügers tell someone that I was there. Walczak phones someone. The Riedls, Janisch, when he was still alive. Then a few more calls to Jena and wherever else, then Seibert makes his way to western Germany. Have you looked at Janisch's two phones?"

"They're still with the technicians."

"Get them."

Mats Benedikt came in and put the photograph of Lothar's girlfriend on the desk along with the printout of a newspaper article.

In the centre was a photo: neo-Nazis at a demonstration in Lörrach, half a dozen faces clearly recognisable, including the girl's.

"Pure coincidence," he said. National security had the faces in its database but no names.

When Mats Benedikt left Louise said, "Have you got anything on Maria?"

"No," Natalie replied, she wasn't known to the Federal Criminal Police Office. She'd printed out a list of Freiburg women who might fit the bill, Maria Schmidt, Schmid or Schmitt. Two officers were doing the rounds with the photographs Birte had taken in Colombipark.

Graeve called her, furious, then came down. "You were going to speak to a sixteen-year-old? Without informing his parents?"

"Not exactly," Louise said.

Although he believed her and calmed down, at least a little, Graeve still read her the riot act. He would never sanction any of his officers intimidating a sixteen-year-old, intimidating *anyone* for that matter. Louise pointed to the photo of the girlfriend in the paper. He nodded grimly and said, "They're still underage."

"Who made the complaint?"

"The grandfather. You know about Janisch's body?"

"Being driven to Heidelberg."

"Being *flown* to Heidelberg, by helicopter. Enders is driving."

"Enders is driving to Heidelberg? What's the point in that?"

"He wants to be there when they cut open the body. I think he's furious. Maybe he's after some respect."

"And you're giving your backing to this?"

"It can't hurt. Freiburg showing its face."

"We need him here."

Graeve shrugged. "He wouldn't have been here this afternoon anyway. He's got to go to Stuttgart later, a meeting at the Ministry of the Interior."

"They're getting serious."

"Well, they're trying to at least."

Gerd called. Kabangu and the woman had just left the archive. "If they separate, I'm to stick with him, right? Not her?"

"That's right," Louise said.

Natalie's phone rang. Rubbing the sides of his head, Graeve said, "What chaos," before leaving the room.

"We've got a visitor," Natalie said. Waiting downstairs was a colleague from Karlsruhe, Stefan Bremer. He'd asked to speak to Boni.

"Never heard of him."

"He says it's urgent."

"Keep me posted about Maria. I want to know the minute they've identified her."

As Louise went downstairs she ran the name over in her mind. Stefan Bremer from Karlsruhe, it vaguely rang a bell.

When she got to the ground floor she remembered: Stefan Bremer and Timo Kahle. April 2004, the shooting in Karlsruhe. Timo Kahle died on the spot; Stefan Bremer was left in a coma for weeks, if not months. She could picture the police photographs: the patrol car parked at an angle, the driver's door open, the window shattered, bullet holes, streaks of blood, helicopters over the city all day long.

Timo Kahle's funeral took place soon afterwards, and amongst the hundred or so police officers from all over Baden-Württemberg were half of D11, Rolf Bermann, and her.

20

"Months," Bremer said. "Two. Then a year in rehab."

"And now?"

"Only desk work. Half days, I can't do more than that. But I'm not going to complain. I'm alive." He was about thirty years old, one metre eighty in height, and his speech and movements were slow. His left hand shook faintly, his voice was soft and his eyes were restless. The scar, which was above his left temple, seemed to have healed well, most of it hidden beneath brown hair; presumably this was why he didn't keep it short. A small rucksack hung heavily from his back.

They were still standing by the security doors, not the right place for this sort of conversation. Louise touched his arm. "How about we meet up this evening? I'll have more time."

"My train leaves at six. Just half an hour, please."

"No chance, sorry."

Bremer thought for a moment. "Don't you want to know what this is about?"

"Of course I do. Tell me."

"Parallels to your case."

"Such as?"

He moved his head close to her ear. "Neo-Nazis."

Bremer didn't want to go to her office; he insisted on talking outside the police station. So they left the building and wandered towards the old town. There was a Vietnamese restaurant just a few minutes away. He walked cautiously, almost hesitantly, and she sensed his fear. A fear of everything – noises, passers-by, vehicles, cyclists – even of the few people in the restaurant. He pointed to a table in the corner, far away from the nearest customer and the entrance, and near the toilets.

Louise took the opportunity to have a bowl of rice noodle soup; Bremer drank water. Even his drinking was slow, almost stiff, as if he found it difficult to coordinate his muscles, bones and thoughts.

"I don't know where to begin," he said, tapping the side of his head. "I've got problems concentrating. That's why I made lists." He gave an embarrassed smile.

"Lists?"

"One for the chronology. One for those involved. One for the lines of investigation. And so on."

"One for the parallels to my case as well?"

"Yes," he said, removing some folded pieces of paper from his rucksack. He unfolded them and placed one on the table in front of him.

Louise saw numbers, spidery letters, crossings-out, underlinings. "Just read it out," she said.

"Parallels to Boni's case," Bremer said so quietly that she could barely understand, and ran his right index finger under the words. "One: Contract killers from neo-Nazi groups? Two: Camper van from Thüringen. Three: National network of right-wing extremists. Four: Verfassungsschutz informers. Five: Ministry of the Interior involvement." He pushed the list to one side and looked up.

"You know a lot about my case."

"I know the file," he said with a fleeting smile. "Friends in data processing. And I sit at my computer day and night. I . . . I don't do anything else when I'm at home."

Louise nodded; she'd realised by now that he couldn't escape that day at the end of April 2004. The attack had become an obsession; those few minutes outside the Lebanese takeaway had dominated his life ever since.

She could understand.

She could also understand that he was ignoring the findings of the investigation.

"What about the gypsy?" she asked.

"I think you'll find they're called Roma people."

"Whatever."

Right after the attack on Kahle and Bremer a witness had seen a man running away from the scene of the crime, and soon after recognised him from a European mugshot, a Roma man wanted in France for grievous bodily harm. The fugitive was arrested two months later in Paris. After interrogation by officers from Karlsruhe, the German authorities applied for his extradition because a cigarette butt had been found beside Timo Kahle's body with a DNA match to the Roma man. As far as Louise knew, he was transferred to Germany after he'd served his sentence in France.

Because the regional department of public prosecution was unable to exclude terrorism as a motive, and a foreign country was involved, it quickly became a matter for the federal department. Until now it had been assumed that Kahle and Bremer were accidental victims, either because the suspect and his unknown accomplices had wanted to get hold of more firearms, or they'd wanted to launch an arbitrary attack on the state and had targeted a couple of police officers.

Nobody who had been following the case in Freiburg's D11 shared this view. *Sounds like a load of rubbish*, Louise had said. *More like politicking*, Bermann had said. They'd spent hours discussing possible masterminds behind the scenes. They hadn't doubted that the Roma man was the culprit.

"The Roma isn't important," Bremer said. "The witness who identified him is. And Timo."

"Timo Kahle?"

"Yes, he . . ." Bremer flicked through his lists.

"One thing at a time, please. Let's start with the witness."

"A neo-Nazi, was a Verfassungsschutz informer at the time, code-name 'Amadeus.'"

"Has that been confirmed?"

"Unofficially."

"Meaning?"

"Meaning that I've got a brother-in-law in the department of public prosecution. Or did have. He's not my brother-in-law anymore."

She nodded and tried to get to the bottom of her scepticism. Bremer might be obsessive and more intensively involved with this case than was good for him, but he didn't give the impression he wasn't compos mentis.

He was searching for the truth. Any truth, not a particular one.

"There was an informer at the scene of the crime?"

"It's what he says, at least."

"You think he's lying?"

"And that he was paid to say it."

"Can you prove that?"

Instead of answering Bremer took a plastic sleeve from his rucksack and put it in front of her. A photograph of a gaunt man from behind, around thirty, bald, black leather jacket. Plus newspaper articles, web page printouts. She pushed it away – too much to read – and asked Bremer to summarise.

He picked up one of his lists and read out the key information on "Amadeus". In a witness protection programme since 2004, new secret name, used to live in a neo-Nazi flatshare in Dortmund, Verfassungsschutz informer since 1999, multiple convictions for inciting hate, giving the Nazi salute, bodily harm. Bremer looked up and his fingers tapped the list edgily. "On 30 April he was in Dortmund, not Karlsruhe. Someone saw him in *Dortmund* on the morning of 30 April. He *can't* have been in Karlsruhe."

"Who saw him?"

Another rummage in the rucksack, another plastic sleeve, another

neo-Nazi, also an ex-informer, this time for the Hesse Verfassungsschutz, codename "Witiko". He too was – Bremer cleared his throat –
"virtually unreachable". Louise saw a blurred picture of a man in
his late fifties, tousled white hair standing on end, a zealous grin
on his lips.

No, she thought, don't say it.

"He's, erm, been in psychiatric care for the past eighteen months."
Flicking frantically through the papers, Bremer gave her a summary.
Witiko lived in sheltered accommodation in Rhineland-Pfalz, serious
depression, anxiety, drug addiction, acute risk of self-harm.

She rubbed the back of her neck, feeling tension everywhere under
her fingers. "Great. One informer in witness protection, another in
psychiatric care, and mine dead."

"Yes," Bremer said, and then laughed despondently.

Witiko had been an active Verfassungsschutz informer until the end
of 2004. Like the distinctly younger Amadeus, he'd lived in Dortmund
and they'd been active in the same organisations. Then he left the
neo-Nazi scene, no doubt against the wishes of the Verfassungsschutz,
or at least that's how Witiko could be construed. He and Bremer had
had a long conversation when he visited him in the clinic a year ago.
Most of what he said wasn't helpful, but some things were, such as
the fact that on 30 April he and Amadeus had taken part in a far-
right rally in Dortmund. Amadeus had pushed him in a wheelchair
because Witiko had sprained his ankle in a night-time "operation".

"Why is he called 'Witiko'?"

"His parents are Sudeten Germans and he spent some time asso-
ciating with the 'Witikobund'. In his youth he was probably a member
of the 'Jungen Witikonen' too." When she asked, Bremer explained
that the 'Witikobund' was a Sudeten German organisation, a mish-
mash of historical revisionists, members of far-right organisations
like the NPD, Holocaust deniers and representatives of the New

Right. When founded in 1950 it was riddled with former members of the Nazi Party, and until 1967 it was officially classified as a right-wing extremist group.

"How did you come across Witiko?"

"Don't ask."

"And who paid Amadeus to lie?"

"That," Bremer said, "is what I've got to find out."

The restaurant had filled up; Louise spotted the odd colleague having a late lunch or an early post-work beer. Bremer's eyes kept darting to all the other customers; he couldn't relax.

"The Roma man," she said. "You must've seen him."

He nodded. "I must have seen both the attackers."

"But you don't remember?"

"No."

"Nothing at all?"

"The whole day has gone from my mind . . . The morning, everything gone. Even the night and evening before." Bremer picked up his glass, noticed it was empty and put it down. He picked out another list with the heading "TIMO".

The phone rang: Gerd. Louise answered and the anxiety was back at a stroke.

Kabangu and the woman had parted company in Kaiser-Joseph-Strasse. The woman was just getting onto a tram; Kabangu was going into Kaufhof. "I *hate* department stores. Department stores, supermarkets and stations, pure hell, Bonì. You don't stand a chance if—"

"Yes," Louise interrupted him. "Shout if you need help." She put her phone down and explained, "A colleague from surveillance." Bremer muttered something, his eyes fixed on the list, and she suddenly realised he wasn't interested in what was happening here in Freiburg, what was going to happen today, or maybe tomorrow.

Only the parallels mattered, only whatever helped him bring some light to the darkness of two years ago.

"Hang on a sec," she said, picking up her mobile and calling Natalie.

Nothing new on Maria Schmidt, Schmid or Schmitt – their colleagues hadn't identified her yet. There was one left to check out: Maria Schmitt living in Vauban.

Only one left, Louise thought. What if it wasn't her? Keep looking randomly in Emmendingen, Breisach, Kirchzarten and Bad Krozingen?

"Excuse me." Bremer got up and went to the toilets, vigilant, prepared, his fingers stroking backs of chairs, the doorframe, his head moving from side to side.

The phone still in her hand, Louise called Enders. Engine sounds, a distant voice almost drowned out by the noise. "For God's sake," she said, "I need you here."

"They've called me into the ministry, what should I do?"

"Maybe say no?"

"No," Enders said.

"Find a computer, but not in the ministry – try an internet café or something. Natalie will e-mail you documents. Karlsruhe, 30 April 2004, one officer killed, another seriously injured. There may be links to our case." She finished the conversation with a strange thought. Why today, why has he been called to Stuttgart today? Who wants to prevent him from being in Freiburg *today*?

The answer was obvious: she was becoming paranoid.

Bremer came back to the table.

"OK," she said. "Now Timo, then I've got to go."

A list containing dynamite. And perhaps a motive, without actually revealing it.

Timo Kahle, born 1980 in Brandenburg an der Havel, military

service after school, then police officer training, first posts in Frankfurt an der Oder and Königs Wusterhausen. As a teenager he had his first contact with right-wing extremism through an older cousin and his friends, going to neo-Nazi gigs, putting up posters for the NPD. His cousin was a known neo-Nazi, active with the Brandenburg Heimat Guard, though Timo hadn't been a member. A string of girlfriends, some from the far-right scene, most not.

In 2003 the cousin was murdered, knifed in a dark side street and the killer was never found. That same evening, Timo disappeared, although he was never officially a suspect; a girlfriend had given him a credible alibi. A few weeks later he turned up in Karlsruhe to start his job there. Because the transfer was so quick and easy, Bremer assumed that influential people had helped.

Eight months later he was shot dead.

"Do you think it's got anything to do with the cousin?"

"I don't know. I . . . I'm not getting any further."

Bremer had talked to everyone who knew Timo and was prepared to speak, in Karlsruhe, Brandenburg and Berlin. He'd been to see the parents, colleagues, ex-girlfriends, friends, neo-Nazis, dropouts, Witiko, other witnesses, army comrades. He'd accumulated kilos of material, heard dozens of stories, run through all kinds of theories, been warned by colleagues, superiors and public prosecutors that his private investigation was being viewed with suspicion and must be terminated at once; and despite this he'd gone on. Eighteen months later he still hadn't found out exactly why he and Timo had been shot at.

"All I know is . . ." He reached for his lists, picked one out headed "FINDINGS" and read it.

One: Contract killing.

Two: Client from the neo-Nazi scene.

Three: Motive in Timo's neo-Nazi past.

Four: Informers involved, know more, lying.

Five: Verfassungsschutz involved.

Six: Baden-Württemberg Ministry of Interior and federal government involved.

Seven: Investigations manipulated, leads pointing to regional and national far-right structures not followed up, Timo's mobile data not analysed thoroughly.

Eight: The Roma man is innocent.

"They didn't analyse Timo's phone properly?"

"Not for the weeks before the shooting."

There was silence for a while. Louise thought she could have drawn up a similar list for the Kabangu case.

This didn't feel good.

With careful, limp movements, Bremer gathered together his documents, finishing with a five- or six-centimetre-high pile in front of him – the day on which one life was extinguished and another destroyed.

"Can you arrange a meeting with Witiko?"

He tapped the pile. "Everything he knows is in here."

"Everything that was useful?"

He nodded.

"Then we need what wasn't useful."

Outside, Bremer said, "We haven't talked about the camper van."

She nodded. "Jena?"

"Erfurt."

"OK, but be quick about it."

The camper van had been captured by several security and traffic cameras in Karlsruhe: the evening before at a campsite in Durlach, and that morning in Südstadt, where it was parked five minutes' walk from the scene of the shooting. According to a witness, at 12.15 a man with a blood-smeared hand climbed into the van and then it drove off, a woman behind the wheel and a second man beside her.

No link to the attack, the federal prosecution office said. The traces of blood on the tarmac that the witness had seen hadn't been secured. There was no manhunt. Nobody made a call to Erfurt apart from Bremer himself, one year after the shooting.

"And? Who rented the camper van?"

"It's on the list," he said.

"Matthias Seibert?"

"Yes," Bremer said, and she saw relief flash across his face. "Matthias 'Matze' Seibert!"

Her phone again: Gerd. She shook Bremer's hand and thanked him. "Think about Witiko. Tomorrow would be best."

He nodded, tears in his eyes. Then he turned briskly and left.

"Gerd?"

"Christ, Boni, you'll never believe who's here . . ."

Janisch's comrade, photographed by Gerd two evenings ago, had appeared after Kabangu came out of Kaufhof.

And now the man was following him.

21

"So? What do we do now?" Gerd had guided her into Herrenstrasse, and where it met Münsterplatz she waited in the entrance to a building, mobile to her ear. At that moment she saw Kabangu walking right beside a runnel, head bowed as if he were following the water with his eyes, as if only the water existed and nothing else. He slowly wandered in her direction, hands crossed behind his back, one pedestrian amongst many, and yet he looked absent, shut inside a different, inaccessible, inner world.

She wondered if he was having a dialogue with Mabruk. A city with lots of little rivers, look, here's another one, you were right, and I found the city. But I have to leave you here, Grandfather Mabruk.

"Bonì . . ." Gerd said urgently.

She took her eyes of Kabangu and spotted the man she recognised from Gerd's first photos: Janisch's friend. Jeans, black hoodie, sunglasses, but the baseball cap from Tuesday evening was missing. Ordinary haircut, keffiyeh around his neck, tattoos on the backs of his hands. He was less than ten metres from Kabangu, walking diagonally behind. She could understand why Gerd had thought he was Antifa; the dress codes were bewilderingly similar, which was the Autonomous Nationalists' intention. Only the sticker on his hoodie showed he was a neo-Nazi: two black flags on a white background inside a black circle.

Bonì could see Gerd now too. Jacket over his shoulder and sweat patches on his shirt, which his small round belly had worked out of his waistband.

The three men crossed a road, one after the other, and strolled through a broad swathe of deep-yellow sunlight.

"Have you noticed anyone else?" Louise asked.

"No."

"Let's get him, then."

Boni sensed the man had been expecting them, had been given orders.

She approached from the side, holding up her police badge; Gerd came from behind. Stopping abruptly, the man held up his hands, fingers splayed: I'm not going to put up a fight, I'm not a danger to you. "What's this about?" he said.

"A night in the cells," Louise replied. She made him show his ID: Torsten Schulz, thirty-eight, born in Stuttgart, resident in Heilbronn. "Been in Freiburg long?"

"Visiting my brother." Voice relaxed, thick Swabian accent, his eyes totally hidden behind the dark glasses.

"Shares your views, does he?"

"I don't know what you're on about."

She glanced over at Kabangu, who didn't seem to have noticed a thing and had continued on his way. He was just disappearing around the corner of a building. "Gerd," she said, motioning to him to follow.

Two patrol cars arrived and the officers took over. She walked beside him to one of the cars. "The woman," she said. "Maria. Who is she?"

"I don't know any Maria."

They stopped by the car door. "Sunglasses, please," Louise said. A policewoman carefully removed the glasses from Schulz's nose. Small, hard eyes appeared, fixed squarely on Louise. He smiled scornfully as if to say: This is a game and we're winning.

"What about you?" Louise said. "Were you meant to be tailing him?"

"Who?"

She gestured to her colleague to manoeuvre Schulz into the back. He offered no resistance and made himself as comfortable as was possible wearing handcuffs. "Aren't you worried you'll end up like Janisch?"

He didn't look at her. "I don't know any Janisch."

"Yes," she said, shutting the door.

Paralysed by a sudden fury, she watched the two patrol cars drive off. She'd thought she was on it, and now found herself limping three paces behind, not getting anywhere. A man like Janisch disappears, no evidence against him; a man like Schulz turns up, there would be no evidence against him either. And what else was he doing apart from following Kabangu, perhaps without knowing why? To ring a number at some point and say where Kabangu was going, without knowing who he was speaking to.

She turned around to follow Gerd, who was no longer to be seen.

What a clever plan. Nobody knew enough to be able to jeopardise themselves or those giving the orders. The Krügers, who simply had to park a car in a certain place, maybe leaving the key in the ignition. Ricky Janisch, who had to pick up a box in Baden-Baden and – presumably – hand it to Walczak. Walczak, who passed the package to two night-time visitors and the following day gave an envelope to Janisch, in neither case knowing anything about the contents. Paulus Riedl, who was instructed by a stranger called Andreas not to make a note of a camper van from Jena in his register. Who might have heard from his wife that Kabangu would be "sorted" and who wouldn't say a word. Matthias "Matze" Seibert from Jena, who had to hire a camper van again, perhaps without knowing why or for whom. Who had to make an unplanned trip to Aachen and report the camper van as stolen.

None of them knew which tasks the others had to do. Or even who else was involved. Apart from Janisch, who'd seen the Russian Niko and Walczak. But Janisch had "gone to sleep peacefully".

So peacefully that his post-mortem wasn't going to take place in Freiburg but in Heidelberg, under the aegis of the Baden-Württemberg Criminal Investigation Bureau and the Ministry of Interior.

And the mysterious Maria . . .

Louise called Natalie.

The last possibility, Maria Schmitt from Vauban, wasn't a match for the woman in Birte's photo. "Maybe Kabangu got the name wrong. Or she lives out—"

"Yes," Louise said. "What about Janisch's phones?"

One private, no suspicious names or numbers. The other had been new, a cheap model with a pre-paid card, never used.

"Nothing, then?"

"Nothing."

Quickening her pace, Louise turned into the street Kabangu had gone down, but didn't see him or Gerd. The mysterious Maria, she thought, who was maybe just supposed to be nice to the visitor from the former colony for a few days, show him Freiburg, be his companion. Occasionally ring the number of an unknown person and pass on information.

At the beginning of the chain must be Erik Willig, the historian from the university archive who was unruffled and would always lie. Willig, she thought, was a key figure. He'd set everything in motion by telling someone – presumably a member of his small circle of right-wingers – about Kabangu's demands. Someone who may have informed a third party, and maybe a fourth and fifth were involved too.

Or maybe not.

Still no sign of Kabangu and Gerd. Boni stopped at a small crossroads, Kaiser-Joseph-Strasse up ahead, Münsterplatz to her left. She dialled Gerd's number and listened impatiently to the ringing. Finally Gerd's heavy breathing and a jittery apology: he'd dropped his phone, had to bend down to recover it and hadn't quite got up again . . .

You're not going to believe this, Bonì, the African's gone, I can't find him, I've been searching for five minutes and can't find him, and your number was engaged, I bet he's just gone shopping, he'll have got hungry, he'll turn up again soon.

Kabangu didn't turn up again.

They searched for a whole hour – Gerd, Louise, officers from Freiburg North – questioned passers-by, shop owners, enlarged the radius and returned several times to Herrenstrasse, at the corner of which both Gerd and Bonì had last seen Kabangu. They kept calling the hotel, got them to check his room, but he wasn't there either.

Ludwig Kabangu had vanished off the face of the earth.

22

"Utter nonsense," Reinhard Graeve said.

They were standing in Natalie's office with Enders on loudspeaker. Both Graeve and Enders were of the view that Kabangu had "vanished" accidentally or on purpose. They didn't believe he'd been abducted and killed, but that he was alive.

"First they organise everything meticulously and then they just pounce spontaneously?" The volume and clarity of Enders' voice varied; he was back in his car on the way to the ministry.

"I really can't imagine it either," Natalie said, as coy as ever when Kripo boss Graeve was present.

Louise stood at the window, looking out into the evening. A reddish light above the streets, a few grey clouds, in the distance a narrow line of shadows: the Vosges hills. The brown Escort was parked in the wrong direction, cigarette smoke billowing out of the window. Gerd was inconsolable; because of Janisch he'd wanted to help and, as with Janisch, he'd failed, or at least that was how he saw it.

She turned around and let her gaze wander from Graeve to Natalie. She knew they were just trying to be friendly, consoling. Why would Kabangu have disappeared accidentally, or even on purpose? And how? They'd covered every open space north of Münsterplatz, talked to dozens of people. No-one had seen him; it was as if he'd never been in this area at all. He must have been abducted just beyond the crossroads.

Enders apologised – a call was coming through, so he hung up.

"They had to pounce spontaneously," Louise said. "We got too close to them. Torsten Schulz was the decoy and we fell for it. *I* fell for it."

Natalie opened her mouth, closed it, shrugged. She already had her coat on, was about to leave, freshly made up and perfumed. A social being, happy, with more to her life than just her job.

She had everything ahead of her, Louise thought. The disappointments. The dramas. The failure. The surrender.

Another phone rang, Graeve's mobile this time. "In a minute," he said. "I'll call you back." He lowered his hand and looked at Louise. "Enough for today, Frau Bonì."

"What about Willig?"

"Tomorrow. And no arresting him, just a friendly chat at his work. The same goes for the Krügers, the Riemers . . . I mean Riedls, and Walczak." He was already on his way out when Natalie's landline rang. Enders again, sounding annoyed. The appointment at the ministry had been postponed.

"Half seven tomorrow morning," he said. "I'll have to stay the night here."

Graeve rubbed the sides of his head. "They only come up with this half an hour before?"

"Politicians."

"They want to keep him away from Freiburg," Louise said.

Two pairs of eyes were on her; three voices were silent.

There was a long pause before Graeve said quietly, "Those are *our* people."

"They know more than we do." She smiled and tried to fathom the sudden relief that outweighed the surprise at Stuttgart's role.

A relief she was only beginning to understand.

Some of the strings, but not all, were being pulled in Stuttgart, for whatever reasons and whatever purpose.

She nodded. *Our people.*

Who didn't want Leif Enders in Freiburg that night or the following morning. Who knew that Kabangu was alive because they knew when he was going to die.

Bonì went down to Gerd and braced both hands on the doorframe of the car. There was a reddish glow on his tired, round face, his eyes were darting about restlessly. She wanted to say something, but waited. Platitudes were to be avoided when someone thought they were to blame.

"And what if he doesn't reappear? I mean, if he reappears like Janisch?"

She couldn't help but smile. "I think he's playing with us. Ludwig Kabangu is a stubborn man. Maybe he thought he'd take back control of his life for a few hours."

"You're not being serious, Bonì?"

"I'm being perfectly serious."

"So why don't I believe you?"

"Because of Janisch?"

"Really?" he said, stubbing out his cigarette in the ashtray and knocking a few other butts onto the floor. "I've got to go, Marek's waiting. St Georgen, some guy pushing drugs."

Bonì stepped away from the car. "Thanks for your help."

Gerd nodded as if to say: Great help I was, botching it all up. "What about you? Going back in?" He nodded at the building.

"No. I'm going to wait on some bench by the river for Kabangu to turn up."

"Bloody hell, Bonì, you and your ghosts. In the end you're right again."

She laughed.

"Will you let me know if you hear anything?"

"I will," she promised.

*

Louise parked behind the Ufercafé and sat in the grass on the bank of the Dreisam. The last rays of sun lingered on her face for a few moments, then it quickly got dark. She leaned back and put her hands beneath her head. The relief was still there. A miraculous moment of peace, relaxation, even though in truth the idea was completely absurd. That someone from the ministry didn't want Leif Enders in Freiburg that night or the following morning to avoid him getting in the way of the attack on Ludwig Kabangu – it was all very far-fetched. Did a section head on the ground spell trouble, or was he being protected?

What about her? Could she now be sacrificed?

She couldn't help smiling.

A world without Louise Bonì? Unthinkable. Even more unthinkable than a world without Rolf Bermann.

The thoughts of an utterly exhausted woman, was the last thing that went through her head. Then she fell asleep.

The message came at 8.20 p.m. from an officer at Freiburg North. Ludwig Kabangu was sitting on some steps in Augustinerplatz, a bottle of beer in his hand and two more beside him, alone amongst dozens of other people enjoying the warm evening.

Alone? Louise thought. Not completely. Another Krüger or Schulz would be nearby.

And Grandfather Mabruk, of course.

23

"Good," she said, sitting down beside Kabangu. "Are we friends again now?"

He smiled. "You're late. Your beer's warm."

"No alcohol for me, Herr Kabangu. I used to be addicted."

On the steps above and below them sat dozens of people in the darkness. Someone was playing a guitar and a girl was singing along. A melancholic voice that didn't hit every note, but whose artlessness and abandon was touching. Down on Gerberau the patrol car drove off. Antifa up by the museum, the officer had said. Louise had spotted them, three or four lads, genuine Antifa.

"Addictions . . ." Kabangu murmured. "I had a few myself. Cigarettes, women, fights. One of the worst was escaping. I was addicted to escaping."

"From what?"

"Myself."

"I'm familiar with that. Do you want to talk about it?"

"Another time."

"If there is another time."

He smiled again, his face youthfully mischievous for a moment. "You're here, Madame Boni. You're protecting me."

"The others are here too."

He put the bottle to his lips, took a swig, his movements relaxed, his expression unperturbed. "Why haven't they done it already, then? Here, for example, where they wouldn't stand out?"

"They must have another plan."

"But one you don't know?"

"I think they'll make an attempt tonight or tomorrow morning."

Kabangu looked at the bottle and ran his thumb over the opening. "You're really sure, aren't you? That someone's out to kill me?" He gave her a friendly, but distant look. He'd uttered the word "*tuer*" again without any emotion. In his voice and eyes there wasn't even a hint of the bewilderment or fear that Louise would expect from a person in whose everyday life *tuer* played no role.

She wondered if he'd ever been in a similar situation. Whether someone had tried to kill him before.

"Yes," she replied.

"And you're going to protect me. Tonight and tomorrow morning."

"Until you leave."

"I'm not leaving."

"For as long as you're in Freiburg, then."

"You'll lose me occasionally, like today."

"I can live with that if you turn up again."

He looked at her pensively. "And what if I were a very different person from who you think me to be?"

"Are you?"

A stiff smile, then he leaned over to her. "Do you think killing can become addictive too?"

"Yes."

He opened the next bottle of beer with a lighter, took a swig, then lit a cigarette. She waited as she was enveloped by the same unpleasant acrid smell she'd noticed in his room. After a silence she said, "We can't find Maria."

"If she knew you were looking for her, she'd call you."

"She doesn't exist. Not in Freiburg at least."

"So many worries, so much mistrust, Madame Bonì! You can't see the good things because you're only thinking of the bad ones."

"Better that than the other way around."

He laughed. "I'm meeting Maria tomorrow morning for breakfast. Have a word with her and everything will sort itself out." A café just off Münsterplatz, he said, hidden away in a side alley, famous for its cakes, they'd been there the first afternoon. The Black Forest gâteau was a dream, no doubt for breakfast too. He got up, holding the necks of the three beer bottles between the fingers of his right hand, and stretched. He wanted to go to a supermarket to get German cigarettes and German chocolate – his soul and Grandfather Mabruk needed comforting until Dr Arndt could be persuaded.

Louise got up too. "What time are you meeting Maria?"

"Eight thirty."

"She won't come."

"She will, Madame Bonì, believe me."

They head west along Gerberau, streams of people like in summer, the occasional glance at Kabangu and at her. The odd bald head shone in the light of the streetlamps; at one point a few metres ahead of them she thought she spotted the man in black from Colombipark with Gothic writing on the back of his hoodie. Other people slipped in-between and then the black hoodie was gone.

For the first time since she'd met Kabangu Louise thought of the war in Rwanda in the early nineties. The Hutu massacre of the Tutsis, or had it been the other way around? She'd never been able to remember.

"Were you addicted to killing, Monsieur Kabangu?"

"What a gloomy topic . . ." He touched her arm. "Shouldn't we be cheerful in the face of death? Shouldn't I go dancing? Surely you know how agile we Africans are? How well we move, how well we dance. I bet you'd love to have the chance to dance with an African!" He laughed, raised his arms, moved his pelvis and shoulders awkwardly, his arms jerking about, and one of his joints kept creaking, though it sounded more like a cracking. He stopped. "I wish I could dance.

My wife was a wonderful dancer! It was amazing to watch her! It was always my dream to be able to dance. I imagine that dancing must allow you to shake all the bad things out of you. All the thoughts that would otherwise stay, making your body and soul ill."

As they crossed Kaiser-Joseph-Strasse the stream of pedestrians swelled, then it got quieter, darker. Thoughts that make you sick, Louise wondered, and asked Kabangu, but he just gave one of his fleeting, mechanical smiles.

Birte called and said, "I'm available now for a few hours."

"Outside the hotel," Louise said. "Thanks."

They took a circuitous route back to the hotel. Kabangu told her about his second conversation at the university archive, which hadn't gone well either. Dr Arndt was friendly but uncompromising, he said. He let politics and money win rather than people. He was afraid of the individual, because many more could follow. And so long as the Rwandan embassy didn't get involved . . . *I'm sorry, Herr Kabangu, we cannot meet your request at this time.*

They went into the supermarket diagonally opposite Colombipark. Louise stayed at Kabangu's side, her eyes frantically scanning the other shoppers. Despite everything she had to be vigilant, despite the meeting at half past eight the following morning. *Department stores, supermarkets and stations, pure hell, Boni. You don't stand a chance . . .*

Back outside, Kabangu said, "The embassy wants me to leave too." The Rwandan ambassador had rung him personally the previous evening. He was worried about diplomatic complications. Irritation on the part of "Germany, our partner". One had to understand that people here didn't like talking about bones from former colonies. Our partner had to be forgiven. With all respect to the dead, my friend, what counted was the here and now, not the remote past. Rwanda had to live and become stronger *today*. *Today* our people must be united and forgive the former enemy next door. Face up to our *own* guilt, for isn't Rwanda itself responsible for killing enough people? Shouldn't we first tell their stories, burying *their* bones and comforting *their* souls before we start preaching morality?

Be gracious and tolerant, my friend, the ambassador had continued. Go back home. Your country is begging you.

"He told you *that*?"

"Not verbatim. He's not a good talker. What he says needs to be translated into a language you can understand."

She smiled and nodded.

"Everything that happens has a story. If it happens to me, it is my story. If I talk about it I give it my voice. Tell it in my words."

"And the story becomes a fairy tale?"

Kabangu raised his thick grey eyebrows. "Not at all! The core of the story is always true and only the core is important. If you give your children a present, you wrap it in pretty paper. Does this mean the present is a fairy tale? Does it not exist? No, it's real! It's just beautifully wrapped."

"Is Grandfather Mabruk a beautifully wrapped story too?"

"Did you hear that, Grandfather Mabruk? She thinks you're a figment of the imagination!" Kabangu cupped an ear to the sky, smiled and finally said, "Yes, I know, Grandfather . . . No, Madame Bonì, he's real. But instead of the ugly story he represents, I've told you the beautiful story he represents too."

Outside the hotel he paused. "I'm assuming you want to come up to my room."

"Any objection if I sleep on the sofa?"

He clicked his tongue to say no. "In my room you'll no doubt be able to best look after yourself. But there isn't a sofa."

"In the armchair then. Or on the floor."

"Yes, on the floor! Like us Africans!" He laughed heartily. "And I'll sleep in the bed like you Europeans. But I'm warning you, I have nightmares and often get up."

"The dead?"

A look of surprise, then he said, "In my dreams they disguise themselves as the living."

They took the stairs as he wouldn't go in the lift: too small, too uncontrollable, Kabangu explained. They had their moods and weaknesses as well, he said, and sometimes they decided to stop halfway to think or rest. You had to understand this and forgive them, which was why he preferred stairs. With a contented laugh he placed a hand on the banister and began walking up.

They stopped on the third floor.

"I don't have children," Louise said.

"Nor do I. And I'm afraid there isn't any beautiful wrapping for this story either."

As they entered Kabangu's room her phone rang: Ben.

She turned around. "Finally!"

He'd just arrived at her flat and wanted to talk. It sounded . . . final.

Not today, she thought. Maybe tomorrow . . . or in a few weeks, a few months. You needed to take your time when things were final.

And surely it doesn't have to be final right now...

"I can't leave now, Ben."

"I'll come to you, then."

24

Ben arrived half an hour later.

He was waiting for her outside in the yellow glow of a lamp on the wall. Unshaven, his hair down to his shoulders again and curly. A handsome man at second glance, which was how she'd been seeing him for the past eighteen months, with the dangerous second glance that cannot be forgotten.

A brief, ungainly kiss.

Louise sensed at once that he wasn't in a good way, she sensed the dissatisfaction, the doubts, the longing. She recalled Osijek in December 2004, her first meeting with Ben Liebermann on the bridge over the Drava. He'd looked so free and content. Months earlier he'd left the police, thrown it all in, and was surviving by helping out with a security firm. He'd been at peace with himself.

And distanced . . . She remembered how long she'd waited for a smile that first time.

Life is odd sometimes. Amazing, all the things that've come from the Breisgau to Osijek.

You ought to smile when you say things like that.

It had begun the following day. Molecules had leaped between them even though they hadn't even touched by accident. From the start she thought this man would suit her, maybe he was the only one. He'd silently allowed her to descend into her abyss, and he was there when she came up again.

The problem was his abyss.

"Have you got to go again? Back down to the Balkans?"

"I don't have to, I want to," he replied. "Yes, I must."

"That's what I meant."

"Come with me, Louise. To Sarajevo or Osijek."

She'd never understood this and nor had she really taken it seriously: Ben Liebermann needed a city marked by war, had to see war in the walls of buildings and people's eyes, to be calm. Only in a damaged city and amongst damaged people did he feel he belonged; everywhere else he was always searching, and felt a failure. *Achieved nothing, never felt at home anywhere, never started a family, drifted from city to city.*

In 2003 the border protection force sent him to Sarajevo as part of a UN mission and the search came to an end.

But she was searching too, wasn't she? Maybe she had to leave Freiburg to find out.

But not for Sarajevo, Osijek or Pristina. No, she thought. She was only a somebody here, in Freiburg. Only here could she be what she was. She shook her head. "I can't. I belong here."

"Yes," Ben said.

He'd tried Freiburg for seven or eight months. He'd sat in a glass box at night, guarding an almost empty car park. Then he'd handed in his notice and spent his days wondering what could become of nothing. Later he told her that Freiburg had been particularly terrible. Far too pretty, too sweet. An unreal place, an island outside of reality. Those who didn't share in the happiness here and couldn't find themselves were flushed out.

Ben had been flushed away to Potsdam. An administrative job with the police. "International affairs, European cooperation" – his field of expertise, at least.

Now, four months later, he was standing opposite her, on his way to a new life without her.

Out of the corner of her eye Louise detected a movement, a pale face in a black parked car, a hand moving at the wheel. Only now did she remember that Birte was here. Watching everything, the awkwardness, the finality.

But she'd turned away, not wishing to be indiscreet.

"It doesn't have to be . . . final," Louise said.

"I can't see another solution."

"We could have a baby. Become a family."

He put his hand on her arm and spontaneously embraced her. "You're going to be forty-six in August."

"But I look thirty-six."

She heard and felt him laugh, more a spasmodic muscular twitch, and thought that this was new. Ben Liebermann was fighting back the tears.

"For fuck's sake I want a child," she said. "Don't you want one too? A small family?"

"No . . . Not here, in Freiburg."

She leaned back and looked at him. "What? But in Sarajevo you would?"

"I didn't mean it like that."

"That's nuts, Ben. Not in Freiburg but maybe in Sarajevo or Osijek? Completely nuts." Anger shot through her veins, a therapeutic fury that restored her strength. Loving nobody meant losing nobody, and especially not losing oneself. Too late as far as Ben Liebermann was concerned, she thought, becoming even more worked up. "I introduced you to my mother, for fuck's sake!"

He looked at her in surprise, now far away, unreachable.

"OK, that's not a good point," she admitted and thought: point for what? Against what? It was getting ever more bizarre.

She was getting ever more bizarre.

"I've got to go back up. Back to work."

He nodded and gave her a peck on the cheek. "I'm here till tomorrow lunchtime. In case you want to talk again."

Talk again, she thought.

So it was final.

25

A long night, perhaps the longest of her life, and certainly the strangest. She didn't sleep for longer than fifteen, twenty minutes at a stretch, waking with a start before the sad dreams and nightmares could begin. Sometimes Kabangu would be sitting crookedly in bed, sometimes standing at the window, sometimes bent over beside Boni, staring at her face. She was convinced he wasn't thinking about sex even though he was wearing nothing but green boxer shorts, and sixty-five wasn't an age you didn't think about sex, and though she was herself thinking about sex. No, he had something else on his mind, something unfathomable. He looked at her with searching eyes, as if expecting answers – was she asleep or not?

Sometimes she awoke because he was speaking in a foreign language to her, to himself, or to Grandfather Mabruk. Sometimes she woke up because she was talking. What she was saying to whom was forgotten the moment she opened her eyes.

After midnight she got a text and, much later, a second: Birte had gone, Gerd had arrived.

On one occasion a lucid thought tore her from her sleep and when she saw Kabangu bent over in front of her she said, "It's all made up, it has to be. You wouldn't have been able to read records about Feldmann and Koch. They would hardly have been written in French or Rwandan."

"On the contrary, yes I could," Kabangu replied in German, very slowly and with a strong accent. "Fortunately it was the heartfelt wish of my grandfather as well as father that I should learn the language of our brother nation. I'm well aware that as the years have passed I've been afflicted by a loss of words and meaning, something I may be forgiven for. Fräulein Louise, I trust you might permit your humble acquaintance to return to French from here."

"Bloody hell!" Louise said, and Kabangu laughed with delight.

When it began to get light she couldn't sleep anymore. She waited until Kabangu woke with a groan, then said good morning and started talking about her dead and a few of the living too, in a mixture of German and French, beginning with Ben Liebermann who'd offered to talk and had meant "farewell". Just don't fall in love, she said, you'll never get away, but you know that already. The immortal Rolf Bermann wandered through the room, Taro the monk, Germain, both the dead and living incarnations, so confusing to have two brothers with the same name, little Germain the successor of the young, wild Germain from an earlier life, one of them only alive because the other had died, how can you get your head around that and still manage a smile?

The final apparition, as reliable as clockwork, was René Calambert. It was snowing, she said, I couldn't see anything apart from his silhouette, the abducted girl in his boot and my fury. The silhouette had a gun, perhaps it raised the weapon and aimed it at me, but that's irrelevant – it was a fair distance away and had my bullet in its leg. What's relevant, Monsieur Kabangu, is the fury, I'm assuming fury fired a second shot, but I don't remember exactly, and do you know who brought order into this chaos, wrapped the story in pretty paper and protected *me*?

"I did," Rolf Bermann said. She just nodded.

At half past seven Louise took a shower. There was no hairbrush, but at least reception had provided her with a toothbrush.

She went back into the bedroom.

Kabangu was dressed, a piece of chocolate in his hand, and looking at her as if he'd been expecting her for a while. "Why did you tell me that?" he asked, his tone not unfriendly. "Do you think I can comfort you? Because I'm Rwandan, an African? Do you believe an African should know how to deal with suffering and loss? With the dead who don't speak or who say too much? An African offers comfort, makes connections and is at one with everything – is that right? He questions oracles or a lump of wood or the dust in the road and this is how he finds answers? Does he have metaphysical contact to the afterlife? I can't help you, Madame Boni. I can't even help myself."

She picked up her coat and put it on. "Good, that's that cleared up, then. Just one more thing. Were you addicted to killing? I'd like to know before I save your life."

"I was," Kabangu said, putting the piece of chocolate in his mouth and going over to the door.

26

Another mild day, albeit overcast. The smell of rain and summer was carried on a gentle breeze. Gerd, who was standing outside the hotel, leaning against his Escort, put two fingers to his forehead as a greeting. Louise saw the birdcage on the passenger seat. *I'm bringing Willi with me*, he'd texted. *He'll keep me awake, you should hear him sing, Boni*. He moved away from the car and started walking level with them.

Marek wanted to come later too, at least to the café, but he couldn't promise anything. Officers from Freiburg North were stationed near Münsterplatz. With priority given to the World Cup preparations they hadn't been able to organise more protection. Hubert Vormweg – Cords – was sceptical. *The relentless criticism from Stuttgart*, Graeve had said on the phone a few minutes earlier. *Besides, there wasn't much hard evidence that she was right, to put it mildly.*

Right about what? she'd asked.

Even that's hard to pinpoint exactly, Graeve had replied.

Especially as the Sky Wave from Jena had been found, along with the thief. Belgian officers had found the camper van at some motorway services near Liège early that morning. The thief, a scruffy casual worker from Aachen, had confessed. But not only that, he'd identified the official renter of the vehicle, Matthias "Matze" Seibert from Jena, as the man who'd got out of the car just before it was stolen.

Must be a very well-organised network, Graeve had said.

It is, Louise said.

Kabangu walked alongside her, lost in thought. He hadn't said a word since they left the room. The reverberations of the night, maybe of her questions too. She'd have liked to chat to him so as not to have to think about Ben.

Talk, she thought.

I'm here till tomorrow lunchtime, she thought.

Lunchtime today.

Colombipark appeared to their left. No sign of any suspicious-looking characters.

Enders called. He was on his way back to Freiburg; the conversation at the ministry had lasted only half an hour. A junior minister, a federal prosecutor and an intelligence officer. Between them the three had taken up twenty-nine of the minutes; he'd had just the one to say hello and goodbye. The upshot? News blackout, investigation to be taken over by the Criminal Investigation Bureau, Freiburg off the case, *and for God's sake* – Enders laughed angrily – *keep a tight rein on Chief Inspector Boni*. All very delicate. State secrets could be revealed. Informers could be exposed, undercover operations put at risk. Speculation was rife, look at Ricky J's death. A second set of proceedings to outlaw the NPD would come at some point, and so they had to proceed with extreme caution and always keep an eye on the bigger picture. Besides, there wasn't a neo-Nazi network in Baden-Württemberg or any nationwide structures. And the World Cup! If the international press got hold of this, it didn't bear thinking about . . . "And so on."

"Have they done Janisch's post-mortem yet?" Louise said.

"Last night. Graeve is about to be notified."

"And?"

"No idea. But we're not going to like it. And let me repeat: we're off the case. The investigation team is being disbanded."

"The line's really bad," she said.

"I can't hear you anymore," Enders said.

"Leif?"

"Louise?"

They hung up.

Narrow Rathausgasse. The footfall you'd expect on a Thursday morning at 8.15, no more, no less, no different.

Ben, standing on a bridge, looking out over a river.

Offering to talk, but in truth going away.

Kabangu was walking right beside the runnels, Louise a couple of metres away, making sure that nobody squeezed between them. She kept looking around at Gerd, who was a few paces behind and signalled that he had everything in his sights. They crossed Rathausplatz. Nobody in the least bit conspicuous. She wasn't expecting to see anyone either. Kabangu's destination was known. If they were planning anything this morning, it would be there.

Kaiser-Joseph-Strasse. Two patrol cars: one parked, one cruising. Then Münsterplatz. Louise remembered the market too late. Although there wasn't an excessive crowd of people here, there were still too many for her liking. She moved right beside Kabangu, put her left hand on his arm and guided him between the stalls.

He pointed up at the belltower. "Too high for me. I'd feel dizzy that high up. You see too much. You look at the small space you're moving in and realise how complex and varied it is. You understand you can't control anything. Only if you're up there the whole time can you be in control. But then you wouldn't be down here, and you couldn't take part. Like Grandfather Mabruk."

The alley the café was in came into view. Louise held Kabangu back while Gerd passed them and dashed into the narrow street. Two minutes later he sent a text: inside the café was empty and there wasn't anyone sitting outside it either. Two entrances, one on the alley, the other leading to the neighbouring museum.

"Could we have breakfast somewhere else, please?" Louise asked.

"No," Kabangu replied.

They left Münsterplatz. Four or five buildings, the last of them

184

the museum, then a recess. A tree, a few tables, at one of which a woman was now sitting. When she noticed Kabangu she raised a hand and waved.

"Maria," he said.

Maria had a logical explanation: she lived in Kirchzarten. For simplicity's sake she'd told Kabangu she was from Freiburg.

"*Kirsch-sarten*," Kabangu said.

"No," Maria said. "Kirch-zarten. The first town if you're heading for the Black Forest." She spoke with a strong Baden accent and laughed coyly. A neat elderly woman, dainty and educated, with the scent of lilies.

She seemed believable as far as Louise was concerned. Nonetheless, she asked her for some ID. Maria gave an embarrassed grimace. "I'm afraid I left my purse at home. It must be on the kitchen table." Turning to Kabangu, she said, "Would you be able to lend me ten euros, Ludwig? I'll give it back to you this evening."

Kabangu gave her a friendly smile. Of course.

"This evening?" Louise narrowed her eyes; the mistrust had returned.

"We're going to the cinema."

"Would you mind if I came home with you later?"

"To Kirchzarten?"

"To where you live."

Maria smiled. "In a police car?"

"If that's what you would like."

"Lovely. How exciting! And extremely practical."

"Madame Bonì is very sceptical and very thorough," Kabangu said cheerfully.

"A detective must be like that, mustn't they? But why is . . . *the police* involved?" Maria had lowered her voice, the last few words almost a whisper. Her eyes were open wide, full of curiosity. Her slim fingers trembled faintly and there was a hint of red in her cheeks.

"The bones," Louise said. "There—"

"Grandfather Mabruk," Kabangu explained.

"There are criminal implications."

A waitress came and took their order. Gerd ambled over from Münsterplatz and sat a couple of tables away. He had a different view of the alley from Louise and sat at an angle which also allowed him to see the entrance to the café if he turned his head slightly.

Humming, he studied the drinks menu.

"Criminal implications?" Maria's whitish-blonde hair was dyed, her light-grey roots shimmering through. The artery on her neck throbbed in a gentle rhythm and the collar of her blouse was buttoned up tight. All of a sudden Louise felt the curiosity and coyness were a contradiction. They didn't seem to fit with the buttoned-up blouse.

"Madame Boni." Kabangu nudged her when she didn't answer straightaway.

"The remains of Grandfather Mabruk may have been illegally removed from his grave, but I suspect you know that already."

The waitress brought the drinks. In the distance, church bells rang out over the clatter, followed by the bells of the minster. Nine peals.

The ringing had died away, leaving a buzzing. A buzzing in her head because the blood was now rushing faster. Three hours till lunchtime, she thought. Maybe four. Depending on what Ben meant by "lunchtime".

A fine film of sweat had formed on Maria's brow. The artery on her neck was now pounding much faster. Louise watched her lift the cup and drink, closing her eyes for a moment. She put it down with both hands. A smile, a murmured apology, then she got up and went inside the café.

Two entrances, Louise thought.

Two exits.

She froze, her muscles paralysed, her hands ice-cold. "Gerd!" she called, pulling her gun from its holster.

Before Gerd could react, his upper body was flung forward, hitting the table. Blood poured from the side of his neck, then more blood spurted in a fountain from his lower back. Once again Louise hadn't heard a shot. Kabangu let out a cry, more an expression of surprise than fear. As she dragged him to the ground she saw render fly from the wall behind, then she yanked the table over and pulled it in front of their bodies.

Two shooters, she thought, one in the entrance to the café, hidden by the tree, the other from the alley – she'd detected movement out of the corner of her eye.

The fingers of her left hand digging into Kabangu's forearm, she ventured a glance at Gerd. He appeared to be alive; his arm was twitching in a jerky dance.

A shadow slithered across the ground; footsteps approached from the café. She pulled back the slide and cocked the pistol. This time she did hear the silenced shot, the bullet knocked the table against her and ricocheted off with a whine.

Another projectile hammered into the metal.

Then came a muffled shout and suddenly she heard lots of footsteps in the street. They fired without warning, cries of pain mingled with the shots and splinters of glass rained down on Louise; the window of the café had shattered.

Our people, Louise thought.

"Stay down," she said, getting up.

The two attackers were both dead. One lay outside the entrance to the café, the other by the building opposite, having dragged a bicycle to the ground with him. A dozen special forces personnel in balaclavas stood as still as statues over the bodies, their weapons aimed at them;

others secured the immediate area. Through the shattered window Louise could see commandos inside the café too.

Gerd, half lying on the table . . . A man and a woman were bent over him, trying to stop the bleeding. His left arm twitched like a fish washed ashore.

Sirens sounded in the near distance, coming ever closer, police cars and ambulances just a few streets away. Everything perfectly prepared, Louise thought. Only with Gerd had they been at a loss. Hadn't been able to make allowances for him.

A masked man approached her, the officer in charge, medium height, brawny, powerful thighs. "Get your man out of here, Boni," he barked, nodding at the overturned table that Kabangu was still cowering behind. She didn't recognise the voice, no name badge on the bulletproof vest, of course not.

At that moment Gerd's arm went limp.

"Colleague of yours?"

Louise nodded and thought: Gerd Rehberg, surveillance squad, divorced, no kids, just a budgie, Willi.

"I'm sorry."

"Yes."

She couldn't get the budgie out of her head. It was singing away in the front of the Escort, waiting for someone who was not going to come back.

No more trips to the park on Sundays.

Ben, she thought.

She missed Bermann, he would bring order into this chaos.

Stay calm, Boni. Hang on in there.

She turned to the officer in charge. "Have you got the woman?"

An indifferent shrug. "Sorry."

She understood. No information. Freiburg was off the case.

Louise looked at the body beside the tree. He was lying on his back, numerous entry wounds in the chest and stomach area, his right

cheek shot away. She still recognised him at once. Camping in paradise, the man with the rucksack. The face that Gerd had photographed
outside the hotel without noticing it.

If only he had, she thought. Yesterday or today. He would have
just had to turn his head.

"Forward march, Bonì!" the commander said.

She went over to the other shooter. He'd ended up lying across
the bicycle, his head supported by the wall. The second man Riedl's
surveillance camera had captured that night. Similar wounds to the
first man, legs unscathed. They'd only aimed at the upper body.

Kabangu came over to her. "It's over," he said wearily.

"No, it's not," she replied.

III

27

An hour later the case had been concluded.

They were sitting in Cords' office on the fourth floor, squinting at the sunlight: Graeve, Vormweg, Louise Boni and a federal prosecutor, Heinrich Behr, a grandfatherly type around sixty years of age. Louise had come across him several years ago, finding him friendly and harmless, but also a little divorced from reality. He smiled a lot; she thought him more likely to be sitting with grandchildren around the Christmas tree rather than at a table at police HQ, discussing terrorists and right-wing extremists.

But she suspected he could also be different.

"Congratulations," Behr said, his gentle eyes wandering across their faces. "It's thanks to you that the attack was thwarted."

None of the Freiburgers responded. They'd lost a colleague; accepting praise was out of the question.

"And not only that," Behr added. "The cell's been broken."

"Rubbish," Louise said.

Behr nodded and touched her knee with a grandfatherly hand. "I'm sorry for your loss. Gerd Rehberg was a good man, I hear."

Cords cleared his throat. "Thank you."

"You can breathe easily. It's over."

A text arrived: Enders, stuck in traffic on the A5.

"If you wouldn't mind giving us a summary," Louise said.

Behr cocked his head and blinked, focused. "As tragic as it was classic. Two young men from the former GDR, in the machinery of reunification they lose direction and status, become radicalised.

At some point they plan their revenge for what they haven't achieved and what they've had to put up with."

"What about the others? Those who helped?"

"A sympathiser here, a comrade there. If we can prove it, they'll be brought to trial."

"Torsten Schulz?"

"He's out," Graeve replied. "His lawyer has just lodged an appeal against his custody. Christopher Rophe. You know him."

Louise nodded and looked back at Behr. "What about the person behind all this?"

"Who do you mean?"

"The one who wanted Kabangu killed."

"Died in the attack." Fatalism crept into Behr's expression. "There was nobody else involved besides those two men, nobody ordering the killing. You've got to accept this, Frau Bonì."

She hadn't expected to hear anything different. The federal prosecutor's priority wasn't facts or the truth, but the whole picture. In Germany as a whole there could be no national far-right networks. The danger from the right was isolated, located in just a few deprived areas. There might be the odd sidekick jumping around the place, but that was all. A democratic state through and through, with a few extremists.

Louise looked at Graeve. "How did Janisch die?"

"Diabetic shock."

"He was diabetic? Did we find an insulin pen in his flat? A glucose meter? A prescription?"

"No."

"Perhaps he didn't know he was diabetic?"

"I suppose that's how it was."

"Quite a story, isn't it?"

Once more Behr's eyes shifted from one to the other. He smiled meekly and Louise guessed what was going through his mind: I'm out of here in a few minutes and I'll be done with Boni. But you've got to keep putting up with her.

She looked at Graeve. "Is it lunchtime yet, boss?"

He glanced at his watch and shook his head. "Just before eleven."

"When is lunchtime for you? Half eleven, midday, one o'clock?"

"Boni?" Cords muttered irritably.

She got up. "Ludwig Kabangu's waiting for me."

"Please get the file ready to hand over to the Criminal Investigation Bureau," Cords said.

"The *complete* file," Behr added.

Louise went to the door and turned around. "The file is incomplete until we know who was behind this."

Kabangu was standing by the window in her office, his hands crossed behind his back. When she closed the door he turned to face her. He looked exhausted, perplexed. He raised a hand in which there was a mobile. "Maria's not answering. Was she arrested?"

"I assume so."

"You don't know?"

"Stuttgart's in charge now. The Ministry of the Interior, the Criminal Investigation Bureau. Public prosecutors working for the federal government."

"What does that mean?"

"It means that this is now about politics rather than the truth."

"Like in my country."

"I suppose so," Louise said.

He smirked briefly before turning back to the window and asking about the mountains on the horizon and the course of the border. She joined him there and spoke about the landscape, the Vosges in the mist, well into France, the border between the two countries was the Rhine. Further to the right was the Kaiserstuhl, mostly in fog, and protruding from the fog was its highest peak, the Totenkopf – the skull.

Which brought them back to the matter in hand, she thought.

"Who thought of calling a mountain that?"

"I imagine there were a few executions up there a thousand or so years ago, and that's how the name came about." She looked at Kabangu. "There's only one Maria Schmidt in Kirchzarten. She's thirty-seven. Is your Maria thirty-seven?"

"No."

"She did the dirty on you."

Kabangu raised his eyebrows as if not altogether convinced. As if to say: Many things are possible, entirely different scenarios too.

There was a knock at the door and an officer entered, carrying the cage with Gerd's budgie.

"On the table, please."

"And a message from Mats Benedikt. The last official act in this case, he says." The officer put a piece of paper beside the cage and left. The newspaper article with the photograph of Lothar's girlfriend, the demonstration in Lörrach. *Her name is Kristina Gendrich*, Mats had written underneath.

Louise looked at the cage. The budgie had a light-blue chest and narrow, dark-blue cheeks. It was sitting on the floor in a corner, staring at her with large, round eyes. It looked as if it knew that everything would change from today, presumably for the worse.

Willi, she thought. What a name for a bird.

Willi and Gerd.

She took the empty water bowl from the cage, filled it from the sink and reattached it. The budgie still had food: grain and something unidentifiable.

Kabangu had come over to her. "Would you like me to make him sing? You must know that we Africans can talk to birds. We talk and sing to them, but not only that. We understand them and they understand us."

Louise brushed this off. "Please, not another story, Monsieur Kabangu. You tell too many stories. They stack up inside my head, blocking my reason."

"Maybe it's the other way around."

"Whatever." Louise picked up the cage and they went to the door. Kabangu wanted to walk back to the hotel – without "protection" – to get a little rest.

Without "protection" was a bad idea, she told him.

"You're always worried."

"We still don't know who's behind all this. Maybe . . ." She didn't finish her sentence. The paranoia had taken root in her head.

They wouldn't try again after that disaster.

In the corridor, Louise said, "You weren't afraid. You were surprised, but not afraid."

Kabangu's eyes widened. "No, no, I was really afraid. Terribly afraid! I was afraid of falling onto Grandfather Mabruk, who was a small, almost delicate man. Anyone falling on him would squash him to death! And I was afraid of spilling coffee on my trousers when I fell. I've only got this one clean pair, you see, they're my favourite trousers. I was terrified of ruining them."

Louise managed a smile. "I'd like to hear the whole story this evening. The story without the pretty wrapping."

"You won't like it."

"That's irrelevant."

They went down the stairs slowly and through the security doors. "Your dinner?" the porter asked, pointing at the bird and laughing.

Outside, Kabangu said unexpectedly, "I don't like this country. Many people here aren't what they appear to be. Like Maria they say one thing and think or do something different. Dr Arndt says there aren't any bones from German East Africa in his archive, but he's acting out of fear and he knows it. The police say they want to protect me, but then they use me as bait. The government says it wants to find out the truth, but they're only concerned about the politics. You, Madame Bonì, are different, but that isn't much help." He looked up at the sky for a moment, then said, "No, Grandfather Mabruk, this isn't our brother nation – or at least not until we can be of use to it again."

At twelve o'clock she was in her flat, listening to the deafening silence. Bloody hell, she thought, twelve o'clock is lunchtime, Ben, you can't say you're staying till lunchtime then leave before twelve . . .

Down in the Balkans twelve o'clock was lunchtime too. Or was twelve too early there? Was lunchtime only at one in Osijek and Sarajevo?

She could've asked Thomas Ilic, the Croat, if she'd still been in touch with him.

Or she could call Ben Liebermann.

But of course that was impossible.

Louise looked at the budgie squatting in its corner. "Say something, Willi. Sing, for God's sake."

Willi was silent.

She flopped onto the sofa and waited until one.

Waited until two. No Ben, no message, and the bird wasn't singing.

When the silence became painful she fell asleep.

At half past two she was woken by her phone ringing.

"We can go and see Witiko," Stefan Bremer said.

28

"Is that them?" Bremer took a closer look at the two stills from the surveillance camera at Riedl's campsite.

Louise shrugged without taking her eyes off the road. She couldn't say for certain but yes, they might have been the men who'd shot Timo Kahle and seriously injured Bremer two years ago in Karlsruhe.

Far-right contract killers. Today they had died themselves and would never testify.

She'd picked up Bremer at Karlsruhe central station and joined the A65. They'd now crossed the Rhine and left Baden-Württemberg.

"Stirring any memories?"

"A strange memory," Bremer said. In his mind he saw a man with a bicycle. The man was standing beside the bike, head bowed, browsing a magazine. A peculiarly familiar and comforting sight, as if he'd often seen the man on their daily patrols through the city.

"One of the killers had a bicycle," Louise said.

Bremer was bent forwards, rummaging in the rucksack between his feet. He sat up without having found what he was looking for. "A witness said she'd seen a cyclist. He was standing by the takeaway, holding a magazine."

"An official witness?" Out of the corner of her eye she saw him shrug.

"Can I keep the photos? For my file?"

"They're yours."

He bent forwards again, looking for the right plastic folder for the photos. Louise sensed his excitement. Finally, some new clues; finally, faces that might one day hit upon concrete parallels in his memory. Finally, answers to questions that had been torturing him for two years.

Unofficial answers. None of the authorities involved would ever confirm them because they contradicted the official line. A Roma man, not far-right contract killers, had attacked the two officers.

If lies stuck around for long enough, she thought, the truth expired.

They came off the motorway at Kandel and headed west, before turning north at Bad Bergzabern. Bremer was looking increasingly edgy. He said he didn't know what state Witiko might be in now. Would he remember him and their conversation a year ago, or the NPD demonstration in Dortmund on 30 April 2004? That Amadeus had been pushing him in a wheelchair, and so couldn't be a witness for what had happened in Karlsruhe?

"We'll see," Louise said. She was less interested in what Witiko remembered. Memories were stories you told yourself to look back in the way you wanted to.

Much more interesting, she thought, were Witiko's fantasies.

A long, light-coloured building in front of the woods. Main house, two wings, other small buildings, parking places under trees, lawns in the late-afternoon sun. Footpaths led through a lush garden in which the first rhododendrons, lilacs and laburnums were flowering. The odd bench, a few people, some on their own, some with companions. Three years ago Louise's therapist had given her a prospectus for this clinic and she'd imagined staying in this place for a few weeks or months, beginning a new life here. In the end she chose Oderberg for her detox and the Zen monastery Kanzan-an in Alsace for her withdrawal.

As she and Bremer wandered up to the main entrance she wondered what and who she would be now if she hadn't opted for the isolation of the Kanzan-an, but had come to a place of interaction like this clinic. Here, she thought, she might have been able to achieve withdrawal from herself too, rather than becoming even more Louise Bonì in the woods around the monastery.

A taciturn young doctor, Dr Verhagen, met them at reception and took them down long, deserted corridors to Witiko's room.

"No light," he said, "then it might be possible."

"A year ago it was OK with light," Bremer said.

"Not anymore."

"Why no light?" Louise asked.

Verhagen shrugged and scratched his nostril. "Maybe he thinks it puts him on a level playing field. More and more he's living in a sort of permanent darkness, taking visitors out of the bright world they're accustomed to and into his." He knocked and opened the door without waiting for a response.

It was almost pitch black inside the room, the curtains drawn, none of the lamps on. Louise found the air fresh and cool; a window must be open. Music was playing in a corner, tinny and flat, like that from a seventies portable radio. The singer was a throwback to the seventies too: Daliah Lavi. When he was fifteen or sixteen, the first Germain was totally in love with her, until real girls became more important.

"Your visitors," Verhagen said.

"Visitors?"

"Stefan Bremer, the police officer, and one of his colleagues."

"Close the door," Witiko said. His voice sounded high-pitched and reedy, a head voice, far from the chest, Louise thought, from the core of the body. Too close to all the faulty wiring that had crept in over the past few years.

Verhagen had shut the door. She sensed him right behind her; Bremer stood to her right. Bonì closed her eyes and opened them slowly. Bit by bit she could make out a rectangle of lighter darkness, the window; the curtain wasn't cutting out the daylight entirely. She couldn't see Witiko. Presumably he was standing or sitting to their left, where the music was coming from. She recalled the man in Bremer's photograph – early fifties, shaggy white hair, an excited if not crazed grin.

"I'm not expecting any visitors."

"Stefan Bremer, the policeman who was here before," Verhagen said impassively but patiently. "And a colleague of his from Freiburg."

"Can't they speak themselves?"

"The murder in Karlsruhe," Bremer said, sounding unsure, as if he didn't know which way to face. "Remember? We talked about it a year ago."

"Is the woman able to talk too?"

"She is," Louise said.

Witiko laughed, a high-pitched rasping sound, almost asthmatic, which broke off abruptly.

Raising a hand, she found Bremer's arm and gave it a quick squeeze. "Keep talking," she whispered.

"The killing of the police officer on 30 April 2004. My colleague, Timo Kahle, was shot dead. I was there and I . . . survived."

"Congratulations. I know nothing about it."

"Oh yes, you do," Bremer muttered.

"Oh yes, you do," Witiko mimicked him, then laughed again.

Louise stepped in. "You said you were in Dortmund with Amadeus that day. You'd broken your ankle—"

"Sprained," Bremer corrected her weakly.

". . . and you were in a wheelchair, being pushed by Amadeus."

"I don't know any Amadeus."

"An informer."

"And I never had anything wrong with my foot."

Louise turned around and asked Verhagen to leave them alone.

"Your responsibility," he said.

A bright rectangle of light when he opened the door, then darkness again.

"Has the doctor gone?"

"Yes," she said.

"Won't make any difference."

Will you come along with me, Daliah Lavi sang, *if my path leads into the darkness? Will you come along with me, if my day hints at night-time starkness?*

Witiko hummed along and nobody said anything for a while. Louise instinctively thought of Ben and the silence in her flat. She thought that her path might lead into the darkness too one day. That one day she might also be sitting in the dark, listening to music to avoid having to put up with the silence generated by the absent and the dead.

But hadn't her path led her into the darkness already?

Louise couldn't help smiling. She actually really felt good about herself in the dark.

"Good times, they were," Witiko said. "Money galore, women galore, fucking for the German revolution. Fuck me, I'm the soldiers' girl, I'm the pure girl of the promised Aryan race. We'll dance in the white circle and undo Stalingrad, we'll undo Berlin, we'll undo Dresden, we'll undo Nuremberg and there's money every few months. I need a tip, the fool running me says, my golden goose, who should we take a closer look at? And I say, him, him and her too, we'd drawn up lists of some people and people who couldn't be trusted. And in a week's time someone's going to torch a foreigners' hostel somewhere in Stuttgart. And so we go and torch a foreigners' hostel somewhere in Stuttgart, and the golden goose is happy, he claps me on the shoulder and hands me a few notes. Good times, they were, so much money for the cause, for the eagle's fight. Organisation costs, planning costs, the German revolution costs, even if we're just talking about CDs for schools, recruiting young people, training young people, concerts, we dance for the eagle, we dance for the Reich, we arm ourselves for the white day, and you know nothing about it, you mustn't know anything, your fools in the top jobs, your bosses and politicians make sure you won't find out a thing. You won't find out that we drill in the camel jockeys' training camps and with our true friends in the States and in Russia, abroad and at home with the German army, that we spin our webs in barracks and prisons. That costs money, the preparation is expensive, you need an army, you need soldiers able to fight, we do our military service, we sign up for a time, we build an army to conquer the internal enemy, the white wolf is patient, waiting for the great day, now and then launching an attack from the National Socialist underground to baffle you, sow fear and work through the lists. It's a great life, in secret and not, a great family, a great game, and soon it becomes serious."

"I thought you'd dropped out," Louise said.

"Camouflage," Witiko whispered. "That I was with them and wasn't, that I'm here and not here, what I say and what I don't say. It's all camouflage, the white wolf knows how to camouflage himself."

Bremer took off the rucksack, apparently to fish out some documents. "I need light, can I turn—"

"No!" Witiko bellowed.

Bremer bent to put down the rucksack, then straightened up. "Before, you said you hadn't been able to see the point anymore. Only violence and hatred but no point, no—"

"Before?"

"When I came to see you a year ago."

"You've never been here. I'd recognise you if you had, but I don't."

"If I could just turn—"

"Are you deaf?"

"I've got photos of both of the attackers, please at least take a quick look."

Silence.

Will you come along with me, shadow and light we'll see.

Witiko began humming again.

"Does the white wolf just attack like that?" Louise asked. "Or does somebody give him an assignment?"

"Where does the wolf live? He lives in the forest, in his secret hideaway, that's where he lives. So how can he know where in the world to attack, where it's necessary to attack to sow fear and make the family happy and test the seriousness for the great day when the avalanche begins to slide?"

"Who does he get his assignments from?"

"One here, another one there."

"The murder in Karlsruhe?"

"Never heard of it."

"Yes, you have!" a distraught Bremer interjected.

Witiko burst out laughing. Afterwards there was silence.

Bremer shifted around, becoming increasingly agitated.

"The person giving the orders, Witiko," Louise said.

"There's more than one."

"Friedrich Krüger?"

"No."

"Julius Krüger?"

Witiko giggled.

"Do you know Julius?"

"I don't know any Julius."

"Thomas Walczak? Paulus Riedl?"

"I fucked Charlie. Good times, they were, so many women wanting to be fucked for the Aryan cause. Charlie was always the first one on her back, opening her legs wide and moaning 'for blood, honour, for the Fatherland, come inside me, my Rudolf, my Adolf, my white, white wolf'."

A click, a button had popped up, the song had come to an end.

Bonì heard Witiko moving. A cassette rewound and started again from the beginning. *Will you come along with me, if my path leads into the darkness?*

"Erik Willig?"

"Don't know him."

"Ricky Janisch?"

"Don't know him."

"An informer like you. Like Amadeus."

"The guy with the wheelchair? There was never anything wrong with my foot." He began singing along softly. "'*To stop me roaming and save me from more strife, you build my house and we'll take a rest from life.*' Erik, Erik," he whispered. "You rarely see him, he's mostly under the hood and so you don't know if he's there or not. He's a Christian knight, like the small, anxious flower man with the dog. Erik's very highly regarded, they say, because he knows the important people, the silent white eagles far above who nobody sees and nobody hears."

"Does Erik give assignments?"

Witiko coughed, then croaked, "No more cigarettes, my dear, that's all over, good times they were, now you're not going to smoke anymore, doesn't matter. Erik who? Eric Bloodaxe? Eric the Red? Eric Clapton?"

"I've had just about enough of this," Louise said.

"Me too," Witiko retorted. "And finish." The click of the button; the song stopped halfway through.

"The man who gave the orders, Witiko."

He didn't reply.

"I want a name. I'm not leaving here without a name."

The seconds passed, Witiko said nothing, Louise felt for the wall behind her and pressed the light switch.

Nothing happened.

She took a small torch out of her coat pocket, turned it on and searched for Witiko with the beam. When she found him he began howling and showered her with curses. A deathly pale face shot through with tiny red blood vessels, bushy brows above eyes wide with fury, his hair standing up in every direction as in the photo.

"Turn it off!" he screamed. "Now!"

"Lock the door, Stefan," Louise said.

Bremer dashed behind her. "There isn't a key!"

"Then keep it shut."

She heard him grunt; he must be bracing himself against it. There was a knock, followed by the sound of Verhagen's muffled voice.

"Another minute," Louise said.

"Another minute!" Bremer called out.

Verhagen's voice, soft, no more knocking. He wasn't making much of an effort.

"Witiko, I want a name. An address. Something!"

"Light off!"

She lowered the torch. "So?"

"Erik, Erik, Erik who? Eric the Red? Eric the Dead?"

"Erik Willig, works in Freiburg University archive."

"Don't know him. I only know Charlie who wanted to be fucked five times a day, shoot the pure inside me, the eternal, purify me, my white wolf . . ."

Louise raised the torch; Witiko howled and put his hands in front of his eyes. She went over to him slowly. "Today your comrades in Freiburg tried to kill a man, and I want to know who gave the order."

"Turn it off! Turn it off!" His voice was cracking and he tensed his fingers like claws, as if about to scratch her face.

Louise switched off the torch and took a few silent steps to the side. Not a moment too soon – she felt the movement of air as Witiko leaped forwards and went sliding into an empty space.

"Fucking whore!" he hissed.

The torch went on, its beam crept across his skinny back, caught thin arms, his white shock of hair. "A name, then you'll be rid of me."

Witiko slumped to the floor, crossed his legs and didn't make a sound. As she moved the beam away she thought she could see his eyes follow the bright dot. The light picked out a round table, a cassette recorder, a red plastic cup and a chair. On the wall behind were colourful posters of old singers: Daliah Lavi, Nana Mouskouri, Lena Valatais, Mireille Mathieu, Vicky Leandros, as well as others, German and foreign, including Jewish singers. Witiko's views stopped at music or beautiful women.

She turned off the torch.

"Today, did you say?" he asked.

"Yes."

"Then they'll be dancing tonight, the white knights, as they always do when the white wolf has attacked. Follow the flower man, he'll lead you to them."

Outside she called Enders. Her gaze wandered across the rhododendrons, lilacs and laburnums. Finally, she thought, they were able to pin down Julius Krüger.

The flower man was a white knight.

Like Erik Willig.

"I won't get any officers for that," Enders said. "We're off the case."

"Do it yourself, then," she replied.

They got into the car and drove back to Baden-Württemberg. Bremer looked depressed; he'd been hoping for more. More answers, perhaps even an explanation for everything that had happened on 30 April 2004. Not just parallels that couldn't be proven, attempts at a cover-up by higher authorities. Matthias "Matze" Seibert who'd hired a camper van back then and again now, and hadn't used it to go on holiday. Two men who back then and again now had come to the south-west to kill. The same background, the same motive, the same death list. White knights, white wolves.

So long as not everything Witiko had said was nonsense.

"What did he mean by 'white knights'?" Bremer asked.

"The Ku Klux Klan. From another source we have indications that a German chapter is involved."

"First I've heard of it."

"Time for a new list." She smiled.

Bremer was not in the mood for jokes. "I'm going to Jena to talk to Seibert."

"He won't talk to you. And it's dangerous."

"For me, doing nothing is more dangerous."

She understood what he meant. Doing nothing would mean giving free rein to self-destruction.

The same was true of her to a certain extent.

They parted company at Karlsruhe station.

"Will you call when you know more?" Bremer said.

She nodded. "You too."

Louise watched him walk to the tram stop, a young man still, hunched under the burden of the rucksack, the burden of an inexplicable, forgotten day two years ago, which might never end.

29

Louise was back in Freiburg by half past seven. On the way she'd called Ludwig Kabangu to postpone their meal and the truth until the following day: *Breakfast, if that's OK with you.* They'd arranged to meet in the hotel at half past eight.

Then she spoke to Reinhard Graeve and asked what he wanted to know about her trip to a psychiatric clinic in the Rhineland Palatinate.

It's best you don't know too much, boss. You wouldn't believe most of it anyway.

Tell me what I can believe.

They've got rhododendrons and lilacs in the garden.

Close to the main station she got two takeaway doners. In Haslach she saw the young footballers again, joined by a considerably older man who seemed to be having more fun than everyone else put together. She pulled over and called through the passenger window: "Dinner!"

Leif Enders had some news.

The Thüringian Verfassungsschutz had denied the request from their "esteemed colleagues" for information on Matthias "Matze" Seibert. Their own ongoing investigations made this "impossible".

Also, the former PhD student invited by Erik Willig to join his "small circle of socially conservative intellectuals" had been questioned in Berlin. "He doesn't remember," Enders said with his mouth full. "Either the conversation or Willig."

"Do we know where he stands politically?"

"Far to the right, the Berliners say." He was publishing articles in right-wing papers, writing a blog along similar lines, making no bones about his views.

"How can they keep all that up?" Louise said. "Lying, staying silent, knowing nothing."

"They learn from politicians."

They were sitting in her Peugeot at the end of the street where the Krügers lived, making a mess of their coats and trousers. They had a clear view of the Krügers' building, of the father's windows down below and those of Julius' family on the first floor. The flat on the ground floor was in darkness, the one above brightly lit. *They're having supper*, Enders had said.

"Does Graeve know you're here?"

He shook his head. "I'm not on duty."

Enders got a text, announced by a soft gong stroke. He answered with one finger, glanced briefly at Louise, then went on eating.

"Wolfgang from Aachen?"

"Something like that."

One of the windows on the first floor opened and Julius' wife shook out a tablecloth. Wearing a pale-blue blouse and with her hair plaited, she looked ready to go out.

"Maybe she's going with him," Enders said.

Another text and another reply.

"Can you stop that now, Leif, it's getting on my nerves."

He growled and said, "Mine too." He stared at his mobile, which he'd obviously muted, and wrote another reply.

"I'm being serious."

He scrunched up the paper and aluminium foil, then looked at her. "Can we talk?"

"Can we do it tomorrow?"

Pointing to his phone, he said, "It's about this."

The front door opened and Julius came out with his wife, both dressed up as if they were off to the opera or some fancy reception. They came towards Enders and Louise in the evening light and stopped beside a mustard-coloured Opel Corsa, a slightly older car. They got in and drove off.

Louise started the Peugeot and kept a safe distance.

"My wife's drinking," Enders said.

Shit, not *that*, Louise thought.

"The problem is, she's denying it."

"I don't want that, Leif. Looking after other people."

"All I need is some advice."

"How to get her to admit it?"

He didn't reply.

They'd followed Basler Strasse to the west, then turned north and passed police HQ.

The main station, straight on, Herdern.

"Can I explain quickly?"

"Can I stop you?"

"No."

They'd grown apart, and after twenty years of marriage had been on the verge of separation when they decided to make another go of it, somewhere else. A new beginning, it didn't matter where, just not in Aachen where everything was familiar and tainted, or Berlin where they'd lived for a few years. Enders heard about the section head vacancy in Freiburg and submitted his application. They moved, but it didn't work. Nothing but arguments, accusations, nights apart, booze.

"Zähringen," Louise said. The mustard-coloured Corsa had turned east and was driving slowly down the narrow side streets of Zähringen. "What do you mean by 'grown apart'?"

"I had flings."

"And then she started drinking."

"It was the other way around."

She laughed bitterly. "What's her version?"

"She doesn't drink, or at least no more than I do."

"And if she does occasionally drink too much it's because you're cheating on her."

"In the past she . . . doesn't matter, that's not the point."

"Who's Wolfgang from Aachen? One of your flings?"

"A therapist we see three times a week."

"Is she suicidal?"

"Maybe."

"And she's in particularly bad shape today?"

"Apparently."

"Go home. Look after her. You're her husband."

Up ahead the Corsa stopped and Julius Krüger made a meal of parking while Louise and Enders waited in a garage driveway. They watched as the Krügers crossed the road, were greeted by a woman at a garden gate, and went into the house.

"Sixteen," Louise said.

Enders made a quick call to HQ. "Weinmann," he said. "Bert and Hannelore."

They drove past the house. The door was open and they could see people in a large hallway, glasses in hand. Another arrival was just entering the front garden. Louise stopped, parking half on the pavement. *Tonight*, Witiko had said. What did that mean, exactly? Ten o'clock? Eleven? Or two in the morning? If lunchtime wasn't twelve o'clock, how was she to know what "night" meant?

Ben, she thought. Right now he was in Osijek or Sarajevo, sitting by a river in the mild evening air, with *her* on his mind – she'd bet anything on it. He wouldn't find the finality of it easy either.

"Here," Enders said, showing her his phone. Ten missed calls. Fourteen texts. "She's drunk."

"Go home, Leif."

"Why? We talk every evening, argue every evening, get drunk, then she cries and chucks me out of the bedroom."

"She needs you now."

"And I need . . ." He pointed at the Weinmanns' house. "This."

"Split up, then."

"It's not that simple. I'm not good at leaving."

"She should be leaving *you*. You're cheating on her!"

"Not so easy, Louise, after twenty years. A new start in your late forties, well—"

"Others manage it." She opened the door. "Wait here." She got out, went into the next side street and took another turn. Hedges, gardens, backs of houses. In one of the gardens hubbub, voices and laughter, candlelight shimmering through the branches – the Weinmanns' house. In the fence was a small gate; a barely visible path led through the hedges and shrubs to the house.

It took a while for her to find Julius Krüger amongst the guests.

She notified Enders, looked for an observation post on the other side of the street partially shielded by trees, and listened to what Rolf Bermann had to say.

You started drinking when your husband walked out on you.

I'm not drinking, for Christ's sake!

When her mobile vibrated, she listened to what Leif Enders had to say.

Just before half past ten a car turned into the street and stopped near the garden gate. The headlights went out, but the engine kept running. A man at the wheel, nobody else.

It's kicking off, Louise texted.

Seconds later a shadow appeared at the gate. Size, outline, movements all matched Julius Krüger.

He got in and the car, a Daimler A-class with a Lörrach number plate, drove off.

Seconds later Enders arrived in her Peugeot.

30

"France?" Enders mumbled.

They'd come off the A5 about twenty kilometres north of Freiburg and were heading towards the Rhine, having just passed the last town before the border, Sasbach am Kaiserstuhl. They could still make out the Daimler's taillights; with hardly any traffic on the road Louise was keeping as far back as possible to avoid detection.

"There might be bureaucratic problems."

"Absolutely not," she said.

Enders laughed softly.

She knew he wasn't really in the mood for laughing. Thirty-four text messages by half past ten, nineteen missed calls.

A glow in his hand: the mobile. Call number twenty.

"For God's sake answer it!"

"I can't, I'm on duty."

"I can't work like this, Leif." She braked hard then came to a stop. "Sort that out, then follow on after."

"You're not serious!"

"I am. Get out, boss."

Leif Enders wasn't Rolf Bermann, he didn't growl, bark or get furious – a pleasant change sometimes, Louise thought. Realising she wasn't going to back down he undid his belt, opened the door and got out.

A few seconds later the darkness in the rear-view mirror had swallowed him up.

*

France was just a smokescreen. Half an hour later the Daimler drove back into Germany at Rhinau, Louise far behind. South of Lahr they crossed the A5 and entered the foothills of the Black Forest. In Ettenheimer they turned north, following a narrow road through dark woods along the hillsides.

Eighty minutes after Enders had got out, the journey seemed to be at an end. The Daimler stopped by the side of the road in the middle of the forest and the headlights were extinguished. Doors slammed shut.

Louise reversed the Peugeot onto a forest path and took off her red coat. The black jumper beneath it was perfect for the night. She hurriedly texted *North of Ettenheimmünster* to Enders, who'd been taken home in a patrol car and messaged every fifteen minutes that he was leaving "soon".

Leaving now, he replied.

She got out.

The Daimler was parked beside two other cars: Julius Krüger and the other man were nowhere to be seen. Boni was just about to make a note of the number plates when she heard the engine sounds not far away. Two pairs of headlights were approaching from Ettenheimmünster.

She waited under the cover of the trees.

A Golf and a Ford parked by the other cars. Strapping on rucksacks, three men and a woman stepped onto a path and disappeared into the darkness. Louise didn't recognise any of them. She hurried over to the cars and texted Enders the makes, models, colours and registrations: two from Freiburg, one each from Lörrach, Karlsruhe and Strasbourg.

Then she followed the six people into the forest.

For minutes Boni didn't hear or see anybody. In fact she saw next to nothing – clouds hung above the trees and there was no moonlight, just the dark night. The path led uphill to begin with, then along the hillside. She walked slowly, going as quietly as she could and so made little progress.

At a sharp turning she stopped and listened. Footsteps, but *behind* her.

She found a hiding place at the last moment. Holding her breath, she squatted amongst some bushes, her face half hidden beneath the black jumper, her eyes free.

A tall man panted as he wandered past her with heavy, large steps. Like the others he was carrying a rucksack. Walczak? She wasn't sure, couldn't see him clearly enough.

No, she thought, not Walczak the lone wolf.

After giving the man a decent head start she slipped back onto the path. The tang of male sweat still hung in the air.

Shortly afterwards the path forked. One way seemed to lead up to the crest of the hill, the other downwards. Louise plumped for the former. A few minutes later she found herself at another fork and went up again, reaching the crest. The path ended in a meadow extending across the entire hilltop. In the darkness she couldn't see where it continued. She waited behind some trees for a while, but nothing happened. None of the seven people appeared anywhere and no-one else came up behind her.

She'd lost them.

Boni hurried back to the first fork and took the other path, which went down briefly before climbing sharply and crossing a wider path.

She squatted beside a tree trunk and closed her eyes. She could hear night birds, the gentle breeze in the trees, the odd creak of a bough, snapping of a twig. Diagonally above her was a strange sound it took a while to identify, *whup, whup, whup.* Wind turbines.

Nothing else.

Gerd arrived, Bermann arrived, Grandfather Mabruk. Ben, who'd seamlessly slotted into the phalanx of the dead.

Louise pushed them aside. Watch out, now, Boni. This isn't the moment for railing against life, or for self-pity.

Just the woods and the night. The birds, the rustling of the wind in the trees, the smell of damp earth, of nature.

And somewhere nearby, seven, eight or fifteen people, Witiko's white knights.

Assuming he was telling the truth.

Fifteen minutes later the time had come – her nose picked up another smell, sharp and spicy: burning wood.

Louise got up, followed the smell and a few minutes later saw the glow of fire in the darkness of the woods.

The cross, which wasn't particularly tall, about a metre and a half, was blazing fiercely. Held by ropes, it stood in the middle of a small clearing that was shielded from the north and west by vertical rock-faces and on the other side by the woods. Eleven people dressed in white cowls and hoods stood in a circle, each of them holding a burning torch, saying nothing, doing nothing, seemingly just looking at the flaming cross in the middle, the light of Jesus Christ, as Louise had read – the Klan was a radical Christian association. On some of the hoods she saw round red, sewn-on badges, on others red crosses. Some had red seams.

She crouched at the end of the path behind huge tree roots, barely ten metres from the nearest Klansman, following the proceedings. She ventured the occasional photo with her mobile.

When the flames began to run out of fuel, she heard the dulcet tones of a man from the circle. But what he was saying was still obscured by the crackling and sizzling of the fire. A murmuring began, they were all speaking at once, reciting something. Jumbled at first, then the individual voices fell into a chorus and became intelligible, obviously a passage from the Bible: ". . . in chains they shall come over, and they shall fall down unto thee, they shall make supplication unto thee, saying, Surely God is in thee; and there is none else, there is no God."

The man's voice spoke once more, a couple of sentences. The others responded with words she couldn't make out.

A pause.

Then the man again, several times, the chorus always responding, this time more loudly and clearly: "White Power!"

The man then struck up a song, the others joined in, a sort of hymn sung in bad English.

Two options, Louise thought.

First: wait until the horror show is over and investigate the owners of the vehicles tomorrow. That wouldn't yield much. The fact that the cars were here wasn't proof that their owners were. And even if this could be proven, what would they accuse them of? Infringement of the Baden-Württemberg forest code by starting a fire? And how could they proven that Julius Krüger or Erik Willig were members of the Ku Klux Klan? Even if this worked, what would the outcome be? The Klan wasn't outlawed in Germany.

First wasn't an option, she thought.

Second, then.

She texted the photos to Enders, then skimmed his messages.

Bit longer

A friend of hers is coming over

Ten mins

On my way

Where are you

Boni put her phone on the ground, covered it in a few leaves and stood up.

Second: show that she was here. That she wasn't going to give up, but fight, because there had to be someone who didn't give up.

Police badge in one hand and pistol in the other, she left the protection of the trees and made for the clearing.

219

The Klan members were still singing their hymn, the cross was still burning.

She slowly approached the circle. Nobody noticed her until she was less than three metres from the nearest person in a hood. A cry rang out, the first few stopped singing, followed by the others.

Bonì entered the round, stopping in the middle of the white figures. Now the only sound still to be heard was the fire. Holding up her badge, she turned around once and said out loud, "Louise Bonì, Freiburg Kripo. If you would be so kind as to remove your hoods."

Seconds passed, nobody reacted.

Then a man behind her began chanting aggressively, "White Power!" The others gradually joined in. A few fists were pumped into the night sky; others held their torches aloft.

"White Power!" over and over again, not even loud, but relentless.

Louise went over to the nearest Klansman, standing so close that she could see the reflection of the flames in his eyes. His expression was full of contempt, he held her gaze, somewhat scornfully as he knew she couldn't do much.

She began inspecting the white phalanx, one by one. Julius Krüger had to be here, maybe Erik Willig too. She would recognise Krüger's eyes and his posture; with Willig she wasn't so sure.

A woman, then two men, one too fat, the other too short.

Another woman. The tall man who'd been behind her in the woods; she could smell the stench of his sweat. Someone she didn't know, his eyes fairly neutral, she thought, pensive. She sensed his authority, a long-time member, someone with lots to say.

"Show yourself," she demanded.

There was movement in the corners of his eyes; he seemed to be smiling beneath the hood. Calmly he replied, "White Power."

Moving along she came to a man of medium height whose posture was reminiscent of Krüger. The eyes were right too, unable to hold her gaze. He managed a whispered "White Power", then broke off.

Louise nodded at the others. "Are these more acquaintances rather than friends too, Herr Krüger?"

He didn't respond.

Four Klan members to go: three men, one woman. All of them looking at her, waiting.

She continued her round. A man, definitely not Erik Willig, shock in his eyes and a hint of fear. They seemed vaguely familiar, but she could have been mistaken. "Hood off," she said.

The man flinched backwards and the torch moved; he'd raised his hand slightly. In the same moment she saw rapid movements out of the corner of her eye: something white was lunging at her from behind. She spun around, yanking her pistol upwards. A metre away was the man she'd first gone up to, torch above his head and about to strike. Now he froze.

Boni aimed the barrel of the gun just above him and fired. With a cry of horror he fell back and the torch dropped to the ground.

"Attempted assault on a police officer," she said, retreating to the line of the circle to have as many of the group as possible in her sight. A moment of anger, fear. "Hood off!" she roared at the man. "Hands up! You're under arrest. Come over to me. I said, *come over here!*"

Boni just had time to see he wasn't moving a muscle before something blisteringly hot hit the side of her head. She staggered to the side, stumbled and fell. Cursing, she caught herself with both hands. A boot stepped heavily on her hand with the pistol, fixing it. A kick to her back threw her forwards.

A man in white bent down and took her gun. Others dragged her arms back and put her in her own handcuffs.

The smell of burnt hair, heat stinging her scalp.

I'm on fire, she thought.

A gush of cold liquid hit the side of her head: water. The pain subsided.

Then she felt a hand on the seam of her coat and she was wrenched roughly upwards.

"White Power," a voice whispered in her ear.

The hand let go. Unchecked, she fell forwards, hitting her head. "Shit," she said, before passing out.

31

Dark dreams, and this time she was at their mercy. She was ablaze, surrounded by her dead, Bermann, Gerd, Germain and the others, all dressed in white, not talking, just watching her burn. She screamed in anger, disappointment and pain. Then she saw someone scamper through the woods, a woman in his arms, and hurry down a slope. In her slumber between dreams she remembered the woods around Oberried a few years ago. Bermann had carried her, saved her, or, better put: she'd let herself be carried and saved by him. Then suddenly Kilian, bent over her, shaking his head as if to say, It's all over, finished, farewell. In her dream she said, You too, Kilian? and began to cry.

Later, in the artificial light, white coats again, two women, one of whom she knew: the Indian doctor who'd given her first aid back in Oberried. Everything was getting mixed up now, she thought, but everything had been mixed up in the life, thoughts and feelings of Louise Bonì for a long time, and nobody would be able to disentangle it all.

When she woke at dawn, Kilian was standing beside her, the living Kilian rather than the dead one. He'd tied his hair into a ponytail and was deathly pale, hollow-cheeked, a shadow of his former self.

"You need to sleep," she said.

He pointed at the wall, where there must be another chair or bed. "I did, two hours."

"Have another lie-down, I'll keep an eye out."

"I need to go."

She nodded, which hurt her head a little. "I'm assuming this is a hospital?"

"Yes."

"Freiburg?"

"Yes."

"I got burnt, didn't I."

"Wasn't so bad."

She felt her head – lots of dressing, not so much pain. "How did I get here?"

"No idea."

"How did you know I was here?"

An exhausted smile instead of an answer. Which probably meant: We're better informed than the rest.

Unpleasant thoughts surfaced. Kilian was, somehow, one of *our people* too. He knew more, was turning up unexpectedly, pulling strings.

"How about you lot? What's the score?"

He shrugged. "Intervention postponed. A few days, a week max."

"What about our informant."

"Battling bravely." He stroked her shoulder and left the room before she could thank him for coming to visit. At that very moment Enders came in. It may also have been an hour or two later as the room was now as light as day.

"Tell me," she said wearily. "Last night over in Ettenheimmünster."

"You first." He pulled up a chair, rubbed his face, another ghost. It was clear he hadn't slept a wink all night.

Louise spoke as she looked at the photographs she'd sent him from her mobile. Most of them were useless, of course – either blurry because of the darkness or showing nothing but a bright, blazing fire. The technicians would sort it out and conjure up a few of the Klan members at least.

Then Enders talked. He'd driven around the area to the north of Ettenheimmünster for ages and only found her car by chance. After that he'd run through the woods for an hour, following the smell of burning wood, which had virtually dissipated by the end. Finally he'd heard her voice.

"Was I awake?"

"You were sitting on the ground, swearing."

Louise contorted her mouth into an angry smile. The memory gradually returned. The white hood . . . An image for eternity. Louise Bonì squatting on the ground, wearing a Ku Klux Klan hood.

Enders shook his head for several seconds. "I'm sorry it took me so long. I should've been there earlier." He sat there, shaking his head again, beating himself up.

"Oh well, at least you were able to save me up on the meadow. Are my eyes deceiving me, haven't you brought me flowers?"

He laughed, briefly cheerful again. "I've brought work."

"Much better than flowers."

Enders had run a check on the five registration numbers. He read out three names Louise had never heard before, including the owner of the Daimler from Lörrach that had picked up Julius Krüger the previous evening.

Then the fourth, Hans Gendrich, Freiburg.

"Gendrich? That's familiar."

"Lothar's neo-Nazi girlfriend. Kristina Gendrich."

"Yes. His daughter?"

Enders nodded.

"Bingo."

"It gets better. Or worse. The last car is registered to Michael Ahlert in Freiburg."

Thoughtlessly, Louise shook her head, then grimaced with pain. "Can't be."

"His car was there."

"Ali Ahlert?"

He nodded again, frowning. "Organised crime squad. D23."

"Ali Ahlert is a member of the Ku Klux Klan? Fucking hell!"

Michael Ahlert was a senior inspector from Breisach who must have been with Freiburg Kripo for eight or nine years now, on and off. A rather unassuming and reserved colleague, early fifties, who had not stepped out of line as far as she knew. Divorced, two children. Bermann used to go for the occasional beer with him after work.

"Let's bring him in," she said.

"Already have. He's in my office, handcuffed, and has a bit of time to think things over. To decide if he's going to keep denying it."

"The denial makes them strong. It's how they get around us."

"Yes," Enders said, turning around as Louise was trying to get up. "There's a big hearing at nine o'clock. Graeve, Vormweg, the public prosecutor, you, me and Ahlert."

His phone rang. Natalie. He held it out to her. "She can't get hold of you."

Louise flopped back down on the bed. From the tiny speaker came music, Falco, unmistakable: "*Amadeus, Amadeus, oh oh oh, Amadeus, Come and rock me, Amadeus.*"

"I'm not in the mood for jokes," she said.

"It's not a joke," Natalie said.

The chorus of "Rock me Amadeus" was the ringtone of Ricky Janisch's prepaid mobile.

32

"Is that possible? Janisch was Amadeus?"

"No idea, I can't make head nor tail of it anymore," Enders growled. Half past nine, they were in his car and it was agonising stop-start traffic on Bismarckallee to police HQ: there had been an accident up ahead. The sun was shining too harshly; although the blow to her head hadn't been that bad, the pain centre was sensitive to light. Louise screwed up her eyes even though she knew this would add a few more wrinkles to her face. All of a sudden she was desperate for two days, five days, five weeks doing nothing but focusing on herself, her body, having a close look at her body again, making plans for her appearance, getting out of it what she could. Exercise, meditation, manicure, pedicure, hairstyle, counting wrinkles. After all, she thought, these were the only certainties in life: getting more wrinkles, hair turning white, flab accumulating on the hips. Everything else was unfathomable and uncontrollable.

Janisch had been Amadeus, but maybe he hadn't. Connections became apparent, but probably they had to live with the fact that they could never be absolutely certain. Too many interests at stake.

Our people.

Louise felt her head. It was hurting a little, but more inside than out. The outside would quickly get better, whereas the inside might never again.

She'd called Kabangu and postponed their conversation again. No problem, he said; he had to stay over the weekend at least. Dr Arndt hadn't yet been persuaded, *there's still no gentleman's agreement.*

And she'd texted Kilian: *We might have a leak.*

Name?

Someone from D23 was there last night.

"Emergency light, please," she said.

Enders put the light on the roof, pulled out of the traffic and drove half on the tarmacked central reservation. He smelled different today, unkempt, of testosterone. Something was happening inside him, his movements more aggressive, his tone harsher, as if he were increasingly losing his composure.

"Were things bad at home last night?" she asked.

"Let's talk about Janisch and Amadeus."

Leaning back, she closed her eyes. "In the nineties Amadeus was in a neo-Nazi flatshare in Dortmund. In 1999 he was recruited by the Verfassungsschutz. In April 2004 he was allegedly in Dortmund with Witiko, and that same year he entered the witness protection programme, then disappeared. Janisch was in Freiburg from 2004, at the time he was already active in the Southwest Brigade, then the serious assault in August. Do you remember what the guy said who'd wanted out?"

"Yes."

Bonì half opened her eyes. "They look similar, at least from the back. You can't see Amadeus's face on Bremer's photo."

Now at the end of the traffic jam, Enders carefully swerved around the site of the accident. "Could be right."

"It could," she said, then thought: another visit to Witiko, torch on, force him to look at a photo of Janisch. Make him remember what really happened. Get him to tell the truth.

A pretty hopeless undertaking.

As they were hurrying from the car to the entrance, Natalie called. There was in fact an anomaly in Ricky Janisch's biography. The official information was correct: schools, training etc., even the parents existed, on paper at least, and cars had been registered and deregistered. But a family of four had been registered at a flat at the same time as Janisch and his parents. Natalie had just been speaking to the daughter. They'd all lived there and she hadn't heard of a Janisch.

"Intelligence services make mistakes too," Natalie said, chuckling contentedly.

One glance at Michael Ahlert was enough to tell Louise that he'd be ready to make a deal sooner rather than later. You talk, get sent off somewhere in the provinces and we'll cover up. His eyes were darting back and forth, his breathing rapid.

But for now he was still holding out.

Hubert Vormweg had begun; his disbelief and naivety were almost touching. Worlds were colliding. On one side Cords, the old '68er who still harboured a few ideals; on the other Ahlert, who had surely never been interested in such ideals. Who was thinking only of himself, pigheadedly, of how he could lie or negotiate his way out of this delicate situation.

"Ali, you represent the state, this city, you—" Cords said.

"Boni made a mistake," Ahlert interrupted quietly. "My car was never up there."

Cords smiled, a sad smile as if his officers were like his own children or siblings. "How often have you had to listen to such excuses in interrogations?"

"My car was in the garage."

"The model, colour and registration number all tally."

"It's not possible, Herr Vormweg."

Ahlert was sitting on his own on the wide sofa. Facing him on one side were Cords and Enders in armchairs, on the other Graeve and Louise. Marianne Andrele, the public prosecutor, had not appeared.

Louise hadn't seen Ahlert in a long while. She recalled him being bloated and pale; now he seemed to be at his ideal weight and looked as if he worked out. On some Klan website she'd read that self-defence courses were offered for "German Christians of German descent". Fitness was important; you had to be prepared for the defence of the West.

"What about the remnants of burnt fabric in your garden, Ali?"

"A curtain, I had . . . maggots in a curtain."

Cords touched his steely-grey beard. This morning he was looking older than ever. "What do you get out of these people? Comradeship? Recognition? It's the *Ku Klux Klan* for goodness' sake! A secret racist society! You, a police officer!"

Ahlert didn't reply immediately, then just said, almost in surprise, "I'm not a racist."

"Where's Andrele?" Louise whispered to Graeve.

He shrugged.

"If you've got questions, Frau Bonì . . ." Cords pointed wearily at Ahlert.

"What role does Hans Gendrich play in the clan?"

Ahlert looked at her for the first time that morning. Examining his eyes, brows, nostrils, she fancied she remembered. The last man she'd been looking at before she was knocked to the ground.

The same fear in the eyes.

She smiled.

"How should I know?"

"Was he there yesterday?"

His head shot forwards. "Time to do the dirty on another colleague, eh?"

Now Reinhard Graeve spoke in a low voice. "What else are the technicians going to find in your house, Herr Ahlert? Torches? That silly . . . Kloran? And what about your laptop? Mobile phone? You know what's going to happen. It's amazing what they can recover these days."

Ahlert lowered his gaze and stared in silence at his crossed hands, his fingers twitching back and forth.

They had him.

Louise reached for her water glass and drank. Her phone vibrated: a text from Marianne Andrele, the public prosecutor. *Behr's taking over. He'll be with you in 5.*

Five minutes, she thought. Five minutes, then they were out of the game. Stuttgart would do a deal; Ahlert would be untouchable, beyond jurisdiction.

"You had access to the case file," she said. "Did you pass on information?"

Cords groaned in horror, making no effort to suppress it.

Ahlert continued to stare at his hands, unable to look anyone in the eye. He'd hardened his body, hidden away his soul.

"Last chance, Herr Ahlert," Graeve said. "Talk, or we'll drop you and go down the normal route, including press release, custody and so on. Accessory to an assault on a police officer, breach of secrecy – in the end you'll confess to get a few years off your sentence. If you talk now we can do more for you."

Ahlert slapped his hands in front of his face, then abruptly looked up. "Like what?"

"We can request a more lenient sentence."

"That's not enough. No charge, no imprisonment."

Graeve shook his head. "You'll be brought to trial."

"It's true then . . ." Cords mumbled into his beard.

Ahlert hesitated briefly, then said, "Make sure the sentence is less than a year."

Louise snorted. Less than a year meant he wouldn't be dismissed from public service. He would work again, albeit in the remotest corner of Baden-Württemberg, and keep his pension rights. He'd get off lightly.

But they had no other choice.

"We'll try," Graeve said.

"Alright," Ahlert muttered.

"Who's Gendrich?" Louise asked.

"He founded the chapter. In 2002 or 2003."

"When did you become a member?" Graeve asked.

"2005."

Louise touched his arm impatiently; there were more important things they needed to know. "Did Gendrich order Kabangu's murder?"

"No idea. Only heard about it incidentally."

"Do you know Erik Willig?"

"Not personally."

"Isn't he a Klan member?"

"Not in our chapter."

"Are there neo-Nazis amongst you?"

"Gendrich has got contacts to the far right, and some occasionally take part in ceremonies."

"Like burning a cross?"

"Cross lighting, yes."

"Did you pass on information from the case file?"

A knock, then the door opened and Heinrich Behr came in with two other men in tow. He introduced them, colleagues from the Criminal Investigation Bureau. With regret in his voice he said, "We need Herr Ahlert in Stuttgart."

"Ali, did you pass on information?"

Ahlert looked at Vormweg. "What do they want?"

Behr strolled over to them slowly, as if he had all the time in the world. A smile on his lips, he handed Vormweg a piece of paper. "This interview is over. Herr Ahlert is being transferred to the CIB."

"What about our deal?" Ahlert asked Graeve.

"Invalid," Behr said.

Enders, who'd been silent until now, listening attentively, leaped to his feet and growled, "This makes me sick!" With both hands he grabbed Ahlert's coat, lifted him up and pushed him as far as the wall, shoving him hard against it. Louise, who had got up like Cords, heard him whisper, heard Ahlert groan with pain and mumble a few unintelligible words.

Again Enders spoke and again Ahlert replied.

Now the two men who'd come in with Behr hauled Enders back and led Ahlert, who looked beseechingly at Cords, out of the room.

"Let's all calm down," Graeve said tensely. He'd stayed in his seat.

Heinrich Behr hadn't moved either. "I wholeheartedly agree. And Freiburg Kripo should be concentrating on other cases from now on. Order from the Ministry of the Interior, and I'm talking about Berlin here rather than Stuttgart."

Ignoring him, Enders was already heading to the door. "Come on," he said to Louise.

33

Hans Gendrich lived and worked in Rieselfeld, to the far west of the city. He owned a cleaning firm and his office was a couple of streets away from his apartment. He had a son, a daughter – Kristina, Lothar Krüger's girlfriend – and had been a widower since 2002. No prior convictions, on the contrary, his social engagement made him a pillar of the local community – treasurer of a free church, member of the parent–teacher association at the school his children attended, rifle club, and he also sang in the Rieselfeld choir.

"Tenor," Natalie said.

"Is he politically active?" Louise was sitting beside Enders in his car, phone to her ear, listening as Natalie typed away.

"He's involved in a few action groups . . . Against Fessenwald nuclear power station, in favour of Mooswald—"

"Take that exit," Louise whispered.

Enders indicated and they came off the B31a.

"A moral crusader," Natalie giggled.

They hung up.

Louise looked at Enders. "I'd never have imagined you could lose it like that."

He shrugged.

"I'm getting to the stage where I've had enough."

She had an inkling of what he meant. Like this, the job was no fun, there was no point to it. Being squeezed out by *our people*, who weren't interested in solving the case, just controlling the information. Who knew what was really happening, what had happened in Karlsruhe in 2004, in Freiburg in 2006? Who was involved, what was the role of politicians, a second ban on the NPD? What were the Verfassungs-schutz and its masters prepared to do to prevent their dodgy deals with neo-Nazis coming to light? Who knew the extent to which the state was involved in wrongdoing? How stable or dangerous were German neo-Nazi structures, how contaminated were the army and prisons, and how criminal was the host of paid informers?

A text message interrupted her gloomy thoughts. Kilian.

Who?

She'd warned him before they set off, confirmed the leak. Even though Irina wasn't mentioned in the case file, she was in danger. Anyone who read the documents carefully would find clues pointing to a source amongst the Russians in Baden-Baden.

Later, she wrote.

Give me a name.

I can't right now.

The idea of Kilian paying secret visits to Ali Ahlert too . . .

"It's not that nothing came of it."

"Losing control usually brings results."

In Enders' grip, Ahlert had talked.

The morning before he'd had a call from an unknown Andreas. As requested, he'd accessed the case information in the computer system, put the printout in a brown envelope, driven to Ehrenkirchen to the south of Freiburg and gone shopping in a particular supermarket there. He'd placed the envelope in a shopping basket beneath an advertising brochure. Ahlert didn't know who'd picked it up.

The same Andreas who'd also phoned Paulus Riedl? Andreas from Baden Heimatschutz?

They might never find out.

Soon afterwards they arrived in Rieselfeld, one of Freiburg's newer areas, clean, tidy, peaceful. They drove down pretty streets, past modern housing developments no more than five storeys high, airy, painted in a variety of hues and lots of green space around them. This was where the city's sewage used to trickle out, beside which Sinti families had lived in hovels they'd built themselves. Some had been driven out of Freiburg by the Nazis and had returned after the war; the others were those who'd survived the camps. Years later the city put them up in nearby barracks, then in social housing. The land was needed; Freiburg was expanding.

Hans Gendrich's firm was in the centre of the Rieselfeld, its glass office front next to a car park entrance with company vehicles in light blue. Through the windows Louise saw men and women wearing tops in the same shade of blue. Light blue like the morning sky, light blue like forget-me-nots, light blue like holiday.

Like the chest of Willi, the budgie.

They got out and entered the building. A receptionist in light blue announced their arrival and a colleague in light blue took them up to the first floor.

"Let me do this," Enders said.

"So long as you pull yourself together."

"Are you being serious?"

She carefully rubbed the thick dressing on the side of her head, which had begun to itch. "I don't know yet."

Hans Gendrich was wearing a light-blue top too. He was of medium height, stocky and muscular. The seams of his T-shirt sleeves were close to bursting when he offered them his hand. His cheeks were similarly rounded, the entire man inflated to the hilt. What remained of his hair, cropped short, made his face appear almost monk-like.

"Sit down, I'm all ears," he said. Louise held her breath then exhaled slowly, suddenly exhausted, relieved almost, not a spark of anger inside her, just an odd feeling of pleasant fatigue: the same dulcet tones that had addressed the other Klan members the night before. She didn't recognise the eyes; he might have been one of the men at the end of the circle she hadn't come face to face with.

She shot Enders a glance and nodded.

"The Ku Klux Klan," he said. "Tell us more."

Gendrich, who'd just sat at his desk, now got up. "Just a moment, please." He went into the next-door room and returned with a man who was in less casual attire, wearing a tie with his light-blue shirt. "Erich Karmer," Gendrich said. "Colleague, family friend and in-house lawyer."

Karmer shook their hands without saying anything, then retreated to the window seat, his arms crossed. He was around fifty, lean, with sunken cheeks, joyless lips and round glasses with silver rims. Louise, who knew a host of lawyers in the Freiburg area, had never heard his name.

Gendrich sat back down behind his desk, waiting impassively, having passed the initiative to Karmer.

"When did you found the Baden Klan chapter?" Enders asked.

"Are you interrogating Herr Gendrich as a witness or as a suspect?" Karmer's mouth remained a line, unwilling to open properly as he spoke.

"Suspected of what?" Enders retorted.

"As a witness, then?"

"As a suspect."

"What's the charge?"

"Incitement to murder and a few minor things besides: setting up and supporting a criminal organisation, failure to render assistance." He rattled off the caution.

Karmer rubbed his eyes beneath the glasses.

"Ask your questions."

"When did you found the Baden Klan chapter?"

"No comment," Karmer said.

"Sorry," Gendrich said.

"Did you set it up on your own or with others?"

"No comment," Karmer said.

"Sorry," Gendrich said.

"Last night, with ten members of your Klan chapter, you took part in a cross burning to the north of Ettenheimmünster. You—"

"No comment," Karmer interrupted.

"Sorry."

"Your car was there and a witness has confirmed your presence. What—"

"Me," Louise said. "I'm the witness."

Karmer's gaze was fixed on her, sharp, clever eyes. "You claim to have seen Hans Gendrich last night wherever it was?"

"Heard."

He waved a hand dismissively. Hearing wasn't seeing. Hearing meant: no danger.

"How long has Michael Ahlert been a Klansman?" Enders asked.

"No comment."

"Sorry."

"Do you know Erik Willig?"

Karmer said nothing.

"No," Gendrich said.

The first lie, Louise thought.

Enders put four photographs of the two attackers in front of Gendrich - the night-time images from Paulus Riedl's surveillance camera as well as police photos of the body. Gendrich didn't even pretend to glance at them. His elbows were on the table, his hands crossed and his eyes were fixed on Enders.

"No comment," Karmer said.

"Sorry."

Enders rubbed his face with both hands, looking increasingly impatient, disillusioned. "Are you married?"

"Widowed." Gendrich still wore his wedding ring, faithful beyond death. Louise didn't think he looked like a husband capable of love; he was too uncompromising, self-centred. A man who determined the directions everyone else had to go in, his own family included.

"What happened?"

Gendrich glanced at Karmer, who shrugged, pursed lips, serious expression, focused. Then he said, "She had a car accident."

"Through no fault of her own?"

Gendrich gave the slightest shake of the head, his eyes remained distanced. "She was drunk: 0.12%. My wife was an alcoholic, Herr Enders."

"Welcome to the club," Enders said, grinning, and Louise wondered whether he was thinking the same as her: that Gendrich already knew all about his wife. Knew his opponent better than his opponent did him.

"Look after her, then. Do what I didn't do."

"Which is?"

"Take responsibility."

"Responsibility," Enders said, nodding thoughtfully. "Do you know Julius Krüger?"

"Yes."

"Is he a Klan member?"

"No comment," Karmer said.

"Sorry."

"Ricky Janisch?"

Karmer seemed to have lost interest in speaking; he just shook his head.

"Sorry."

"Ludwig Kabangu?"

"Another man who's lost his wife," Louise added.

Karmer said nothing, seemingly surprised. "Kabangu," Gendrich said, "sounds African. I love Africa. Safari in Kenya, the beaches there. Namibia. I was there last year with the children. A black mamba crawled into our tent but we were lucky. My son wants to go back, but my daughter still dreams of the mamba. It was in her sleeping bag. Ah, well. Life can be over from one second to the next, you have to be so careful. Keep your little home clean. Coffee?"

"No," Enders said.

"With sugar," Louise said.

Gendrich sprang energetically out of his chair, left the room and returned carrying three espressos.

"*Were* you being careful?"

"Take a stick, use it to bash your sleeping bag, I drummed into them beforehand. I often go, I've got friends down there. Bush hunters."

"Black friends?"

"Ethnic Germans."

They drank in silence. Karmer emptied his cup in a single gulp, not hiding his growing impatience. Wasted minutes, pointless conversation, his body language and facial expressions signalled.

"Time for a story," Louise said. "How it might have happened."

Gendrich turned to her. "I'm all ears," he said, now sitting upright, arms on the armrests, showing off his relaxed muscles.

"In March you find out that Ludwig Kabangu is coming to Freiburg at the end of April, probably from Erik Willig or one of his elitist right-wing acquaintances. A black man from one of our former colonies is making demands, you think. The world is getting worse and worse. You want to set an example, give a warning, for once get out of the woods where all you do is stand around a burning cross, shouting, 'White Power!'

"So you activate the network. A contact can help, maybe Andreas from Baden Heimatschutz. Andreas rings around. Comrades in Jena, Freiburg and wherever else become active. Other Heimatschutzers, 'Blood & Honour' people, members of the Southwest Brigade. Most of them you won't know. For example, the two men who end up with your assignment to kill Ludwig Kabangu, who aren't perhaps quite as professional as you'd expected. They don't have weapons, or at least not the kind they need for this sort of mission, a Makarov and a Tokarev.

"The network relays the information back to you. What now?

"You call a friend, Mike – American Ku Klux Klan, frequently in Europe, residences in Moscow and Vienna – and outline the problem: you need to get hold of a Makarov and a Tokarev, from somewhere, somehow. No problem, Mike says, giving you the name of a contact and vouching for you. Let's call him Niko.

"You order the weapons.

"Meanwhile, a certain Matthias Seibert hires a camper van in Jena. The two contract killers and their female companions need their trip to the Breisgau to be comfortable. More telephone calls follow: on Monday evening, comrades from Jena arrive, a Sky Wave, don't put it in the register – Paulus Riedl, camping in paradise. And: we need a car for the night, Eschholzstrasse, Saturday evening, nine thirty – Julius Krüger, the flower man, member of your Klan, I recognised him last night. And: a white Golf, parked in Eschholzstrasse, key in the ignition, you drive it to Baden-Baden, pick up a box at 'Iwan and Pauline' restaurant – Ricky Janisch, ex-informer for the Verfassungsschutz in the witness protection programme, codename 'Amadeus', is no longer alive, diabetic shock, apparently. You might have known him, he was one of the more important guys.

"Janisch picks up the box and gives it to a man I doubt you know, Thomas Walczak, lives with nineteen dogs in the forest near Bollschweil. At night Walczak goes off, meets the two men from the Sky Wave, hands over the box, probably without knowing what's inside: the Makarov and Tokarev. The weapons are now in the possession of Stuttgart CIB. Both men were shot dead yesterday morning. But we're getting ahead of ourselves.

"Janisch meets Walczak again and receives an envelope full of money, which may have come via a supermarket in Ehrenkirchen –

we don't know yet. Our colleague, Michael Ahlert, sadly a member of your Klan too, was at this supermarket yesterday morning. He also got a call from Andreas. The same Andreas? Doesn't matter. Ahlert drives to Ehrenkirchen, a few hours later you've got hold of the investigation file and know what we know.

"Have I forgotten anything?

"Oh yes, one more little job for the so-called Maria Schmidt. Meet a black man in Basel. When you're both in Freiburg go for a coffee, a walk, to the museum, can you manage that? On Thursday morning at half past eight, meet him at a café behind Münsterplatz. When the bells stop ringing, go through the exit to the museum, keep going, keep going and don't stop."

Louise took a sip of her coffee. She sensed the eyes of the three men on her, and sensed too that Gendrich wasn't in the least impressed, let alone unnerved. She cleared her throat. "On Thursday morning, Maria Schmidt is sitting with Ludwig Kabangu and me outside the café, a few tables away is a colleague of mine, Gerd Rehberg. Rehberg dies shortly after nine but his killers, the men from Jena, die too. Because there's another player you weren't expecting Herr Gendrich, whereas at that stage I was. Experts in such situations. But I'd been expecting them twenty or thirty seconds earlier, a massive mistake. Why did they arrive on the scene too late? I don't know. Twenty seconds earlier and Gerd Rehberg would still be alive, just like Ludwig Kabangu is still alive. You wanted to set an example and sent four people to their graves, but the one person you meant to have killed, because he sullies your delusional view of the world – you didn't get him.

"What's more, you've left lots of little traces behind. Telephone calls, the odd comment. Your car was in Ettenheimmünster, *you* were there, and maybe you were elsewhere too. In the supermarket in Ehrenkirchen, for example, where there's CCTV. Your daughter is friends with Lothar Krüger, a connection that one day might leave you vulnerable. Young people can't be controlled, even if they've got a far-right mindset.

"Someday someone's going to blab, Herr Gendrich, maybe one of the children, maybe Julius Krüger, who's weak and can't look me in the eye. Or the Riedls, managing their sad paradise, a disastrous marriage – she cheats on him, he's in despair. It won't be impossible to pry one of them out of the network, I've already made a start. Or Maria Schmidt, who's in police custody and is looking at a charge, which wasn't the deal, was it? She lied to me, a police officer, about her identity. All the others – Torsten Schulz from Heilbronn, Matthias Seibert from Jena, the man in Aachen who supposedly stole the Sky Wave – will they withstand closer investigation or intensive questioning? Will they stick it out? No, I'd bet my life on it. We will get them. *I* will get them. Not today, not tomorrow, but perhaps the day after."

For a few seconds, silence prevailed, tension was in the air. For those few seconds possibilities materialised, there was hope, stupid, irrational hope at the end of some arduous days and nights . . .

Then Karmer yawned and said as his mouth closed again, "A police officer at her wits' end. Are we finished here? I've got stuff to be getting on with."

Gendrich stood up with a meek smile, pointed to her cup and said, "You haven't finished your coffee. Columbian beans, I have them imported specially. It would be a shame not to. Don't you like it?"

They were standing outside by the car, exchanging glances without words. Police officers at their wits' end indeed. Louise had never felt so helpless.

The ring of her mobile broke through the torpor.

"Some more info on Ahlert," Natalie said.

Ali Ahlert was with Karlsruhe Kripo for two years from 2002, in the section for national security, responsible, amongst other things, for politically motivated crime such as right-wing terrorism. At the end of 2004 he returned to Freiburg.

"And?" Louise said. Her gaze fell on the glass building. At the floor-to-ceiling window of his office stood Hans Gendrich, hands in trouser pockets, watching her. She heard Enders' phone ring, heard his voice. He got into the car and closed the door.

"Ahlert was in the police sporting association, the shooting club, pistols and revolvers," Natalie said, sounding tenacious, patient.

"I don't understand what you're trying to tell me." Louise looked back up at Hans Gendrich, who was standing in the same position behind the immaculately polished window. He was perfectly still, not making any move to turn away, as if he wanted to be sure that they really were leaving his territory. A warlord on the hill, seemingly invincible, studying the movements of his impotent enemy. Planning the next gambit, the next list.

But he'd lost too, hadn't he? The attack on Kabangu had failed.

The question was: was Gendrich the sort of man who simply accepted defeat?

No, she thought.

A shiver ran down her spine.

"Timo Kahle," Natalie said. "He was a member of the shooting club in Karlsruhe too. There are photos of him and Ahlert with other people. At a party, some sort of competition. They knew each other."

"Timo Kahle and Ali Ahlert?"

"Yes."

"Shit. Any more on this?"

"No, haven't had the time. I'm meant to be . . . doesn't matter."

"Is Ali still there?"

"No, he's been on leave since this afternoon. Four weeks, it's already been signed off. Herr Graeve says we won't see him again. He's Stuttgart's man now."

Louise opened the passenger door and got in. Her fear for Kabangu was back, but there was another feeling too . . .

That it was hopeless. In the end they didn't stand a chance.

Now off the phone, Enders started the car.

"Ahlert and Kahle knew each other," she told him. "And Gendrich's—"

"One more thing," Natalie interrupted her.

Enders looked at Louise, his eyes, his voice drained. "What about Gendrich?"

"He's going to try again," Louise said.

"What do you mean?"

"Kabangu."

Enders, who was pulling away, turned to her. "He's going to try again to have Kabangu killed?"

She nodded. The shivers got colder and her eyes filled with tears. Kabangu, who wasn't ready to leave. Who couldn't be protected around the clock without surveillance officers, without a team. Without his willingness.

No chance, she thought. You don't stand a chance.

"Louise?" Natalie said in her ear, insistent now.

"What?"

"Herr Enders is being transferred to Lörrach."

"Hmm," Enders said.

"They're transferring a section head?"

"Hmm," he said again.

"Because of what happened with Ahlert?"

He nodded. A section head losing it and assaulting a suspect in the chief of police's office was unacceptable, if that was how they wanted to play it. No lenience, no caution, only immediate transfer. Graeve didn't want it, nor did Cords, she thought. Stuttgart did.

They'd reached the B31a. Clouds gathered over the hills of the Black Forest, turning the woods and peaks black. Freiburg was still in sunlight, as so often. Enders drove slowly as if trying to stall the run of things. Meetings with Cords at HQ, perhaps with a lawyer. Going home, alone with his thoughts, his anger. And later, the conversation with his wife.

"They're just bluffing," she said. "It's all part of it. They threaten you with Lörrach, you promise to improve, and after a week you'll be back at your desk."

"Is that what I want? I don't know."

"It's what *I* want." She saw him smirk. "Hold on a sec," she said, taking out her mobile.

Kabangu was still refusing to leave. He wanted to stay until Arndt had given him the remains of Grandfather Mabruk. He was in his room, sounding sombre, at a loss, as if he'd been thrown off course, back to an unpleasant past. "Let them," he said despondently. "Maybe that's why I'm here. To be taken from this life."

"Rubbish," Louise said.

She heard him laugh. "Are you coming back here to keep an eye on the both of us?"

"I'll be there in fifteen minutes." She put her mobile in her lap and looked at Enders. "I wonder why they're taking you out of action rather than me."

"Taking you out of action has never worked in the past."

They grinned wearily.

"They're cutting you off. Natalie, the investigation team, me, surveillance, all gone. You'd end up on your own."

"Would I?"

Enders nodded. His left hand on the wheel, fingers of the other scratching stubble on his chin ever since they'd left Gendrich's car park. "Time to throw in the towel, Louise."

"Oh, come on."

"Gendrich, Walczak, the Riedls, Willig, you'll never get them, not a single one of them."

"I'll get the Krügers, then. Julius," she said. "Besides, I think Riedl would talk."

"Not Julius and not Riedl. Not now when you've got no support and have to go it alone. All they've got to do is to keep quiet, deny everything and nothing will happen. They know that."

"Meaning?"

He shrugged. "Have patience."

She knew what he meant. Gather evidence, look for holes, ask colleagues from national security to keep her posted while she busied herself with other cases. Work on Graeve and Cords when the time came. If she tried to do it her way she'd be taken out of action like Enders.

"What about Kabangu?"

"He's got to look after himself."

Enders now put his right hand on the wheel too, looking more relaxed, as if accepting his fate. He drove as quickly as usual.

The bridge over the Dreisam, to the north-west the spire of the minster's tower in golden light, a friendly late afternoon in April. Gendrich would be going home soon, she thought, to cook for the children maybe. Make a few more calls.

One call was enough.

The network would be reactivated.

Maybe the next killers were already standing by. This was the problem when *our people* covered things up, when the state lied: the others didn't feel threatened. They spoke a bit more quietly, made fewer calls, kept a low profile for a while.

And ploughed ahead.

They were outside Kabangu's hotel, unable to think of what to say. Another farewell, Louise thought, maybe not for good; they'd see each other again. And yet, in another way perhaps it was final, if Enders didn't come back. Didn't want to, wasn't allowed to.

"Alright, then," she said.

"Keep in touch."

"You too."

"And keep your head down."

"Yeah, yeah."

Louise watched him drive away. She knew he was right: she'd been sidelined. Outmanoeuvred by her own people to avoid damaging the wider picture.

Our people, she thought.

Time to find some new people, she thought.

Time to throw in the towel.

But there were two tasks left.

Talk to Kabangu.

Talk to Walczak.

34

"I came here to bring a dead man home and I'm leaving another dead one behind," Ludwig Kabangu said. "Please explain that to me, Madame Boni. Explain to me the point in that. Do I only get my dead body in exchange for another? Is that the price? But why do *you* have to pay it instead of me? I mean, I didn't listen to you. I didn't take your warnings seriously. No, it was worse than that. I didn't care if you were right or not because I didn't care if I lived or died. And now your colleague has died in my place. Is this the explanation perhaps? My life for his death? Please, I need an *explanation*."

This time Louise sat on the edge of the bed, Kabangu in the armchair. He'd drawn the curtains, shut out the soft afternoon light as if the answers to his questions were easier to find in darkness. She had difficulty making out his features, reading his expression. Again his room was hot and sticky; the stale cigarette smoke irritated her stomach.

"I have no explanation, Monsieur Kabangu," she said.

"Or is this about my death rather than my life? Is the actual purpose of my visit to your city to lose my life here?"

"Why should it have a purpose?"

Bending forwards, he whispered, "Because I also killed in the past. Because I killed so many people that I can't remember a single one of them. Do you know what I did?"

"I can only imagine."

He continued in a whisper, his hands on his knees. "One day we, the Rwandan Hutu, were told that the Tutsi were going to kill us. In the papers we kept reading that the Tutsi were going to kill us, and we heard it on the radio too, day after day. So we had to strike first. We read and heard about the terrible crimes committed by the Tutsi against the Hutu. We read and heard that the Tutsi didn't want democracy but sole power so they could suppress and kill us. We formed militias, we got weapons. The lucky ones got pistols, the less lucky ones machetes, which there were more of. Pistols are expensive, machetes cheaper – it's quite simple.

"But I'm getting ahead of myself. We didn't begin with the killing. Perhaps we'd never have begun at all if our president, a Hutu, hadn't been murdered. In 1994 his plane was shot down in Kigali shortly before landing. Who by? I don't know. There are people who claim it was extremist Hutu. If that's true I have to accept it. Other people say it was the Tutsi around Paul Kagame who governs our country today. If that's the truth I also have to accept it. I respect this man. Under him we have peace.

"Back then the peace broke down, the war began, the slaughter began. I don't want to tell you about it, and I can't because I don't remember. I killed too many Tutsi and Hutu collaborators to be able to count them. In my mind I can't picture a single face of one of the dying. I don't recall a single one of these murders. I know I killed repeatedly, but in my memory it happened silently, in the darkness, as if I hadn't noticed. As if I'd dreamed it and forgotten the dream. I read and heard that we had to kill all the Tutsi to survive and so I killed. I killed strangers, neighbours, friends, indiscriminately and ever faster. I was out of my mind, I was in a frenzy, I was obsessed by the words and voices I read and heard. But I don't remember anyone I killed, any tears, screams, no moment when I was killing.

"One thing I do remember was that I . . . my wife . . . she was also a Tutsi. I was so obsessed by the words and voices that I hit her. I raped her, I locked her up, but that wasn't enough. I was so obsessed that I wondered whether I had to kill her too.

"That evening I got drunk to summon the courage to do it. But in this other frenzy, my love for her prevailed over the hatred. I went to her and said: Go, or I'll have to kill you. She wouldn't go so I hit her again and again and again, and then I chased her out into the night, running behind to frighten her and drive her away for ever."

Kabangu filled a glass of water and handed it to Louise. "Here, have this." He drank too. She thought she could see tears on his cheeks; with a rapid movement he seemed to wipe them away. "I never saw her again, Madame Boni. A few years later, when there was peace in Rwanda, I learned she'd died in 1998 in poverty and all alone." He raised his arms and brought them down again. "That's the story without the pretty wrapping."

"What about Grandfather Mabruk?"

He didn't answer immediately. His eyes flitted about, his hands rubbed his knees. Eventually he said, "Mabruk was my wife's favourite grandfather."

"Is the story about his bones true?"

"Of course!"

"That Mabruk's bones were removed from his grave by Germans and came to Freiburg via Feldmann?"

She saw him nod. "Every word of it is true. Although perhaps not in your understanding of the truth, I mean word for word."

"Mabruk was a Tutsi, wasn't he?"

"You do what you can. It's not much. It's . . . so little. A tiny bit of penance." Leaning forwards he lowered his voice once more to a whisper. "But perhaps my penance won't be taking Grandfather Mabruk back home like I always thought. It's too little! It's no penance at all. It's . . . just a gesture. Perhaps my real penance will be dying here. Being murdered just as I murdered others. Don't you think?"

"I don't believe in such connections."

"Metaphysical connections?"

"Whatever you call such things."

"I understand what you're saying, but I think differently." He leaned forwards yet again and said, "There's a greater connection."

Before the Germans arrived in Rwanda, he told her, "Hutu" and "Tutsi" were used to describe social rather than ethnic groups. The Tutsi were the better off, they owned cattle, practised livestock farming and were the masters. The Hutu were the peasants, grew crops, had a few cattle at most and were the servants. Then there were the Twa, the oldest inhabitants of Rwanda, who lived as hunter-gatherers. When the Germans bought up the land and took possession of it, they needed indigenous governors in the colony. Their choice fell on the ruling Tutsi who they regarded as superior Hamites, migrants from the north and ultimately related to European peoples. They saw the Hutu as a subordinate Negroid people who were servants because as a race they were inferior to the Tutsi. And thus social terms became ethnic ones, the "superior" Tutsi on the one hand, the "inferior" Hutu on the other.

Belgium, which was awarded Rwanda after the First World War, developed this system further. All Rwandans got passports in which it said whether they were Tutsi, Hutu or Twa. Now the ethnic, racial differentiation was officially sanctioned. The Tutsi were again privileged, including in the Catholic schools even though the Hutu formed the majority of the population. Towards the end of the era of colonial rule, Hutu and Tutsi parties came into being. Violent clashes took place and hundreds of people died. What did the Belgians do? They began to support the Hutu. The Tutsi feared they would lose their influence and so the situation continued to escalate.

"You know where the creation of Rwandan ethnic groups led in the end," Kabangu said. "And now I'm sitting here in Germany, one of the killers from 1994, who maybe only became a killer because the Germans and Belgians, through their racist colonial policy, divided us into different ethnic groups."

"That's the connection?"

"Yes. The wheel turns full circle."

"No," Louise said. "It's coincidence. Just stupid coincidence."

"Not from a historical perspective. I'm here because the Germans were in Rwanda."

Her mobile rang: Marek, deep voice as monotone as Gerd's, as distant. Surveillance officers were a breed apart, motionless, patient beings whose strength was in watching, not in acting, not in talking. "I'm here, Boni."

"I'll come down."

She stood up, went to the door and gave Kabangu instructions: no going on walks without protection until he heard from her. Let nobody in. Careful by the windows.

Pack your suitcase.

Later, when she was back, he had two options. Let her take him to some airport and put him on some plane that wouldn't touch the earth again until it was out of Europe. Or let her drive him to Provence to keep a lonely, bitter, fighter of an old woman company until Grandfather Mabruk was released from the basement of the university archive.

Kabangu had got to his feet and taken a few steps towards her. She saw him smile, he blinked, his eyes still damp, or damp again. "You want to save someone who doesn't deserve to be saved, Madame Boni."

"I think *I've* deserved it," she said.

Marek was in his car outside the hotel, his face greyer, his eyes perturbed, everything was more sluggish than usual: his blinking, breathing, nodding. Sometimes he frowned, as if he thought it inconceivable to be in this reality, in a world without his colleague of so many years. He was taller than Gerd and just as round. He smoked like Gerd, there was coffee in the central console and a six-pack of beer in the footwell of the passenger seat.

"I'll take the bird," he said.

"Sure."

"Willi, what a stupid name for a bird." He shook his head. "He just makes a break for it. Surely he knows you've got to look from side to side."

She thought of Gendrich. *Life can be over from one second to the next, you have to be so careful.* Much of what he'd said sounded like a cynical commentary on the events of the past few days.

"Unbelievable," Marek said. "Right, you've got two hours, then I have to be off."

She nodded. "Watch out, Marek."

"No worries, Bonì. We'll take this to the end, in his honour."

35

Wittnau and Sölden in the gentle evening light, to the east the slopes of the Black Forest, the woods. Louise took the turning to St Ulrich with mixed feelings. Right until the last moment she wondered if it was really necessary to go and see Thomas Walczak again.

No, she thought. What for?

But she was following her intuition, not her reason.

The gravel road. She drove through the forest at walking pace. No dogs to be seen, no man in boots and fur gilet. She wound down the window. After Kabangu's overheated room the fresh air felt good.

Louise recalled what Natalie had found out about Walczak in recent days. Not much, but enough for a few conclusions. A bit of provocation.

When she arrived at the clearing it was getting dark. From inside the car she could hear the barking, which became louder the moment she got out. She checked her pistol and returned it to the holster.

The dogs were in their cages, already settling down again. She couldn't see Walczak.

Louise was just about to go to the cabin when she heard his voice. "Late in the day to be coming here."

He was behind her. She turned around, slowly so the shock could subside. He was standing four or five metres away, wielding an axe, its well-worn shaft at least half a metre long. The gilet, trousers and shoes she already knew; his expression was also the same – at once sizing her up and defiant.

Without giving an answer she turned away and made for the dog course.

Muffled footsteps behind her, Walczak was following slowly.

She stopped by the fence. He came up to her, keeping his distance. Most of his face was obscured beneath the thick, unkempt beard; only his eyes were clearly visible. Harsh, cagey eyes.

"Janisch is dead," she said.

"The courier?"

She nodded, and it occurred to her that he knew this already. Her gaze alighted on the cabin in darkness. Perhaps Charlie came in the evenings with news, before lying down on his mattress. "Want to know what I think? Too refined for casual killers, for far-right violent thugs. We're responsible for Janisch. Experts with police badges, colleagues – in the widest sense of the word, I mean."

Walczak didn't react, didn't ask questions. He was still staring at her. She sensed he'd been waiting for her to return.

But why? What did he see in her?

Boni looked at the axe, its head on the ground, shaft leaning against his thigh. With the merest hint of a smile, Walczak seized the axe and threw it over the fence, a flick of the wrist as if he'd thrown a frisbee.

"No idea how they did it," she said. "Officially it was diabetic shock, but that's rubbish."

"Not my problem," he said.

She turned to the cages. A few of the dogs were looking over, but most were focused elsewhere. "Perhaps it is. Janisch knew too much, knew too many people involved. The Verfassungsschutz ran him as an informer. His death is a warning. Look, we'll clear up if needs be. Maybe they're going to do some more clearing up."

"Not my problem," he repeated.

"Help me, Walczak."

"*Herr* Walczak."

"The money you passed on to Janisch, who was it from?"

"The courier? I didn't give him any money."

"Where do you buy your food? What you need for your meals?"

"I eat what the dogs leave."

She reluctantly grinned. "In a supermarket?"

"There isn't one around here."

"In Ehrenkirchen there's one, ten kilometres away. You don't have a car, but maybe a moped, a bike. Ever been there?"

"No."

"You stand out, someone will remember you. Member of staff, customer. Supermarkets have CCTV, you'll be on it."

"Come back when someone has remembered."

"Someone else who was involved was supposed to go to Ehrenkirchen to leave an envelope in the supermarket. Who for, Herr Walczak?"

"You're asking the wrong man."

"Maybe I'm just asking the wrong questions."

He snorted.

Louise looked at his bare arms, the ugly, obscene stick figures. "Those tattoos, where did you get them?"

"Sins of my youth."

"More like youth detention, right? Some of the boys held you down, others did the etching. Biro ink, or they used soot and something sharp, a spring from a lighter. Must've been painful."

Staying very still, Walczak returned her gaze and said, "Someone else has died, I hear."

Louise nodded. "Colleague of mine. One of the good guys. The good colleagues." Her telephone buzzed; the display read "Enders". She put it away. "I suspect you had some help back in youth detention. Right-wing extremists who roughed up the boys with the ink. That's how you came to be on the organised scene. But you're not really part of it. Politics doesn't interest you. You needed an outlet for your hatred, you still do, the hatred is still there. Just hatred. And the dogs. One of the youth workers you beat up is Jewish. You broke his arm. Smashed his arm so many times against a bedpost that it broke."

"Yes," Walczak said.

"Because he was Jewish?"

"Because he was a bad youth worker."

"Then a Pole and two Germans. Why the Germans? Were they long-haired hippies? Communists? Child abusers?"

"Bad youth workers," Walczak said calmly.

"You didn't touch another of the youth workers, even though he used to beat children. Your third or fourth place, a home in Bavaria, right? Hofmann, I think. He was shopped by a colleague and later dismissed after a court sentenced him for having taken minors to NPD rallies. Did he take you too? Was he some kind of substitute father figure?"

"Hofmann? Don't know a Hofmann."

"Rubbish."

He gave a throaty laugh and a slight nod.

Louise recalled one of Natalie's handwritten notes, somewhere deep in the "Walczak" pile. "Your grandfather was half Russian, your father a quarter." She didn't know if this was relevant. A possibility, no more than that.

"Boni, is that a French name?" Walczak now seemed to be standing closer to her, not much, a few centimetres.

"Father French, mother German, even though they'd both rather it was the other way around. Then—"

"The police accept foreigners?"

Louise shrugged and smiled; finally she was getting somewhere. "Then the army. For six years you didn't draw any attention to yourself. But no sooner had you left the army than it all kicked off again. An acquaintance this time, I've seen photographs from the case file.

Before, a passport photo. After, when admitted to hospital. The man is unrecognisable. Twenty years older than you, a weakling, he didn't stand a chance and you tried to beat the life out of him. Why? He's German."

"I've forgotten," Walczak said.

Her mobile again, Marek this time. She answered. A call from the surveillance squad: he'd been summoned to see Cords. No surveillance out of work hours; a written warning was in the offing, a major dressing-down at the very least. He was worried and said, "I'm just going to drive over there."

"OK."

"It's going to go tits up, Boni."

The moment she ended the call Enders rang again, and again she didn't take it. Kabangu without protection, she thought, hastily running through her options. Birte, herself, one of her former colleagues, maybe Enders . . . Suddenly she felt like a feverish patient, deliriously seeking solutions for a problem that might not actually exist.

But the inner voices wouldn't be silenced. Kabangu without protection. Gendrich, who hadn't looked like a man vanquished.

"Five years inside," she said, trying to concentrate. "After that everything was suddenly different. Shall I have a guess?"

Walczak didn't reply. His right hand was now on the fence, and once more the distance between them appeared to have shrunk.

"You moved here, to this isolated spot. No more people, no more hatred, all quite simple. The occasional customer, a woman, other than that just the dogs."

He said nothing. In the fading light she couldn't see his expression anymore. His eyes were dark patches, no longer readable; the beard did the rest.

"Help me, Herr Walczak, I'm running out of time."

A text arrived. Exasperated, she glanced down at the phone in her hand.

Woman's body Baden-Baden. Pills and alcohol. Daria Polionova. Call me!

A photo followed, a beautiful, pale, woman's face, eyes closed.

Irina.

Louise groaned and looked up, her eyes suddenly full of tears, Walczak blurred, moving beyond the tears, a dark, powerful shadow. On impulse she raised her arms to fend him off, it was too late to draw her weapon . . .

But he didn't attack her, he didn't do anything. He was just there, standing very close. Heavily and menacingly he filled her field of vision in which she could no longer make out any contours.

She lowered her arms and head, and suddenly her legs gave way. Catching herself with her hands, she sat there and thought: Irina.

Shaking, Boní wiped her eyes dry, and when she was able to focus again she called Kilian's number.

Only the ringing tone for what seemed like for ever.

A movement beside her; Walczak was on his knees, so close that she could smell him. Booze, dirt, dogs and another note, a good one, spicy, fresh wood. A ridiculous thought ran through her mind: like him she should escape to isolation, back to the Kanzan-an or, even better, hole herself away in the cabin covered in filth, sleep here, get woken by the morning light or dogs, no more people, no more responsibility, no mistakes, no blame.

No more dead.

Irina – not a mistake, but her responsibility.

She pressed number recall and listened to the ringing tone. He must know by now; the elegant villa behind trees and bushes in Baden-Baden was under observation around the clock. Besides, he found out everything earlier anyway, having access to internal systems whose existence she was unaware of.

Louise called Enders.

"About bloody time!"

"Drive to the hotel, will you? Please, he's on his own."

Enders hesitated, then said, "I can't, they're not finished with me yet. Is that her? The Russian?"

"Yes."

"But why?" He almost shouted the words, impotent, overwhelmed.

Louise shrugged. Having read the case file thoroughly, Gendrich must have passed on information to Niko in Baden-Baden. They helped each other out, disruptive elements had to be got rid of, traitors. That was how they generated fear and respect. Informers were killed, weak points eliminated. The other people in the mix found out and kept quiet. People like the Riedls, the Krügers.

Walczak.

She turned to him, his bearded face barely two hand breadths from hers. He looked as if he were studying her. He didn't appear to be listening, only looking.

Enders wanted to know where she was. She hung up.

"Somebody else is going to die today, I hear," Walczak said.

Louise shook her head, unable to hold back the tears. She knew who he meant.

She knew they didn't stand a chance.

Without another word Walczak stood up, stepped over her legs and wandered over to his cabin.

As she returned to her car, on the phone to HQ, Walczak stood by the door watching her. Maybe, she thought, she'd got too close to him in a totally different way than she'd feared – too close for his liking rather than hers.

36

Blue lights at dusk. Half a dozen patrol cars, doctor, forensics and a Kripo van. Enders' car was there too. For several minutes Louise didn't get out, she just stared at the vehicles and officers standing around. She kept glancing at the hotel entrance in the hope that Kabangu might emerge and wander off deep in thought, a gaunt, slightly stooped figure. She lacked the energy to open the car door.

Graeve and Enders hurried into the street, Graeve on the phone. He gesticulated angrily and turned away. Enders spotted her and came over. Leaning his forearms on the frame of the open window, he seemed about to speak, but said nothing.

"How?"

"Do you really want to know?"

"I wouldn't ask otherwise."

"Shot and then hanged, maybe the other way around. It's not yet clear."

"Hanged? Lynched?"

"In the bathroom, from the frame of the shower cabin." There were tears in his eyes which he wiped away. Two entry wounds, he said, in the stomach and head. The receptionist said a woman had appeared around seven o'clock, asking for Kabangu: *Please tell him that Maria Schmidt would like to speak to him.* But the woman wasn't Maria Schmidt, she was younger, early thirties, a different type altogether – "boyish", according to the receptionist. All the same she probably wasn't strong enough to . . . But there was no sign that a second person had been present.

"Did she have a tattoo on her shoulder?"

"She was wearing a coat."

"Ask him. A 'black sun'. On the right shoulder."

Enders just looked at her.

Hanged, she thought. "I'm leaving now," she said.

He nodded towards the hotel. "In case you—"

"No." She started the engine, waited for Enders to move away, then drove off. No more images burning themselves indelibly on her memory, returning in nightmares for months, years. Images that didn't let other stories cover them. Stories about how things might have been, until maybe that was really how things were, stories in pretty wrapping. A man from Rwanda comes to a city with lots of tiny rivers to bring back home his wife's grandfather. One Friday evening he steps out of the hotel, gaunt, slightly stooped, wanders off deep in thought. Comes back around midnight and says, a little too gruffly, "Four fourteen."

Despite everything she couldn't help but smile. The fresh wind blowing through the open window brought with it this story and others, as she drove through the streets of Freiburg without really knowing where she was heading.

When Louise stopped at some lights the image she hadn't wanted to face was suddenly there. She closed her eyes; the image remained. She wished she could see Grandfather Mabruk in it too, but he was missing. Kabangu was alone. Nobody to offer him or her comfort.

There was a hooting behind her; the lights had turned green. She drove on, then turned mechanically and purposefully. Her body seemed to know where it was heading while her mind was otherwise preoccupied.

When Bonì recognised the streets and realised she'd driven to Rieselfeld, she wasn't particularly surprised.

37

Hans Gendrich was working late. From a distance Louise could see that the lights were on in his office, a bright cubicle in an otherwise dark building. She turned into the car park, left her vehicle there and walked back to the road.

Now Gendrich was standing at the window; he must have heard the engine. Just as he had that afternoon, he was looking down at her, hands in his trouser pockets, seemingly relaxed, untouchable, but maybe it was just her impression that this man was untouchable and she powerless because his structures worked and hers didn't anymore. A melancholic smile would have suited his bearing, a sort of empathy with the vanquished. It was almost as if he'd been expecting her, as if he'd studied his opponent so intently that he knew her moves in advance, even moves like these.

Then, she thought, unlike her he also knew how this ended.

Go up and ask him, she thought. Ask him how this ends.

Go up, aim your pistol and ask him. Talk about the beginning in 1907, in the colony of German East Africa, when Grandfather Mabruk was unlawfully removed from his grave, then ask him how this ends. Tell him it's almost a hundred years ago now, how does a story end that began almost a century ago? How must it end? Because I don't know . . .

Go up and ask him, she thought.

Then Gendrich moved abruptly, turned his head a touch too quickly and she could see he was saying something. Clearly someone else was in the room, someone had just entered; Gendrich looked surprised. He pulled his hands from his trouser pockets, all of a sudden not relaxed or untouchable anymore. He took a step forward, his hands raised, muscles tense, ready to fight; there was a mamba in their clean home that they hadn't bashed away because they hadn't been expecting it. Louise realised that only now could he predict the end, just like her.

At that moment Gendrich's head flipped backwards, he staggered uncontrollably until stopped by the window. The mamba bit again, Gendrich's arms crashed against the glass with a dull thud and the light blue of his shirt was stained dark.

He doubled up and collapsed on the floor.

For a few seconds nothing happened. Then the light went out and the dead man by the window disappeared in the darkness.

Louise sat on the kerb, giving free rein to her tears as she waited. Tears of grief, and of relief that she hadn't gone up and aimed her gun at Gendrich. Cars passed, pedestrians, and with them different stories, stories in which Ludwig Kabangu didn't feature, which meant he was alive, somewhere in Rwanda, maybe for a few days in Freiburg too. Stories in which he might have stepped out of the hotel that evening, walked off and come back late. Four fourteen, she heard him say, before he struggled up the stairs because he didn't fancy the moods and foibles of lifts.

Without having heard footsteps she felt fingertips on her shoulder.

"You need to get away from here," he whispered.

Nodding, she took his hand, nestled her cheek against it and begged for forgiveness because of Irina, because of Daria, not a mistake, but her responsibility.

Begged him for forgiveness for what he'd done.

For what lay ahead.

She knew he'd now disappear for ever, somewhere where he could live with what had happened and what he'd done, without having to lie day after day, without having to betray his principles. Where he could accept who he had become, and perhaps forgive himself one day.

"Promise me you'll get enough sleep, OK?" she said, because she couldn't think of anything better.

His hand stroked her cheek, her brow. Once more she heard nothing; she merely sensed that he had gone.

Epilogue

An afternoon in mid-May. For hours now Africa had been far below Louise, one foreign country imperceptibly taking over from another. The journey would eventually come to an end in another foreign country. In the belly of the aeroplane sat a coffin and a white box, both sealed, the homecoming of the dead a highly official act, even though it was all very discreet. Only Louise was accompanying them.

The day after Kabangu was murdered, Peter Arndt sent an army of colleagues into the basement. A week later Louise was standing at his desk in front of a labelled box that "with ninety per cent certainty" contained the remains of Grandfather Mabruk. *If that's not good enough for you we'll keep investigating.*

That will do.

Then take him home quickly, Frau Boni. I've been hearing his voice for days, he's my bad conscience, my memory, my nightmare, if you don't mind my quoting you.

He can really get on your nerves, can't he?

A few days later Kabangu's body was released. Graeve notified her. *Your decision,* he said.

I want two weeks' holiday.

Take four.

Two. After that I'll go on sick leave.

Retreat into isolation. Sleep, be awoken by the morning light or by cats. No more people, or at least no more than half a dozen silent nuns and monks. No more responsibility, no mistakes, no guilt.

Just her and her dead.

Maybe at the Kanzan-an she would be able to make peace with them at last. With herself, her job. And return with new energy.

Graeve had implored her not to throw it in. He'd promised to take all the time it needed knocking on doors and picking up the phone until Enders' transfer was revoked and he was sitting back at his desk in D11.

If that's your condition.

One of many, she'd replied.

I doubt I'll have any influence over the others.

Not without messing around inside my head.

Her head . . .

Her head had made her go back a few days ago to see Walczak again. Tell him you arrived too late, the voices in her head whispered. Tell him how Kabangu died. Shout into his face that you might have been able to save Kabangu if he'd decided to open his mouth earlier. Tell him he can't save himself by helping others to kill.

Tell him what Kabangu's murder means to you.

But Walczak had vanished. He'd turned the cabin into firewood, taken the dogs and left, apparently for France. A patrol car had seen a pack of dogs trotting over the unguarded border one night.

A flight attendant announced they would soon be landing in Kigali. Louise heard Grandfather Mabruk laughing and cheering a few metres beneath her.

She didn't hear Kabangu. Kabangu wasn't laughing or cheering.

Maybe when you lay him beside his wife in the earth, Grandfather Mabruk said. Maybe then he'll find peace, because he's been saved from loneliness.

A nice thought. Saving Kabangu in death because she hadn't managed to in life.

Acknowledgements

I'd like to thank everyone who's helped me with this novel, especially Chief Inspector Karl-Heinz Schmid (Freiburg Police HQ), the social scientist Heiko Wegmann (www.freiburg-postkolonial.de), Roland Braunwarth (Baden-Württemberg Criminal Investigation Bureau, Institute of Forensics) and all those who did not wish to be mentioned by name.

OLIVER BOTTINI was born in 1965. Six of his ten novels, including *Zen and the Art of Murder* and *A Summer of Murder* of the Black Forest Investigations, have been awarded the Deutscher Krimipreis, Germany's most prestigious award for crime writing, and four have been adapted for film. *Zen and the Art of Murder* was shortlisted for the 2018 CWA International Dagger. He lives in Frankfurt. www.bottini.de

JAMIE BULLOCH is the translator of Timur Vermes' *Look Who's Back*, Birgit Vanderbeke's *The Mussel Feast*, which won him the Schlegel-Tieck Prize, and novels by, amongst others, Steven Uhly, Robert Menasse, Romy Hausmann, Sebastian Fitzek, Arno Geiger and Daniela Krien.